The Day Before Thanksgiving

A Harbinger of Change

Steven Ray Elliott

Copyright © 2022 Steven Ray Elliott

All rights reserved. No part of this book may be reproduced or used in any manner without the prior written permission of the copyright owner, except for the use of brief quotations in a book review.

To request permissions, contact the author at
StevenElliott.physics@gmail.com

ISBN 979-8-9871987-0-4 (Paperback)
ISBN 979-8-9871987-1-1 (EBook)

The Day Before Thanksgiving
Steven Ray Elliott – 1st ed.

Cover Image Credit: NASA, ESA, G. Dubner (IAFE, CONICET-University of Buenos Aires) et al.; A. Loll et al.; T. Temim et al.; F. Seward et al.; VLA/NRAO/AUI/NSF; Chandra/CXC; Spitzer/JPL-Caltech; XMM-Newton/ESA; and Hubble/STScI

The turkey photograph was taken by the author at the Hubbell Trading Post in the Navajo Nation.

Dedication

The opportunity to attend graduate school was one of many gifts I received as a result of my parent's life-long dedication to their children.

The love and encouragement from my wife and daughter not only made this effort possible but worthwhile.

Therefore, I dedicate this manuscript to Norman and Barbara Elliott, Mary Elliott and Alexis Elliott. I love you all.

This is a work of fiction. Any similarity between the imagined characters and real persons is purely coincidental. Although there are many scientific studies investigating the possibility of a change in one or more of the fundamental constants, at the time of writing, none has found credible evidence of such.

Contents

Acknowledgments	i
Glossary and List of Major Characters	ii
Prolog	iii
Memorial Day, Fear of Change	1
The Changing Universe Society	13
Lecture on Change	29
Love Changes Things	37
Baseball Never Changes	43
School Begins, Hope for Change	54
Celebration, No Unexpected Change	65
Funding Studies of Change	76
The Day Before Thanksgiving	85
Conversation, Might Rules Change	95
Evidence for Change	106
Consequences of Change	120

"When you have eliminated the impossible, whatever remains, however improbable, must be the truth."

- Sir Arthur Conan Doyle

"Whenever possible, substitute constructions out of known entities for inferences to unknown entities."

- Bertrand Russell

"A common sense interpretation of the facts suggests that a super-intellect has monkeyed with physics."

- Fred Hoyle

"This is rather as if you imagine a puddle waking up one morning and thinking, 'This is an interesting world I find myself in – an interesting hole I find myself in – fits me rather neatly, doesn't it? In fact it fits me staggeringly well, must have been made to have me in it!' This is such a powerful idea that as the sun rises in the sky and the air heats up and as, gradually, the puddle gets smaller and smaller, frantically hanging on to the notion that everything's going to be alright, because this world was meant to have him in it, was built to have him in it; so the moment he disappears catches him rather by surprise. I think this may be something we need to be on the watch out for."

- Douglas Adams

Finances, Preparing for Change	129
Transparency Brings Change	137
Change is the Only Constant	145
Resisting Change	150
Lecture with Changes	167
Yearning for Change	175
Another Change	182
As the World Changes	193
A Message of Change	201
Even More Change	208
Talking about Change	215
Change for the Worse	231
Change of a Change	242
Day of Change	251
Everything Changes	259
The Change Revealed	265
For Further Reading	272
About the Author	275

Acknowledgments

First let me think my beta readers, Wenqin Xu, Fred Jenkins III, Mary Elliott, and Alexis Elliott. Their comments helped clarify many story elements. I would also like to thank others who have read previous stories of mine providing feedback that helped improve my writing; Laura Jenkins, Debra Pohlman, and Robert Montana. The editing efforts of Bernadette Freeman improved this manuscript's prose and added color to the story. I am sincerely grateful for her efforts.

For a book with a physics focus, I would be amiss not to thank the mentors and collaborators I have had throughout my physics career. There are many, of course, but a few stand out as having had a large impact on my personal view of science; Richard Reif (Career Enrichment Center, Albuquerque Public Schools), Prof. Daniel Finley (University of New Mexico), Dr. Michael Moe (University of California, Irvine), and Prof. Hamish Robertson (University of Washington).

Glossary and List of Major Characters

CUS - Changing Universe Society
MUTs - Multi-Universe Travelers
ET - experiment name, E for electron, T for Time
PQW pronounced 'peek-week' - parts per quadrillion per week
NSF - National Science Foundation

Thomas Conrad - assistant professor of physics
Deborah Dana (DeeDee) Champton - physics department chair
Tanya - Thomas' sister
Mark - Tanya's husband
Samantha (Sam) Hendrix - business consultant and accountant
Harold Simpson - Changing Universe Society leader
Jonathan Simpson - Harold's son
Adrian Treadwell - postdoc woking with Thomas
Carl Jackson - new graduate student who works with Thomas
Kathy Dotson - senior graduate student working with Thomas
Fareed Raja - NSF program manager
Cole and Kelly - Mark and Tanya's friends
Arthur Dobbins - alias of Johathan Simpson
Judy Dotson - Kathy's sister

Prolog

A quoted snippet of dinner conversation from the upcoming Thanksgiving holiday;

"Interesting world, turkeys live in," Cole offered while looking at a bite size portion of the bird on his fork. Cole was an amateur philosopher and his speaking style could easily be mistaken for that of a preacher. He had a skill for making a dramatic point through parable and today he had quite a holiday story to tell. "Every day as they grow up, the farmer comes to them and feeds them. He takes care of them and protects them from predators. He makes sure they are healthy and their offspring do well. As they grow, they come to associate the farmer with good things. Then the day before Thanksgiving arrives and their world changes suddenly. They see the farmer coming and they start thinking about being fed. But then the farmer grabs one and wrings its neck. The other turkeys must be shocked by the violence. They can't fathom that the rules of their existence changed with the rise of the new day sun. There are philosophers who think man may be in for a similar fate. One day the conditions of our Universe might just change. We'll be as lost and confused as the turkey who witnessed his friend become our entrée."

Memorial Day, Fear of Change

Thomas Conrad was sitting at his office desk wearing his usual slacks and button-down shirt. He was tapping the keyboard impatiently trying to estimate the laser power required for his proposed next experiment. The door to his office burst open, shattering his concentration. DeeDee Champton, his department chair, stormed in accompanied by three senior faculty members. Two security guards stood behind just outside in the hall.

"Thomas, your work has been awful. Not just sub-par but awful," lectured DeeDee. She towered over him ominously in her dark blue business suit with a floral blouse and flats. She snapped her fingers and his desk, along with everything on it, disappeared. "We have decided to take early action to rid our department of your unsuccessful program."

She snapped again and all the other credenzas and bookcases, with all their books and three-ring binders disappeared. Thomas' backpack was gone. Even the chair vanished. Thomas was now standing in front of her, stiff with fright. "We have talked to the bank and your house and its furnishings have been repossessed. Your car has been towed."

She snapped her fingers one last time and his clothes were gone leaving him naked. He desperately tried to cover himself with his unwilling hands. "This academic life you have taken for granted is over. Good luck in your

1

future endeavors, as if you have any future. Security, escort Dr. Conrad off campus. He is no longer welcome here."

As DeeDee turned, she disappeared along with the other faculty members. Handcuffs appeared on Thomas' wrists and the security guards appeared next to him. Each took an elbow and they began pushing him out the door.

Thomas bolted upright, panting and sweating. The high-thread, organic cotton sheets on the king-size platform bed were soaked. The patterned bed spread was on the floor. Still breathing heavily, he knew what he had to do: following a recently acquired routine, he gathered his senses by scanning the room making visual contact with familiar furnishings. The end tables with the faux Tiffany lamps were where they should be. The boxy mahogany armoire stood tall near the bay window overlooking the yard. The original paintings by local, but well-regarded artists, were hanging where they had yesterday. His modern decor calmed him as he rose to full consciousness with a sense of order restored. His breathing slowed to normal.

He didn't need a therapist to tell him that this recurring nightmare came from his fear of not getting tenure. That insight didn't stop the dreams from disturbing him. After all, the fears were based in reality. His graduate school friends, Sigmond and Evelyn, didn't get tenure at their Ivy League schools. However, they both stepped into tenured positions at state schools. They were disappointed of course, but still in the game. He was already at a state school. He had to succeed here. If he failed, his life would be instantly and dramatically changed. The thought petrified him and the nightmare dramatized it. All he had ever known was science. That was all he ever wanted to do. Last year, he had been offered a job as a process engineer. Certainly it would have paid well, but it sounded horrible. Designing systems to monitor paper thickness at a factory just didn't excite him like doing experiments to unlock the secrets of the universe.

It was early, just after dawn, but he was awake. He had several hours before he had to drive to his sister's house for a family barbeque. "I think I'll get up and use the time to work on that public lecture," he thought. "At least getting some work done will help with this stress." He edged out of bed and stepped into the shower. The bedroom bath was large, meant for a sharing couple, with a separate toilet room. The shower head was a wide ceiling mounted fixture giving the feel of standing under a waterfall. The hot water and body wash were refreshing, and he stood under the flow for much longer than usual. Out of the shower, he took stock of himself in the full length mirror. He was average height. He didn't have a beer belly, but no six pack either. He had a full head of dark hair, which he kept full but trimmed. He shaved any emerging facial hair daily. He recently bought a new pair of designer glasses. "I'm not a movie star," he smiled. "But I do have my good points."

Dressing in recently purchased jeans, a button down collared and wheat-themed patterned short-sleeve shirt, belt, dark socks and loafers, he made sure he was dressed to go to Tanya's, even though he wouldn't leave for several hours. His sister put a lot of work into these get-togethers and he didn't want to be late. He was well aware of his habit of getting deep into a problem and losing track of time. So, he organized his days around opportunities to concentrate. He had established routines intended to diminish the impact of daily decision making. Many of these decisions are made at the start of the day when he was rested and most creative. Since each decision consumed mental energy, he risked losing his most productive hours to the trivial. He wanted his energy spent on his work, not a bunch of grooming, clothing, meal preparing, commuting, or other life management choices. His routines allowed him to prioritize work, even though he was fastidious about his lifestyle.

Thomas walked down the short hallway of his two-bedroom house to the kitchen. He stopped to turn on his high-fidelity sound system, starting up his Tidal music streaming service choosing a playlist with alternative rock. He loaded his espresso machine to make a cappuccino, which he drank from a trusted mug. He put three large spoonfuls of plain yogurt into a bowl, adding some berries along with a small handful of unsalted sunflower seeds.

Thomas had an oak bookshelf that he designed himself while he was a postdoc. With the back supports bolted flush to the wall, the shelves got increasingly narrow with height so the front supports were angled. The bottom shelf was thirty inches above the floor, and it had a four-foot wide leaf that extended three feet from the wall to serve the purpose of a desk surface. The bookshelf itself ran nearly the full length of the wall and the shelves above the leaf were covered by wooden doors. He flicked on the LED light he had installed to illuminate the desk section. He sat down in his executive desk chair which was so cushy that he occasionally fell asleep in it while reading. He opened his laptop to review the presentation.

A feeling of relief swept over him as the pace of the morning finally eased and he began the primary task for the day. Looking at the first slide, however, he knew he had a problem. The title of the talk was OK, he thought. "As the Constant Changes: Is the Electric Charge Timeless?," seemed cute enough to capture the attention of the non-expert. However, the first slide was technical, resembling a seminar for scientists doing competing work, not a survey for those seeking an intriguing discussion topic for the evening's subsequent drinks and dinner. "This was going to take a lot more work," he sighed to himself. He examined every point he was trying to make from the point of view of a lay person, desperately trying to provide the context the audience would need to understand the key concepts. Several hours later, he had a moment of panic when he noticed the time. Realizing that he would be at least a few minutes late, no matter what he did, he carefully saved his presentation files, closed his laptop, turned off the sound system, grabbed his car keys and left for the ninety-minute drive up state to his sister's house.

Thomas was a bit late, but well before the afternoon fare was ready, so all was good. The conversation was lively and the food was delightful. When the party wound down, he helped carry leftovers back into the kitchen as Mark walked the last guests to the driveway.

"Thank-you for the cookout, Tanya. The burgers were delicious. They had much more zest than I usually associate with ground meat." He cringed as he feared his sister would find that comment dismissive, but she didn't seem to take offense. He leaned against the stainless steel refrigerator as she scooped the last of the potato salad into a glass storage container.

"You're welcome Thomas, but I can't take credit. Mark has a secret recipe, although the secret isn't that clever. Don't let on that I told you, but he uses Italian-flavored bread crumbs when mixing the patties. The spices add to the flavor."

"Well Mark is a cooking genius, even if he does lecture philosophically a bit much."

Tanya rolled her eyes and nodded as she moved on to scooping strawberries.

"His views on tenure at research universities was a bit too close to home for me today. I hope he didn't get upset when I lost control." Thomas tried to read his sister's face.

"Are you kidding? He lives for a good debate. If people get emotional, he knows the topic was an important one. But how are *you* doing? Still having nightmares? You have another year, right?"

"I submit my package next spring for consideration the following fall. But I am really stressed about it. Everything depends on the experiment being a success. I need to get it published before I turn in that paperwork. If all goes as planned, I should be OK. But these experiments are hard and something is very likely to go wrong. I don't have a lot of time to rebuild and try again."

"Everything you have said about your team sounds like you all will get it done. They're good at this." She opened the dishwasher to begin loading plates.

"Yes, but there are only three of us and there is a lot of work to do. I also have that public lecture next month. That will be good exposure and the University will like it. But it's also a lot of work to prepare that kind of talk. The public is not expert in physics and this experiment is not simple to explain to non-physicists. I will have to spend a lot of time getting it ready."

Mark entered the kitchen through the patio doors and joined the siblings' conversation. He opened a fresh Stella and offered one to Thomas, who declined. "I'm sorry I got too emphatic earlier, Thomas. I know this coming year is going to be an intense one for you. I didn't mean to add to your stress."

"It's OK Mark. I shouldn't have snapped at you, in any case. By the way, I loved the hamburgers."

Mark nodded thanks for the compliment and took a swig of his beer. "We really should discuss the philosophy of your experiment. The suggestion that the electron's charge might be changing in time is really fascinating. I'd love to hear more about the consequences and what it would mean for us lowly humans if the charge value wasn't stable. Since our last chat, I did look into the anthropic principle as you recommended. I was surprised to see that a fair number of physicists consider it to be a reasonable premise. This could make for a great lecture topic for my class at the junior college."

Mark's knowledgeable interest surprised Thomas. "Mark, the premise that the physical laws and fundamental constants of the Universe *must* allow for the development of sentient beings who are then able to contemplate its existence – well – that seems a bit much to me. The Universe didn't choose values for fundamental constants so that it will have *admirers*. Or at least, I find that preposterous. However, the idea that our Universe is only one of an infinite number of universes is intriguing. The anthropic principle has a plausible interpretation within that multiverse concept."

"But Thomas, then how do you explain that the fundamental constants all must lie within a narrow range for life to develop, and that those constants just happen to be in that range? Doesn't that seem too much of a coincidence?"

Tanya cleared her throat meaningfully and in response, Mark picked up a dish towel and made some swipes on a hand-painted platter.

"I am not a proponent of intelligent design, if that's what you're suggesting." He allowed for a snicker at that comment and continued. "However, I do consider the possibility that there are an infinite number of universes, a so-called multiverse, and within each universe, the fundamental constants might be random. We live in a universe that happens to have the right values for those constants for life to come about. This is the universe with the right conditions for us to exist. With an infinite number of universes, at least one had to fit that bill. That doesn't sound so crazy to me."

"Interesting point, but how would we know if that's the case."

"Ah! You have just hit upon why I'm uncomfortable with the multiverse hypothesis. There isn't any way to test it." Thomas shifted so he could watch Mark's face as he presented his case. "We can't look into one of the other universes and measure the electron's charge there. It's *fun* to think about, but I, personally, don't consider it science if you can't test it. It's more up your alley. On the other hand, there are theories that can accommodate a changing charge in just one universe. It may be very unlikely, but it is testable, and our experiment has the potential to falsify a variety of theories."

"A *fascinating* discussion boys," opined Tanya. "But we have a lot of dishes to wash and empty bottles to take care of. Come help me clean up."

"Good idea, Tanya," replied Thomas. "We can discuss the multiverse while staring a sink full of dishwashing soap bubbles. Each its own universe within a foam of creation."

Samantha Hendrix strode into the Brewers Cup and surveyed the coffee shop for her potential new client. Tall, blonde, with perfect posture and a taste in clothes that drew admiring glances from men and women alike, she exuded confidence and modernity. She carried a burgundy leather briefcase and was dressed in a dark pant suit. The coffee shop was not crowded - too late in the day for the morning rush. Given it was Memorial Day, most everyone would be at family holiday get-togethers.

She spotted the new prospect. Harold Simpson was a young looking septuagenarian in clean pressed clothes, but clearly didn't understand the purpose of a brush. His ear-length white-blond hair was mussed. He wore a tan collared shirt and multi-colored tennis shoes that clashed with his otherwise sharp dressed attire. "Comfort, or a style choice?" she wondered.

When the two made eye contact, Harold rose and waved her over. "Ms. Hendrix," he introduced himself, "I am Harold Simpson. Please allow me to buy you a cup of coffee or tea."

"Thank-you," she answered, savoring the chivalry of a man forty years her senior. "I'll have tea. Decaf English breakfast, please."

Harold gestured for her to take a chair, and as he walked up to the counter, she settled into the tiny booth. He returned with the tea and a couple almond biscottis.

"I'm glad you could meet this afternoon. I know it's a holiday and you probably had more enjoyable things to do than talk business, but I really need to get an account manager started soon. Our organization is preparing for a major change and we need to get things in order." His voice was a strong baritone, with a slightly folksy quality. It was a voice that seemed honed for public address.

Samantha removed an iPad from her case and opened a file to take notes. She sipped the perfectly brewed cup, while thinking she should remember this place. "No problem, Mr. Simpson. I limit my clientele list so I can be available when help is needed. You can be assured I will always do what I can to make time if you require it."

Harold circled his hands around his own cup. "My son runs most of our organization's operations, but I fear he is traveling this weekend and couldn't join us. But I am sure you will meet him soon enough."

"Please, tell me what it is you require." Her fingers hovered about the iPad's keyboard.

"I am the leader of a religious movement, the Changing Universe Society. It is not a recognized religion by the IRS, but we do operate as a non profit to benefit the needs of our members." Harold searched her face for any reaction.

She nodded, making notes and keeping her face expressionless.

Harold smiled and continued. "We were established nearly a decade ago and, as time has gone by, our resources have grown and we need an account manager to help understand our cash flow and bill paying and project oversight. Basically, Jonathan, that's my son, is good at keeping things organized but he says he needs help with the money issues. The paperwork to keep the state and federal governments happy is quite a chore. I'm sure you can imagine." He added in a dry chuckle. "Keeping the money safely invested and accounted for has become a challenge also. I want to hire you to manage that end of our organization. You come highly recommended."

"Thank you, I am happy to hear that. I forwarded my remuneration requirements to you. I know some people think I am expensive but I work hard to make sure my clients think I'm worth the extra cost. How long are you planning for this position? I only ask because I have another opportunity that would be a three month effort, starting mid June. If this has a shorter time frame than that, I may have to take the other option."

"To be honest, Ms. Hendrix, I am not sure how long.

I can say, however, it would be at least six months and likely longer. I would be more than willing to sign a six month contract that includes options for ongoing following quarters.

Sam nodded slightly, to encourage him to continue.

"I'm sure you will learn a lot about our organization as you work with us, but we are closely watching an experimental program at the University. That program is measuring the electron charge to see if it is changing. We firmly believe that at some future point, it will start to change. When it does, that will be the indication that it is time for us to schedule our departure. It will take a couple months to make all the arrangements once that date is set, and we will require your services until our departure."

Samantha typed the word *departure* into her notes and then bolded it. "Fascinating, I never considered that the electron charge might change. But why do you have to depart once it does change and where will you go?"

"If the charge starts to change, living here will no longer be possible. We will join the Multi-Universe Travelers.

"OK, then," Samantha decided to not pursue that logic, but she did make a note of the time scale and that the organization would depart by joining some other group, whatever that meant. "I can begin tomorrow by looking at your books and learn what your goals and constraints are."

"Great," exclaimed Harold as he clapped his hands. He pulled a card case from his pants pocket. "Here is Jonathan's contact information for your reference," he said as he handed her a card. "I will send him a message as soon as I get back to the compound and copy you. You two can take it from there. Actually, I don't really have much interest in the business end of things. I will leave those concerns to you and Jonathan."

She put the card in her case as she stood. "Thank-you for the tea and I look forward to hearing from Jonathan." Harold grinned.

As she pushed open the door and walked outside, she thought, "if nothing else, this at least will be an interesting job."

As Thomas drove back home from his sister's place, he considered his situation at the University and tried to relax. In several ways, the fall semester would be the start of a new life for him, for both better *and* worse. On the good side, his experiment was nearing ready to take data, albeit almost six years into his assistant professorship. His small team had checked all the systems of their basement installation and they judged it should be ready to go very soon. In a few months, he would be able to publish, a critical career milestone. If the experiment produced good data, he was confident he'd be promoted.

Pulling into his driveway, he saw someone standing on the side of the house, looking in the large living room window, but his view was obscured for a moment by the tall pines flanking the window. He refocused on parking for a second and when he looked back at the house, he saw no sign of anyone there. He got out and looked around the window and pines. He saw no footprints on the soft earth and no sign that the window had been tampered with. He checked the front door lock; it was secure. "Must be seeing things. I need to get some rest," he said to himself.

The Changing Universe Society

Jonathan led the new Changing Universe Society members to the common room on the first floor of the old factory. Harold's tabletop podium bearing the placard with the bold CUS logo was set in front of several dozen padded chairs arranged in rows.

"Please everyone, take a seat," he instructed. "Harold Simpson will be here in a few minutes to begin your orientation to our compound."

Jonathan was an average sized guy with dark hair, that he kept cut conservatively, but he procrastinated updating his glasses. He kept himself in reasonable shape. Most often, he wore slacks with a collared shirt, but no tie. He dressed to look professional, but with intent to appear approachable to newcomers; he deliberately omitted his suit jacket.

The inquires about joining the Society were increasing at a rapid pace recently. Most of the recent new members were from out of state, indicating that the group's online presence was broadening. Jonathan noted a substantial growth in interest after CUS posted a description of the ET project at the local university on their web site. He loved the catchy name those scientists created for the project. It had been a great recruitment tool.

He surveyed the assembled group from the front of the room near Harold's podium; yes, a good group. Six families, all with lots of money. Conveniently, the new members didn't seem to care about their money. They gladly handed over all their assets without any thought of taxes, an estate plan, formal paperwork, or even living expenses. All to be part of something bigger than themselves? Yes, that was Jonathan's guess at their motivations. Of course, after joining, the CUS covered their expenses. Certainly, there was a value in that exchange. Although it seemed strange to Jonathan that they were so willing to part with their assets, he wasn't complaining. The lack of financial records provided an exciting opportunity. He found it easy, a breeze, to conceal from oversight much of the money the group raised.

Harold showed no interest in financial issues once he had begun communicating with the Multi-Universe Travelers. As a result, Jonathan had complete autonomy and could move money as he saw fit. The financial advisor Harold found also seemed to take a blind eye. She helped him keep track of the movements, but wasn't too concerned about the details. She didn't judge or question his motives. She just charged a top fee to explain various exotic transactions and help keep the books. Jonathan smiled as he considered the plural of books. All of these unlikely developments just fell into Jonathan's lap and he wasn't going to miss the opportunity.

Jonathan took a chair nearby as Harold entered the room and strolled to the podium; he stood in front of it, not behind, and spread his arms in a pastoral welcoming gesture, to a quiet smattering of applause.

"Dear friends, I want to welcome you to the Changing Universe Society. I am Harold Simpson. This journey we have embarked upon will be the grandest of our lives. The grandest of any lives ever lived in this Universe, the Gaia Anótatos." He paused for the usual applause at the mention of Gaia; Harold knew how to play his crowd. He continued.

"By committing to this journey, you now have a direct connection to the Multi-Universe Travelers or more simply MUTs. They soon will be collecting us to begin the process of starting a new universe. We will all be living in that wonderful new cosmos soon. Our existence will take on a special meaning as we work to populate that universe, even as this one comes to an end."

"In a few moments, we will tour the compound. Does anyone have any questions?" Harold asked.

A young woman in a flowing shirt over jeans with a flower in her hair started the exchange. "You said you would explain some of the MUTs history when we got here. I'm really curious."

Harold smiled, "Yes Deidra, we should discuss that. I will give a quick summary now, but remember that we have weekly discussion sessions and workshops to study and learn the various details."

He paused to emphasize the beginning of his description. "You know that throughout history some peoples have just disappeared, with no explanation. Interestingly, distant groups have disappeared at similar times. There must have been coordination. The ancient Indus civilization vanished about ten thousand years ago. At roughly the same time, the builders of Catalhöyük and Göbekli Tepe also disappeared. The Anasazi left their cities in the thirteenth century. The Mississippians departed their cities at about the same time. Amazingly, the inhabitants of Easter Island and Angkor also departed at that point in history. These coincidences are striking and indicate two primary waves of disappearance. Now most archeologists will claim, with circumstantial evidence and scant proof, that these disappearances happened because of changing rain patterns or some other environmental event. But actually, these peoples were the first waves to be collected by the MUTs."

Harold paused once again to let those facts sink in. He continued, "Although ten thousand years may sound like a long time, it's the blink of an eye to the MUTs. Those civilizations were called home, just like ours is. The big question at this time is, how many of us will join them? It is up to each individual to act, once they learn the truth. By joining the Changing Universe Society, you have acknowledged the truth and have taken that necessary step.

Another woman joined in. "I have heard you mention Gaia Anótatos in some of your speeches. What is that exactly?"

"Good question Janice," Harold began, "The MUTs informed our ancient comrades that our universe should be called Gaia Anótatos. Gaia Anótatos is the founder of all life. She is the source of life."

A young man sitting next to his wife in front raised his hand and asked, "Sorry to ask a practical question when people want to discuss the Multi-Universe Travelers, but where will we be living until they come?"

"As a result of your generous financial commitment to CUS, Mark, you will be given an apartment here in the compound. During our tour, I will show you several examples. After the tour, you will each meet with Jonathan and discuss the options for housing for your family. By this evening, you will know which apartment will be yours. We expect you to either buy your own food or contribute to our operations in some way. Basically if a member of your family works part time to contribute to food and utilities, you will be fine. We cover other costs."

"What about health care? Jonathan told us you cover that but I haven't seen a policy yet," asked a woman in the back. "My daughter has asthma and allergy concerns. We need to see the doctor often and the drug costs are high."

"We do cover health care, Sarah. We have a group policy that we arranged through a local health care co-op. The CUS covers the premium costs and the out of pocket costs are very small. We are proud of that negotiation." Harold waited a moment, but no one else had any questions. Harold smiled knowing that Jonathan had done a good job explaining things before people committed. Harold was proud of his son.

For his part, Jonathan was always amazed at how well his father could remember everyone's name with just a single introduction. He really put people at ease with that talent.

"OK then," said Harold. "Since there are no further questions, let's begin the tour with a discussion of this room. This common area plus the associated kitchen takes up almost the entire first floor. We have an AV facility for larger presentations in Jonathan's office, there next to the kitchen. This room is where we have meetings and discuss the arrival of the MUTs. We also produce web-posted videos of events and lectures here. You can see the cameras and microphones mounted around the room. We also have common dinners here. The kitchen is always open if you prefer to eat here rather than cook for yourself."

Harold led the group to the main entrance and stepped out onto the sidewalk, pointing back to the building. "This structure you were just in used to be fertilizer factory. Built back in the 1920's boom era, this wooden structure is very stout and classic. I fell in love with the architecture and layout. The bottom floor and basement manufactured fertilizer back when this area was well away from town. The upper floors held the national offices for an agro-business. We are proud of the remodel job done on this building." Harold talked in a clear voice, projecting easily as if he were an enthusiastic tour guide, gesturing left and right and sometimes walking backwards to address his audience.

"We took control about six years ago and immediately began making changes. We renovated the upper floors for modern convenience and operation. Admittedly, we still have some work to do cleaning up in the basement. Early on, however, it became clear that this building wasn't going to be enough. Fortunately, the apartment complex across the street became available. We now have capacity for about two hundred fifty people, but we are getting near that limit. We added the canopy over the street joining the two buildings and the city worked with us to have an effective mass transit hub near here. If you look up, you will see a walkway joining the third floors of the buildings. We added that last year. Above that you see we are presently adding another walkway between the roofs of the two buildings. Down the block, there is a sizable parking lot for the complex. There is another entrance near that lot. Let's go back inside and I'll show you the upper floors."

The group returned inside through a separate entrance door behind the kitchen. A short walk down the hallway found a stairwell door. As they ascended the narrow staircase up two floors, Harold informed them, "The basement only houses the utilities, and isn't used otherwise, except the laundry facilities are there."

He stopped at a door not too far from the stairwell. He fumbled with his key chain while beginning his next speech. "This is one of our two bedroom apartments. We have various floor plans with one, two or three bedrooms depending on the needs of the occupants. These floor plans are intermixed so that families, singles and childless couples will interact. As you look around, realize that this is a typical apartment within our complex. The bedrooms, kitchen and living space are similar in all our offerings. The decor and design are modern as these models are only a few years old. Now, if you'll follow me, I'll show you the other building."

The group walked down the hallway and made a left turn. The passageway left the building and proceeded over the street. The view from the overpass was actually rather nice and the group stopped for a second to admire it. Trees lined both sides of the street, spaced evenly in breaks of the sidewalks. The street itself was well paved with no evidence of trash. As they entered the other building, Harold again fumbled with his keys and opened a door to another apartment. "This is a three bedroom model. The decor is somewhat more dated in this building as the apartments are older. But, I think they are still nice."

"Where do the children play," asked a woman who was holding the hand of a young girl.

"Let me show you that, Randi," answered Harold. He led the group back across the street to the factory building and then up two more flights of stairs. They exited a door and walked out onto the roof and into the center of a large playground. The kid's eyes lit up and they ran for the swings and jungle gym. "We have a variety of playground equipment here along with a number of game tables in the play room on the far side of the roof. Also if you walk to the edge here, you will see a park just a couple blocks away. The kids should have plenty of things to do."

With their questions answered, the group headed back down the stairs, and into the basement. "Here we are below the common room," explained Harold. "This room had a fair amount of electric power and natural gas outlets so we have converted it to a laundry facility. You can see we have a fair number of the appliances installed, but that far side area still needs cleaning up."

After returning up to the common room, Harold handed out the CUS tan shirts and arm bands. "Welcome to the Changing Universe Society. I will now leave you with Jonathan to make decisions regarding your apartment choice. Don't hesitate to come find me if you need anything." Harold led the group to a table with drinks and snacks and offered the refreshments.

As Harold said goodbye, Jonathon poked his head out the door to his office near the kitchen. He saw what he expected - the families were trying on their new shirts and helping themselves to piles of granola bars and pitchers of fresh squeezed juice. He raised his voice to be heard over their excited chatter. "I will be starting with the Johnson family. Please come in."

Jonathon's private office was not only large enough to house a massive executive desk with a throne-like wheeled chair, but a twelve-foot long conference table, sleek as a new sports car. He gestured for the couple to take seats in the capacious conference chairs.

"We have iced tea if you'd like some. It is hot today." The couple shook their heads no, so Jonathan continued on. "OK, then. You are a childless couple, I see. Do you plan to have children?"

"Someday, we might," replied Mrs. Johnson. She was an attractive, late twenty-something dressed in a solid blue mid-length dress. "At this point we're still getting settled."

"Then I assume a one bedroom apartment will suffice. You are in a bit of luck there, we have a fairly good inventory of those. There are four to choose from. Two each in the factory and the apartment complex. And there is a choice of floors in both. Any preference regarding floor. Oh and by the way, I know Harold doesn't like elevators, but both buildings have them. They are large and make moving easy."

The couple exchanged a glance and the wife spoke. "We'd like the factory side."

"Excellent, let's go look at the two choices and see which you prefer." Jonathan led them out the back door over to the stairwell.

It took about ninety minutes to get all six families placed. Afterward, Jonathan shut the doors to his office and finished the paperwork. He glanced at the clock calculating he had fifteen minutes till his next appointment, enough time for a bathroom break and a fresh iced tea.

Samantha walked purposefully into Jonathan's office right on schedule. "Hello Jonathan, I'm Samantha Hendrix, but my friends call me Sam. It's good to finally meet you in person."

As Jonathan looked up, he was taken aback. She made a dramatic impression. Her business suit and posture gave a professional aura, but the tailored fit made it obvious that the woman was strikingly attractive. After a pause, he regained his composure and responded. "Ah yes, hello Sam. We have talked by phone or email so often, that I feel like we are old friends. It is certainly good to put a face to our interactions. Can I get you something to drink? We have a fresh pitcher of iced tea." He held up his nearly empty glass. "I can personally vouch for it."

"That would be great," answered Sam. "The weather is warm today. I followed along on Harold's tour of the facility and then took a good walk around the outside grounds while waiting for our appointment. I am a bit overdressed for climbing stairs, but now I have a pretty good idea of your operations here."

"Please have a seat and rest a bit," instructed Jonathan. "My father can certainly overdo the walking. I'll be right back with the tea."

As Jonathon exited, Sam opened her jacket and fanned her throat as she scanned the large office. Every surface was slick and clean, very modern, a bit at odds with the folksy common room adjacent. Internally situated within the building, it was windowless. She could smell an aroma of something simmering on a stovetop from the next-door kitchen. Sam took one of the twelve seats at the conference table and set her briefcase on the table in front of her. She continued her scan of the room. A safe sat in the corner next to an entertainment center housing audio-visual equipment. It looked fairly hi-tech to Sam; clearly Jonathon did a lot of recording of something. A five-shelf case held books with esoteric titles. A treatise on international banking caught Sam's eye. Another bookcase held binders with labels that implied they held information on the residents. The art on the walls was tasteful, but not originals, recalling the décor of generic hotel rooms. Two doors led into the room, the one Sam entered that connected to the common area and one that joined a hallway behind the office.

"The Changing Universe Society is doing very well," started Jonathan as he reentered the room with two glasses of tea. He set one down in front of Sam and one by a chair directly across from her. Condensation from the cold wet glasses made puddles on the polished table surface. Sam thought such a nice table required coasters, but she didn't say anything. "We had six new families make arrangements to move in earlier today," he continued. "We are really growing, but we still have a number of empty apartments, so we can keep expanding."

"Well, the facility sure looks nice and the books are certainly in good shape. CUS is doing well. I agree."

"Thank you, Sam. But I know you are busy so I guess we should get down to why you're here. I have been following your instructions. I have left a fair amount of money in local accounts for operating expenses. But I have been moving most around to make sure it avoids unnecessary scrutiny. Those foreign bank accounts you helped me with are working out great. Although the travel for some of the in-person transactions will be a bit of a pain."

Sam leaned forward slightly and touched his hand, "Love, it sounds like it's all working as we designed. You got the alias passport for the bank churning, right?" Her eyes seemed to smile as she held his gaze.

"Of course. It's all going as we planned. The money is very safe." Jonathan smiled. He wondered if she was flirting and he felt a need to impress her.

"Where did the money come from to start this enterprise?" Sam asked.

"My father doesn't seem to care about money anymore, but ten years ago, you wouldn't have seen that. He invented an effective facial recognition tool for smart phones that was very competitive with that of a leading industry player. They bought him, and his patents, out. That settlement along with the agreed-upon royalties made him rich. He used the money to buy this old factory and remodel it. Then he bought the apartment complex across the street, and still, enough was left over for maintaining this place. In addition, we are raising a lot of money from people joining. They happily donate all their wealth and I want to protect that money."

"What do you need to protect it from?" Sam asked. She was curious about his motives but didn't expect an honest answer. All her work with their books pointed to impropriety. As long as she was uninvolved, she wasn't too worried about what her clients were planning. Maybe she'd crossed a line with this case by giving such specific advice on how to avoid detection during transfers, but the paper trail only showed effort balancing the books. There wasn't any mention of consulting.

"When the MUTs arrive, the CUS will depart. I want to make sure that money goes to the right place."

"And where is that? May I ask?" Sam was thinking that something just wasn't right about this. What was he up to?

"To those who deserve it. Those who have worked hard to make sure everyone is well taken care of between now and when the MUTs arrive," he replied.

That explanation didn't help Sam much. "If everyone leaves with the MUTs, who would remain that deserves the money?"

"Not everyone may leave," he suggested conspiratorially.

Sam nodded thoughtfully. Her suspicions were confirmed. She had seen similar cases in the past; Jonathan was preparing to embezzle the money. Clever scheme he had. She did see one problem, though. "But just because people leave doesn't mean they won't have a claim to the money. What if they come back?"

"To leave with the MUTs, you have to leave your body behind," he answered nonchalantly.

The casualness of his response shocked Sam, giving her a cold chill. She wanted to be sure she heard correctly. She cleared her throat. "They leave their bodies...?"

Jonathan responded with a slow nod.

She was aghast but she hid it well. She couldn't be sure this was a suicide cult, but Jonathan sure made it sound like one. As the surprise wore off, she became intrigued by the possibilities that this situation presented especially now that she understood Jonathan's motives better. This revelation, however, was a bit overwhelming. She needed to collect herself.

"Where is the restroom?" she asked. "That tea got to me and I have a bit of drive after our meeting."

"It's outside this back door and to the right down the hall a bit," answered Jonathan with a vague gesture. Sam stood and walked to the door. She tried to turn the knob, but it was locked.

"I'm sorry," apologized Jonathan as he stood. "This room was where the old factory kept its more valuable or hazardous items. That's why it's so big. The two doors have combination locks on them to keep things safe. I thought this room would make a good office with a safe place to keep money we have on hand. The doors are supposed to open from the inside even when locked from outside, but sadly that one is broken and I haven't had an opportunity to hire a locksmith. Follow me, and I'll show you the very long way to the restroom." He led Sam out the door into the common room, turned left and walked to the end of the wall, turning left again. Jonathan opened the door in front of them to a hallway going left or right. They entered and turned left one more time, where Jonathan pointed out the restroom door. "I am just going to go down and unlock the door to my office. You can return that way."

"Thank you," replied Sam as she opened the restroom

door. After splashing some water on her face and patting dry, she took a couple minutes to compose herself. She stared at herself in the mirror as she reconsidered the conversation in Johathan's office. "Should I tell someone?" she asked herself out loud. "These people might be in danger, although it's by their own choice." She reapplied a fresh layer of lipstick and noted a slight tremor in her hand, which she willed still. She gave a deep sigh, stood up straight, and walked back to Jonathan's office. Once there she stopped and looked at the lock. To her surprise it was not a deadbolt, but a simple combination dial turned to sixteen. This door would lock if it was shut and the dial spun. "Very old school," she said softly to herself, "or very old factory, I should say."

Jonathan had not returned to the conference table; he was seated in his throne-like executive chair, swiveling slightly side-to-side. Sam reached into her briefcase and pulled out a legal sized envelope. She kept her voice crisp and businesslike. "I have the financial reports for the last few months here for you. You are right, this place *is* doing well. The operating fund makes nearly as much as it spends. Your off-shore accounts are growing quickly, nearly three hundred thousand this last month alone. You have nearly ten million in those foreign banks already. We have some paperwork to file with the IRS, but it's pretty routine stuff. I filled out the forms but left the numbers blank, as you requested, so you can fill out as appropriate. They are electronic forms so I copied them to the flash drive in the envelope. My bill for last month is also in there."

"Great! Thank you very much Sam. I'll file the form and make you an electronic payment later this afternoon."

"Take care, Jonathan and I'll be in touch." Sam left through the exit to the common room. She turned right toward the exit walking by a bulletin board mounted by the kitchen. Posted there was an article on an experiment done at the local university. It showed a photograph of three scientists standing by a large collection of scientific apparatus. The caption described the project and also identified the man in the picture as a university professor leading the study. Sam had to look twice at the scientist to convince herself that it wasn't Jonathan. "Wow do they look alike," she thought.

Jonathan read through the contents of the envelope. This is very nice he thought. Sam does good work, but she is expensive. And she asks too many questions. I will have to keep an eye on that. He logged into the bank account that covers operating expenses and made a transfer to Sam's account. As he made the payment, he realized that she certainly knew a lot about CUS. If she would just join, then dealing with her would be straight forward. If we had a member who does books, I could part with her. But Sam knows how to move money in ways that keep auditors happy. She keeps suggesting things I would never think of. As long as I need that help, she would be hard to replace.

Harold never knocked and just walked into the office. "Hi son. Was that Samantha Hendrix I saw leaving?"

"Yes. She dropped off the latest accounting reports."

Harold paused before responding and studied Jonathon's face. "She is a very attractive woman. I hope you aren't having thoughts about her. You know the MUTs are preparing for our departure. I don't yet know when that will be, but it could be soon."

"Don't worry Dad," Jonathan assured him. "My eyes are entirely on the ball."

"Glad to hear that, son. Very glad. CUS is coming to an important juncture. I need you with me." Harold gave his son a long stare intended to send a message.

Jonathan wondered what that message was.

Lecture on Change

Thomas' public lecture was scheduled on an early June Saturday; the last of such lectures for the school year before summer break. He purchased a new, more formal belt of smooth black leather and he polished his black shoes to partner his usual work attire, slacks and a button-down forest-patterned shirt. The hour-long talk was scheduled to start at seven, so he left his house at five and walked to campus. Upon arrival, the audio-visual technician took his USB flash drive with the talk and turned on the projection system. Thomas was experienced giving presentations at the University, so he was compliant while the AV tech spent several minutes going over the system's operation. "Can't have any technical hiccups during a public lecture," she explained. Hearing nothing he didn't already know, Thomas zoned out and hardly heard a word the woman said.

The microphone and remote control tests worked as expected, so Thomas went backstage for a glass of water. He had given a lot of talks during his career, but few to a general audience. Even after extensive effort he still had an underlying fear his talk was too technical. "I should have done a practice talk with Tanya and Mark," he thought. Unconsciously sipping his water, he hoped his nerves wouldn't snap during the coming hour-long wait. Fortunately, Adrian, the postdoc on his team, found him a few minutes later and asked how he was doing. A bit of small talk with the postdoc was just the distraction Thomas needed. The event organizers opened the doors at six thirty and the auditorium began to fill up.

The final minutes before the talk were excruciating, but finally after a pitch by the Dean of Arts and Sciences for the University's fund raising efforts and a brief introduction by the Physics and Astronomy Department chair summarizing Thomas' career, he ascended the steps to a round of polite applause. Thomas did not have to work hard to build their enthusiasm.

"A number of physical constants define our Universe," he began. "The speed of light, the mass of an electron, the strength of the electrical force are just a few of these. Theories that try to explain the Universe in one mathematical description, for example string theories, or theories including extra dimensions, or theories that explain the expansion of the Universe, allow for the variation in time of these quantities that we otherwise consider to be constant. If we can see variation in one of these constants, it could point to an all-encompassing theory that describes the Universe."

Thomas paced back and forth across the elevated platform. He chose to do without a lectern, and although there was a stool at the back edge, he was effectively without obstruction in front of the audience. He remotely advanced his projected slides and used a laser pointer to describe the graphics.

"My research attempts to answer a specific question; does the electric charge change with time? If it does, it must change very slowly otherwise we would have noticed it by now. Therefore any experiment attempting to find

such a change must be very sensitive to small variations. We reach the required sensitivity using the precision of lasers. Atoms consist of negatively charged electrons orbiting a positively charged nucleus. As understood by quantum mechanics, the electrons cannot reside in just any orbit around the nucleus."

Thomas projected a cartoon of an atom and slowly began to describe its structure.

"There are only specific orbits that are possible. Scientists usually refer to these orbits as atomic states. Each possible state is defined by a specific energy. That is, the atom must gain or lose energy to move an electron from one state to another. If an electron moves from one state to one of a lower energy, it will emit light. That ray of light will have an energy equal to the energy difference between the states. If a ray of light of a specific energy impacts an atom, it might move an electron to a higher energy orbit."

Thomas stopped for a second to take a drink from the water bottle the AV tech left on the stool. Although the earlier nervousness had made him thirsty, he now was getting into his groove. This wasn't that different from the hundreds of other talks or class lectures he had given. The audience was enjoying themselves. He had this and he knew it.

"Laser light has a very specific energy, hence the light source can change the state of an electron. Because the energy is so well defined, we can be specific about which state we move the electron to."

He scanned the audience; only a few people were nodding off or acting distracted. Most were attentive. His confidence continued to grow.

> *"Similarly, when an electron moves to a lower orbit, we can measure the energy of the emitted light. From its energy, we can precisely determine which excited state fell back to which lower energy state. Our experiment is designed to measure the energy of certain transitions that depend strongly on the value of the electron charge. We then compare it to a reference transition wavelength that is not so sensitive to the charge. Hence if the charge changes, we will see the wavelength of the monitored transition change. In our experiment, which we call ET, we compare transitions in mercury to those from a cesium atomic clock. The construction of our experiment is nearly complete and we will begin taking data this fall."*

A young man in the front row, probably a student, spoke up. "Why don't the test-transition and reference-transition wavelengths change the same? I would think if they did, you wouldn't see any effect because the ratio between the two would be the same." Thomas was impressed with the student's recognition of the subtlety and enjoyed the engagement.

"That's a good question and that would be the case if the electrical force binding the electron to the nucleus was the only force involved," answered Thomas. "However, the electron and nucleus are moving and they spin. As a result, magnetic forces are also involved. This is a bit subtle so it will take me a while to explain."

Thomas wanted to be careful here as he knew the science was sophisticated. He didn't want to lose the connection with the crowd that he had so successfully established.

> *"The electrons in an atom can be in a number of possible states, each defined by a specific energy. The energy of a given state is determined*

by the force of attraction between the electron and nuclear charges. If that was all that determined the energy of each state, we would have the situation you describe. That is, as the electric charge changed, the energies of both transitions would change in the same way."

Thomas saw that this was getting too technical for his listeners, so he took another drink to let some of this sink in with his audience. As he drank, he watched their faces. He was losing a few, but most still seemed to be with him.

"There is a small correction, however, we need to include because electrons spin. Each spinning electron acts like a small magnet and the strength of this magnet depends, importantly, on the electric charge. This magnet, however, sees a magnetic field due to the relative motion of the electron around the nucleus. Since a magnet in a magnetic field also has energy, there is a small additional contribution that each orbit possesses. The size of this addition is different for different orbits. As a result, the energy of each state will depend on the electric charge differently and, if the electron charge changes, the wavelength from two different transitions will change differently. We pick two transitions for comparison that are very different in this regard so that the ratio will be sensitive to any change."

The student was nodding his understanding and many people in the audience were also responding positively. As Thomas ended his presentation, the applause was thunderous. The non-expert attendees understood his explanation of the difficult topic. Thomas thought to himself, He ended his presentation with a silent wish that the University administration was seeing this. He felt sure this was a successful evening.

Many people from the audience approached Thomas afterwards to compliment him or ask questions. While he was answering, Thomas noticed that a group of ten or so people, all sitting together, were wearing identical tan shirts. His effort to identify them was interrupted by the arrival of the department chair, DeeDee Champton, her hand extended and a pleased smile cracking her face. "Very nice job, Thomas. That is just what we want in a public talk. Science that is advanced enough to excite the community and described in a way that doesn't bury them in jargon."

"Thank you DeeDee. I'm very happy to hear you think it went well." She seemed absolutely sincere, without any of the trace of menace she bore in his dream. Thomas felt confident that he had enhanced his reputation at the University and therefore his chances for tenure.

"It did. You go relax somewhere to catch your breath. I know this has been a lot of work."

"I will. We have a group going to The Gulpers' Guild."

He detected a tiny pause as if waiting for an invitation to join, before she responded, "Enjoy," said DeeDee. As she briskly exited the hall, Adrian took this as her opportunity to join Thomas.

"She's right. You did do a good job. Now we just have to get the data."

"Yes, this fall will be important for us," Thomas nodded to his young colleague as he started packing his things to leave. As he patted his pockets trying to remember where he set down his laser pointer, a voice sought his attention.

"Professor Conrad, my name is Carl Jackson." He was well-dressed, physically fit with coal-black skin. "Do you have time for a short chat?"

"Certainly Carl, how can I help you?" Thomas recognized him as the young man with the insightful question.

"Well I started graduate school last fall. I recently passed my qualifying exam and now I'm ready to start research. I want to pursue experimental science and I am fascinated by your experiment. I was wondering if you had space for a student? I'm going home for the summer, but would like to get started when school starts back up."

"Yes, actually. Our team is only three people at present. Myself, Adrian here who is a postdoc, and a senior student who will graduate in a year or so. Now is a perfect time to join."

As they spoke, Thomas considered that hiring this African-American student would not only improve his team, but would likely also be good for his tenure case. His team would then have two women and a black man. That would not go unnoticed. As soon as he thought it, Thomas felt a bit ashamed considering demographics; The kid asked an astute question. He is clearly very smart.

"Why don't you have your academic records sent to me and let's meet when schools starts in September for an interview," suggested Thomas. "If all looks to be in order, we'll discuss the details of the work. We plan to turn on the apparatus then and it will be a good opportunity to see it running."

"Great. I'll be back just before classes start."

"Perfect, we'll see you then."

"Good to meet you Carl," added Adrian as she ex-

35

tended her hand to shake his and the small group broke up.

Almost no one was left in the hall by that time. "Thanks for coming tonight, Adrian," said Thomas. "Your support was kind and helpful."

"Of course, I enjoyed it. Plus I'm looking forward to the The Gulpers' Guild," she smiled. "Hope Carl works out, he seems sharp."

Love Changes Things

Thomas savored his Maker's Mark, swirling the liquid over the single square of ice. The Gulpers' Guild, was a dark wood-paneled sports bar with extensive memorabilia distributed along the walls and ceiling. The numerous TVs had a variety of sporting events; soccer from South America, track and field trials, and, of course, many baseball games. Thomas was focused on the center screen, two long-time rivals were battling. Adrian and Kathy, the graduate student on his team, joined him for a post-event celebratory sip, but they didn't share his interest in baseball. The game wasn't enough to keep them in their seats and left when it went into extra innings. He didn't plan to sit there drinking till nearly midnight, but it was an amazing game. Both teams scored multiple times in overtime but still, inning after inning was required. Seventeen and counting. Good thing he could walk home from here as the drinks were taking their toll.

Even while focused on the game, he felt a commotion at the bar. Wow, that bright yellow sun dress could not be much tighter and the contrast with the dark wood decor made for a dramatic highlight. She was tall even in her casual slip-on shoes. Her shoe color matched the dress, which told Thomas something, although he wasn't quite sure what. She was leaning on the bar rail, waiting for her order. That she got so close to his seat without him noticing only spoke to his love of baseball or, if he was more

37

honest with himself, his inebriation. She was nearly as tall as Thomas, and her long blond hair suited her height. He was staring at her so hard, he didn't even notice that she had turned and was looking at him. When she raised her drink in his direction, he turned red. "Thank God, I am drunk enough to respond by raising my own drink," was all he could think. When she stepped toward his table, his heart skipped and he straightened in his seat.

She leaned in to speak; he noted her lips were freshly touched with rose. "Didn't you give that public lecture at the University this evening?" she asked.

"Yes, I did. Were you there?"

"Absolutely. I loved it. For a non-technocrat like me, it was very enlightening. My name is Samantha, by the way, but everyone calls me Sam." She took an open chair at the table.

"Hello Sam," Thomas responded. He sat up straighter still and nervously swept the crumpled napkins and the plastic sabers from Adrian's Singapore sling aside. "Thank you very much for the review. Usually such feedback is hard to get. It's only the other scientists who ever comment."

She ran her middle finger along the rim of her martini glass before grasping the stem to raise a salute and take an appreciative sip. She made a perfunctory glance around at the hockey sticks and baseball mitts adorning the walls. "Interesting place, The Gulpers' Guild. But why are you here by yourself?"

"Top of the eighteenth inning," he replied nodding to the screen. "My friends weren't as enthused."

"Got it." Sam reached across the table, casually placing her hand on top of his. "I like a lot of games Love, but baseball isn't one of them."

Thomas turned his hand over so that they held hands. "Would you like another drink?" His heart was racing and he decided this day couldn't get much better.

Sam picked up her glass and tilted it toward Thomas. "I just ordered this cosmopolitan, so I'm good."

Thomas caught the bartender's eye, picked up his glass and tilted it. The bartender nodded and pulled the bottle of Maker's Mark off the shelf.

"Do you think the electron charge might actually change?" she asked.

"Who knows," he answered. "To make progress understanding the Universe, you have to keep testing what you think you know. This is one way to do that. Since some theories predict such things, it seems like a good place to look."

"Have you thought about how the world would be affected if the charge did change?"

"It's not like I am trying to make the charge change. I'm just trying to see if it does. It is also clear that if it is changing, it must be very small and slow. Otherwise, as your question suggests, we would see effects in various places. But let's not talk shop. Tell me something about you. What do you do?"

"I'm a financial manager by education and an accountant by employment. Rather boring actually. I help keep track of the money for businesses or organizations. I usually do project work and am self employed from that view. At the moment I have a number of small clients with about half my time going to a local religious non-profit."

The collective groans and cheers by the few remaining patrons drew Thomas' attention back to the TV. A walk-off RBI single ended it. Thomas had to smile at himself. He had lost track of the game while talking to Sam. "Well the game is finally over," Thomas declared. "And The Gulpers' Guild closes in a half hour or so. Don't suppose you'd like to get out of here, would you? I'd certainly like to see where this conversation leads."

"Love to. What did you have mind?"

"I live within walking distance. One of attractions of this place. We could head over there."

"If you live in this neighborhood, you must have a nice place. I'd like to see it."

The ten minute walk to Thomas' front door seemed to pass instantly. As he was getting ready to insert the key, he leaned in and kissed Sam. She responded so strongly, that Thomas was enthralled. He knew his courage tonight was likely driven by Maker's Mark, but his every move seemed to be the right one.

They broke apart long enough to enter the house. Sam took a few steps into the living room, illuminated by a single table lamp. Everything was in its place. "Would you like a drink?" Thomas asked.

"What are you going to have?" Sam was idly perusing the titles on the coffee table.

"I think I will have a cup of tea. I think I've had enough for one evening."

"That sounds good. I'll have some too. But can you point me to the little girl's room?"

"First door on the left down the hall."

"Back in a sec." She touched three soft finger tips to his throat above his wilted shirt collar and laid a soft feather of a kiss on his lips; Thomas was raising his hand to touch hers, but she flitted away.

Thomas set about brewing the tea and still not believing how well this was going. Once the water boiled, he filled a pot with a chamomile-loaded infuser. He grabbed two cups and went back to the sitting room. While the tea steeped, Thomas turned on Tidal and selected a soft jazz playlist. Then he sat down on his couch.

"I'm back." Sam filled the doorway and Thomas sighed as he gazed at her form. "You really do have a nice place here. For a single guy, you have great taste. I was expecting cinderblock shelves and a mattress on the floor. But your décor is sophisticated, tasteful. The art work is also excellent. I recognize a few of the artists. Good job Thomas."

"Thank you, I do like this place. The ambiance helps me unwind. I think the tea is ready."

Sam walked toward the couch and left her shoes near the coffee table. She then sat down right on Thomas' lap, put her left arm around him and spun so her legs were across the couch. She leaned forward and whispered in his ear, "the tea does smell good."

He turned his head so they could kiss. It was a hard passionate kiss that brought his senses to full alert. She circled her other arm around him. She had a faint floral scent and her lips were gentle and silken. Thomas' right hand was on her knee and it instinctively knew it should softly caress her leg. He slowly moved his hand up the inside of her leg, shocked at how soft and smooth her skin was. She adjusted so that her legs slightly separated. The subtle move was so enticing that Thomas nearly lost control. Even though he wanted to just roughly grab her, he kept his composure and slowly inched his hand upward. When he reached the top of her inner thigh, he realized she wasn't wearing underwear. These continued surprises, not quite lewd but definitely erotic, overwhelmed him. He stood, lifting her with relative ease and carried her to the bedroom.

Thomas woke the next morning and turned his head to look across the pillow. Sam was still asleep and only partially obscured by the bed covers. Her blonde strands were tousled, and her eye makeup was smudged. Neither one of them slept much last night. "She is absolutely beautiful," he thought. "If I have a girlfriend, will the distraction keep me from the focus required to get tenure?"

Sam opened her eyes. She smiled at him and put her hand on his chest. Slowly she slid her hand down his torso and clasped his groin. "Shall we spin one again, Love?" she cooed.

As Thomas leaned back to enjoy what was coming, he reconsidered. "Then again, maybe having a girlfriend will center me and improve my focus at work."

Sam liked Thomas' yogurt breakfast, and said that the cappuccino was a treat. "I need to get home. But how about if I pick up some things at Whole Foods and we cook dinner here tonight? Thai Holy Basil"

"That sounds great," replied Thomas. "Can I give you a lift to your car? You must have left it near The Gulpers' Guild."

"Oh no. Like you I live not too far from here. A number of my clients are in the business district around the U. So it's convenient to live in the area. I can be home in fifteen minutes and the walk will do me good. Shall we say six?"

"Six it is." They shared another long kiss as she walked out the door. Thomas realized he hadn't looked at the clock. What time is it anyway? He wondered if he was late.

Baseball Never Changes

Thomas arrived at his lab in Grunderson Hall a bit after eight. He put his lunch in the fridge, set the box of scones he bought at the Brewers Cup on the counter, and started a pot of coffee. He had been seeing Sam now for over a month and was feeling optimistic. He was gradually becoming convinced that his new life-work balance was a good thing. He smiled as he planned his day. The next goal was to make sure the chamber that housed the optical resonator held vacuum. He was organizing the various tools, pumps, gaskets, bolts and gauges needed for the job when Adrian and Kathy came in.

"Morning you two," Thomas said.

"Good morning," they replied as they too put personall items away. The two women cheerfully poured cups of coffee and grabbed scones, thanking Thomas for the treat.

"What's the plan for today?" Thomas asked them.

"I am making good progress on the data acquisition software," answered Adrian. "There's a bit more work to do on the data blinding algorithm and the output files plus I want to make sure the keys are correct and are hidden properly. Hopefully within a week or two I can proceed through a complete checklist of computer commands, reads, and writes for all our hardware."

"Excellent," complimented Thomas. "And you Kathy, what have you got going?"

Kathy brushed scone crumbs from her lips with a cloth napkin. Her diligence on keeping the lab free of dust and dirt was omnipresent, especially when eating. "I am verifying my analysis code properly reads in the data files that Adrian's acquisition code produces. I'm also doing some more tests of the analysis with simulated data to confirm we're calculating correct uncertainties and central values. I will be writing some online analysis code for Adrian to add to the acquisition so we can quickly tell if everything's working. It's looking good and soon I'll just be adding bells and whistles."

"This is getting really exciting," effused Thomas. "The last laser we need should arrive in September and we should be ready to start very soon after that. Thanks to your hard work, we are well ahead of the game. It will be an exciting fall." He raised his coffee mug in salute.

"Well, it was all three of us, Thomas," said Adrian. "We've been at this for four years with you, and you're right, it is exciting."

"Yes, and the three of us deserve a reward," announced Thomas. "I have bought tickets for our third annual baseball outing to a Cow-Tippers game. Tickets are for Saturday's game."

Both women groaned. "Again," sighed Kathy. "You know baseball isn't our thing."

Adrian raised her hand and pointed her finger weakly to the sky. "Yay. Go Cow-Tippers."

"Perhaps, but it's a chance for us to connect over an activity that isn't work related. We'll have fun. The ballpark's beautiful, I promise good weather, the food is good but not too expensive, and I reserved the same seats we've had the last two years."

"OK, I admit that the brats at the park are really good, especially considering how small the venue is," said Kathy.

"And we get Corn Silk Ale," said Adrian. The local microbrewery, Corn Belt Brewery, won the concessions bid at the park and was popular with the team. "Support our local small business!"

"Most importantly, you will get a chance to meet Samantha," said Thomas.

"Can't wait to meet the woman who tolerates your affliction with baseball," joked Kathy.

"I am looking forward to it. I think you all will like her. She's smart and fun. She should fit right in with this group," concluded Thomas.

Adrian pulled her MG Spider into a parking spot of the stadium. She had inherited the sports car from her uncle; it had some minor rust and the transmission was a little balky, but driving it around the campus let her feel, as Kathy put it, "wicked cool". As the two women exited the vehicle, they felt the envious gaze of other game attendees. They strolled nonchalantly to the will-call window. The day was warm enough for tank tops, shorts and flip-flops, although they carried light sweaters for the anticipated cool-off when the sun set.

"Here we are. Another baseball outing with Thomas," moaned Adrian

"I know, right?" answered Kathy. "The third time. It wouldn't be so bad if this was a real baseball team, but double A? It's almost amateur hour."

"At least today, we have a more entertaining game: check out the girlfriend." Kathy grinned at Adrian.

"Thomas is a decent looking guy with a good job, so it'll be fun to see who landed him," offered Adrian.

Thomas bought game tickets the previous two years and he always bought box seats on the first base line close to home plate. This ensured that the modest press box tower behind home plate shaded them. An appreciated choice for his companions on this hot and humid July early evening.

They picked up their tickets and passed through the turnstile. A man was hawking programs. "Do we want a program?" asked Kathy.

"No, Thomas will buy one and I certainly don't need one. Let's grab a couple beers and then find our seats."

As they descended the steps off the concourse toward the field to the box seats, they saw Thomas and a woman in the two aisle seats, in close conversation. Kathy and Adrian stopped to watch. "Wow, that must be her. She is quite the looker, huh?" commented Adrian.

"That blue tee sure contrasts perfectly with her blond hair. Think she actually likes baseball, or just Thomas?"

With a short laugh, Adrian responded, "I'm guessing both. With looks like that, she could get a guy to do whatever. She wouldn't go to a game unless she wanted to."

They moved down the remaining steps and reached their row. "We're here," said Kathy.

"Hi guys," said Thomas. "Kathy, Adrian, this is Sam. Sam, this is Kathy and Adrian."

"Very glad to meet you," said Sam. "I have heard a lot about you two and the experiment, so I feel like I almost know you."

"Hmmm," hummed Adrian. "I guess we have a lot to ask you about then. Thomas hasn't said much about you other than you exist. So we have some catching up to do."

"Grab your seats, it's getting close to game time. I see you have already got beers, also, so we're set for at least a few innings," said Thomas. He stood in the aisle while Sam shifted slightly in her seat to let the two women pass. Adrian sat beside Sam and settled her bag at her feet. Kathy nudged her, and Adrian glanced to see everyone stand.

The small talk was interrupted by the public address system announcing the name of a local high-school trumpet player who was walking toward the pitcher's mound followed by the ROTC color guard from the same school. They performed a marched pirouette as they positioned themselves to face the center field flag poles. The standing crowd was impressed with the trumpet player's rendition of the Star Spangled Banner. Per local tradition, the crowd's cheers crescendoed with the line 'the land of the free' and continued with enthusiasm to the end. Their cheers were followed by an umpire yelling, "Play ball."

The game started slowly. The first inning was sloppy with a couple of errors and base running mistakes. When it finally ended Thomas announced he was headed to the restroom. As Thomas left, Sam leaned across Adrian and said, "Kathy, Thomas tells me you are doing the analysis for the experiment."

"Yes," Kathy replied. "It's going well, at least on simulated data."

"How do you know your result is right?" asked Sam.

With the more serious question, Kathy shifted to face Sam. Adrian felt awkward, hemmed in between the two; she couldn't raise her arm to sip her beer without jostling one or the other. "We have lots of cross-checks and the actual answer is hidden from us until we are done making sure everything is good-to-go."

"Have you heard of the Changing Universe Society, Kathy?" asked Sam.

"I don't know much about them, but they have a bit of a presence on campus. I heard there was also a group

47

of them at Thomas' talk."

"You should keep an eye on them," warned Sam. "They have strange views on the constants of nature and they are paying close attention to your experiment. I encourage you to get the result out quickly."

Kathy shot a glance to Adrian, who asked, "Have you said that to Thomas? He's the boss. If there is a PR issue, he should know."

"Certainly I've told him, but I think it deserves emphasis." Adrian shrugged; she did not relish the idea of emphasizing an issue that the *girlfriend* brought up.

Kathy went back to the schedule. "We plan to start taking data in late September. We'll run for three months, meaning we should be ready to publish early next year. That's pretty fast."

Sam nodded, then leaned toward Adrian. "So Adrian, what's your role?" Adrian sipped her beer before answering. She found Sam's gaze to be as intense as their lab's lasers.

"Kathy is the computer genius especially with the complicated statistical techniques, so I have focused on the computer control of the electronics that do the work of the experiment. I produce the data files that Kathy analyzes. And I hide the answer from her, so she can't cheat." Adrian looked over her shoulder at Kathy with a big smile.

"I can certainly see why Thomas speaks highly of you two," said Sam. She seemed like she had more to say but at that point Thomas returned with an immense bag of peanuts in the shell. They passed the bag between them, biting the shells and tossing the husks to the floor under the seats, while the next four innings played out.

"Woohoo!" exclaimed Thomas. "A pitching duel!" He adjusted his cap excitedly. He wore a battered Cow-Tippers souvenir cap that contrasted with otherwise-tidy appearance; he wore a pale-yellow collared shirt and long khaki cotton shorts. He explained that the number of grounders and fly balls early in the pitch count made for a quick pace. "This pitcher for the Cow-Tippers has been great this year," said Thomas. Although he wasn't sure his companions cared, he continued. "He has an amazing ERA and I bet he gets called up. If not the big league, then at least to triple A."

Almost as soon as Thomas made this compliment, a loud crack ruptured the quiet chatter of the crowd and the ball looked like it was shot out of a cannon as it sped toward center field. At the warning track, the fielder leapt and caught the ball before it could cross the wall just at the 410-foot label. The crowd stood and cheered as the home team came jogging off the field. " I should mention that the center fielder is pretty good too." His companions giggled at the clever recovery.

Adrian stood. "I'm getting hungry and I'm going for a brat. Anybody want anything?"

"I'll take one and another beer, please," said Kathy.

"And me," added Thomas. "Beer and brat."

"Me too," said Sam. "It's hot out here and those peanuts were salty, so I'm also ready for another beer. I'll go with you. That sounds like a lot to carry."

"That's four brats and four Corn Belt lagers," summarized Adrian. "Back in a sec."

Thomas stood in the aisle to let the two women pass by. Sam gave Thomas a quick kiss as she passed. As they walked up the steps, Adrian quickened her pace to be even with Sam and said, "I love your top. Where did you get it? I thought it was a T-shirt when I saw it, but the material is certainly not cotton. The color is so vibrant."

"Thanks, I get most of my clothes from a couple of online stores that I've grown to trust over time. I've ordered enough now that I am confident about sizing and the online color displays are actually pretty good. It's so much easier than shopping, especially for business wear."

As they got in the concession line, Adrian continued, "Well you certainly know what you're doing. The color really brings out your hair by contrast."

"That's nice of you to say. I was going to say how awesome you look. Those long legs of yours do justice to those daisy duke shorts"

"What would you like?" interrupted the concession worker, sparring Adrian the need to respond.

"Four brats and four lagers, please," answered Adrian.

"K. But I gotta tell ya, we just had to load the grill with a fresh batch," warned the acne spotted high schooler. "You're looking at a five to ten minute wait. Is that OK?"

"Sure," Sam responded loudly to be heard over the noise of the crowd and the play-by-play announcer. She nodded to Adrian and said normally, "We'll just chat for a bit."

They moved over to an empty spot along the wall to wait. Standing close, Sam reached out and touched Adrian's upper arm. "Thomas really appreciates the work you do in the lab."

"That's nice to hear. We are getting close to running and things have gone fairly smoothly. Everyone is in a good mood these days and really anticipating the fall."

"But what about you?" started Sam. "No boyfriend?" She removed her hand and looked directly into Adrian's eyes.

Adrian was distracted by the moves. She darted her eyes away from Sam's penetrating gaze, before responding, "Nope, no present relationship. I guess I'm not that socially active these days."

"I'm surprised. Someone as attractive and smart as

you are must have to fight them off. With your talents and good looks, you should have lots of options. Both with the boys and career."

Adrian chuckled self-consciously and returned her gaze to meet Sam's luminescent green eyes. "Thanks, but physicists don't make that much. I expect to do OK, but I don't think I'll be rich. I am counting on this coming year to get a good result and some exposure. With that, I hope I'll find a good spot somewhere."

"You looking for a faculty job?"

"I wouldn't turn one down." Adrian answered. "But the money and work/life balance are better in industry. So I'm considering both options."

"Ladies, your order is ready," called the server. While the kid charged Sam's card, she handed the beer tote to Adrian. She took the box of brats, grabbing extra mustard packets and paper napkins. "I'd like to get to know you better, Adrian," said Sam as they retrieved the refreshments. "How about we do lunch this week?"

"I'd like that." The young woman felt a glow of pleasure from the attention, and immediately felt she needed to veil her enthusiasm. "Thomas says you're a money whiz. Getting your take on my career options would be useful. Maybe we can combine a little business with our lunch?"

Sam put her hand on Adrian's shoulder and gave it a companionable squeeze. "Of course, it'll be fun. Let's plan on Friday. Let me give you my number." With her hand still on Adrian's tank top strap, Sam leaned forward to whisper it.

"Hang on, hang on!" said Adrian as she put the beer caddy on the condiments counter. She whipped her phone out of her back pocket and instructed the phone to add the contact. She held the phone to Sam who repeated the number, with her lips close to the phone's microphone and then said "Add date to calendar."

Adrian smiled and entered the time for the lunch on Friday. "It's a date."

As they walked down the steps, Thomas and Kathy were having an animated, and seemingly hilarious discussion. "What's so funny?" asked Sam.

"We were just commenting on how the Bisons were beating the Cow-Tippers one zip late. Seems a bit counter intuitive, don't ya think?" answered Kathy.

Sam smiled at the poor joke, but Adrian just looked a bit embarrassed.

As Sam and Adrian distributed the food and drinks, Thomas caught them up on the action they had missed. Adrian couldn't exactly follow everything Thomas explained and found herself lost in thought for the next few innings. But at the bottom of the ninth inning, with the Cow-Tippers down a run with two outs, a bloop fly to short right got the crowd standing again. The right fielder called off the second baseman while running up to make the catch. Characteristic of many double-A fields, the turf wasn't as flaw-free as an athlete might hope. The fielder stepped in a shallow divot and tripped. He fell about three feet from where the ball landed. "Did you see that! Did you see that?" In his excitement, Thomas lifted his battered cap to run his fingers through his hair before settling it back on his head.

The three women nodded their understanding. With this ray of hope, the crowd stood up in unison. Thomas continued, "The field, it's a double-A field, it's not smooth, it's..."

"Bumpy?" suggest Sam. He nodded. With this ray of hope, and only their second hit of the game, the Cow-Tippers were still alive. The crowd stood in unison, cheering loudly.

"Cow-Tippers are still alive!" screamed a fan to their

left. Someone in the stands started the Cow-Tippers chant, a bass lowing for five beats followed by a staccato "Go Tippers!" Caught up in the excitement around them, Thomas and his friends clapped and joined in the chant with enthusiasm.

The next pitch was a ball, but the following pitch landed deep in the parking lot that bordered the left field fence. The walk-off homer provided a moment of excitement, but the sudden ending of the game felt a bit anti-climatic. Some of the Cow-Tipper fans stayed to cheer some more, as this raised their hopes for nabbing the division title, but Thomas' group gathered up their sweaters and bags and headed out of the stadium.

At the parking lot, Kathy and Adrian thanked Thomas for the fun evening, while Sam reapplied her lip gloss. "Good night Kathy and Adrian. It was really nice to meet you," said Sam. As they separated to find their cars, Sam and Adrian hugged. "See you next Friday."

"Friday?" asked Thomas as he and Sam began their walk in the opposite direction.

"We're going for lunch." Sam answered. In the dark walk to the car, she led Thomas between a van and large pickup. She put her left arm around his neck and pulled him in for a kiss. With their lips locked, her right hand discreetly slipped through the back waist band of his shorts and squeezed his left buttock. She slowly eased the kiss and let her lips trail to his ear. She whispered, "Shall we go to your place?" she asked.

School Begins, Hope for Change

Wednesday morning, Thomas left his house and walked his usual route through the college town to campus. Oh, what a late-September fall day. It was just the right kind of warm. You wouldn't get overheated from a long walk, but there was no need for a coat. Unlike today, the weeks leading toward Labor Day were hot and humid and left his shirt sopping wet under his backpack. He picked up his usual black coffee at the Brewers Cup and continued walking up the street, smiling as he walked past The Gulpers' Guild. This school year was off to a good start.

Sam had cooked another great meal last night. Thomas savored having her as a dinner guest, twice this week so far, an exciting lifestyle adjustment. She matched baked salmon with the rice pilaf and wilted spinach salad and paired an excellent Cloudy Bay Sauvingnon Blanc that complimented the fish. The strawberries and angel food cake finished the meal off perfectly. They had finished cooking and eating by eight, leaving several hours for other pleasures, while still letting them get to sleep at a decent hour. Between the great sex and a good night's sleep, Thomas was more than ready for a day in the lab. Today, the team would start data taking and he was full of energy. "Life is good," he thought.

He always loved his morning stroll through campus, especially in fall with the excitement of the new school year. The students were glad to be back on campus, some because they looked forward to their classes, some because they looked forward to parties. Either way, Thomas figured, their enthusiasm made the University feel alive and electric. But it wasn't just the students. The mature trees and shurbs and bright green of the grass contrasted the red brick buildings beautifully. He really loved this place.

On his left, he skirted the edge of the University quad as he entered the garden area abutting Grunderson Hall, the building that housed the Physics and Astronomy Department. He noticed a gathering around a speaker outside the hall, which was not a common sight, so Thomas stopped to listen. The older man was holding court from atop a concrete planter wall and spoke to a small crowd standing on a grassy knoll in front of him. His hair was mussed, but his clothes were well pressed. His casual, yet presentable dress, seemed telling. The speaker wore a tan shirt but Thomas couldn't quite make out the emblem on the light blue arm band. Something about the attire reminded him of the group at his lecture last June, piquing his curiosity as to what the man had to say.

"There are a number of physical constants that define the Universe. These constants, never change. The electric charge of an electron, for example. The strength of gravity is another. But these constants must have the values they do in order for us to exist. A slight deviation and we wouldn't be here. Why *is* that? Don't you find that curious?" The old man paused for the crowd to nod in agreement. He continued.

"Take the value of the electric charge for example. If it was slightly smaller, atoms couldn't hold their electrons. If it was slightly larger, atoms would hold electrons so tightly that they could not be shared between atoms. Either way, molecules could not form and life would not be possible. We are composed of molecules and we only exist because the charge value is just right." Thomas could disagree with the man's basic explanation but he admired his folksy delivery.

"It's not hard to understand this once you realize that things were designed this way. Our Universe has been built and designed by intelligent Multi-Universe Travelers, or MUTs, as I like to call them. The MUTs knew exactly what they were doing. The Universe that we know didn't just appear by accident. The MUTs can move between the infinite number of universes that make up the Multiverse. They set the physical constants to values for our Universe to bring us into existence. The MUTs created us by designing this Universe we live in. This explains why the constants are what they are and why we are here."

Thomas sipped his coffee and rolled his eyes behind his sunglasses. Another Alien Invasion nutter. He counted heads in the crowd and estimated about fifty, with twenty-five people or so were wearing the arm bands. He eased closer to a young man wearing one so he could get a better look; it had an emblem of a small cartoonish space ship against a background depiction of the crab nebula. The organization's name was blazoned below the nebula. He was amazed at the number of people who followed this speaker.

As the sermon continued, Adrian walked up and stood next to Thomas. They exchanged nodded hellos and listened together. "Once the Universe ages to a point that the sentient occupants have reached an acceptable level of advancement, the MUTs harvest their creation and recycle the Universe. The MUTs will start to change the constants so that our Universe, in just a few years, will no longer support life. Soon, however, before the changing constants do their damage, the MUTs will come to Earth and collect all believers. This is the way the MUTs continue their line. We will become the next incarnation and prepare another universe to produce yet new lifeforms!" The arm-banded people began to applaud enthusiastically with murmurs of agreement.

The old man waved his hand for quiet from his followers and continued, "Join our brotherhood and you too will be become one of these MUTs. You will be saved and live in paradise in another universe. I am Harold Simpson and I have founded the Changing Universe Society to serve you, to deliver you to a higher existence. Join us and you won't perish in the coming apocalypse."

"What utter nonsense," quipped Thomas. "Who set the parameters in the MUTs' universe?"

Adrian smiled at the whispered wisecrack. As they turned to leave, Harold stared directly at them, although neither noticed as Thomas asked Adrian, "You're getting in a bit earlier than usual. Anything up?"

"No," she replied. "I saw a flyer for this rally a couple days ago and was interested. These kinds of groups put on quite a show and I get a kick from the free entertainment."

Entering Grunderson Hall, the two coworkers made a quick hairpin turn and started down the basement stairs. They walked down the hallway to door B156, which Thomas quickly unlocked. As they entered, Kathy was already working away. "Hi Kathy," Adrian said cheerfully.

"Hi you two."

Thomas loved this lab. He had built it over the last five years and it fit his every need. With the University's generous start-up package, he remodeled this space and assembled the equipment. A small National Science Foundation grant paid Adrian and Kathy's salaries, and of course, two months of his summer salary.

The lab was divided with a room within a room. The inner room enclosed all the optical equipment and lasers kept in perpetual darkness. The walls, ceiling, and pretty much every paintable surface was flat black. Two optical tables occupied the center of the dark room; they were heavy, being made of metal skin covered non-metallic honeycomb core. The surface of the tables was broad, four foot by eight foot with threaded holes on a two-centimeter-spaced pattern allowing for mirrors, lenses, sample chambers and various parts to be screwed in. Cables wound their way through sealed slots in the wall that separated this dark and clean space from the outer room where the scientists spent most of their time.

In the outer room, computers and electronics allowed the scientists to peer into the dark room and stay abreast of the experiment. This room had plenty of desks and cabinets. Shelves and drawers of this room stored spare optical elements, vacuum system components, and cables. Each member of the team had an ample desk and of course the toys and mementos collected over the few years they had occupied the space. By the door was the obligatory coffee pot and small refrigerator. Adrian and Thomas took their lunches out of their packs and put them in the fridge.

"I think we're ready to start this game," said Kathy, swiveling in her chair to face them. "Adrian and I have been retesting the systems over the last couple days and everything works just fine. The interlocks are working, so we can leave this room without worrying some idiot will try to enter the dark room when the lasers are on. We tested all the alarms."

"Right," interrupted Adrian. "We tested the alarm system several times, over three hours."

"You bet," continued Kathy, "If any of the systems fail, all three of us will get email and a text. We verified the uninterruptible power supply shut-down process works if the power goes out. The filters are working, so the dust levels will be kept below spec. Adrian's control computers and code are working flawlessly. I think we are ready for long-term operation."

"That's great, Kathy," answered Thomas. "I noticed that I got a lot of test messages recently. Did you document the cross checks?"

She nodded emphatically. "Everything is summarized in our electronic log book. I went through the procedure we developed and did the check off's as we planned."

"Let's do it then," declared Thomas. "Let's fire those photon guns." Kathy Dotson was a stellar graduate student. Thomas knew he was lucky she chose his project to work on. He trusted her, not only as a person, but as a collaborator. If she said they were ready, he was sure they were ready. The postdoc working with him, Adrian Treadwell, had graduated from a prestigious university in Germany. She had worked with Thomas for nearly four years and of course she needed a result for her upcoming job search as bad as Thomas needed it for tenure. Adrian had assembled the laser systems almost by herself. Working nights and weekends, she was a tireless scientist who really understood that doing things right the first time was the right way to do things. The two young women were certainly a key strength of his program. He knew the project would not be where it was without them.

Thomas and Adrian watched while Kathy went through the start-up checklist. One by one, switches were flipped, either literally or symbolically on a computer touch screen. Interlocks were set, doors were locked, lasers were turned on and warmed up, vacuum pumps started, source ovens heated, magnets for the atom trap were turned on. After an hour or so, the team rejoiced as the measurements began. Kathy pumped her fist in the air in triumph. Adrian gave the thumbs-up, but their celebration was interrupted by a knock at the door.

Adrian opened the door and found a young black man standing outside. "Hello Adrian. Good to see you again. I hope you remember me. We met at the lecture last June."

Adrian gazed at him blankly for a moment. He put out his hand, and said, "Carl Jackson. I'm looking for Professor Conrad." She stepped aside to let Carl enter and extended her arm toward Thomas.

"Hello Carl," replied Thomas as he crossed the lab and approached the door. "We certainly remember you. Come on in and thanks for coming by. We just turned the experiment on, so we're a little bit distracted and a lot excited. In fact, our ion beam is established and we should have trapped mercury ions anytime now."

Carl's face brightened with excitement as well - he understood the significance. "Excellent!"

Thomas guided Carl over to a series of posters that hung on one of the laboratory walls. "I know these posters don't do the lab justice, but the dark room is now locked up. We won't be able to go in there until we reach a stopping point. At least these pictures, you see here, are recent. This photo shows an oven that heats a mercury sample to boil off a few atoms into a gas," he explained.

"We then use lasers and a radio-frequency field to ionize those atoms. The resulting mercury ions then propagate down a vacuum line until they reach the trap. The trap is formed by a set of lasers that exert forces on the ions to keep them inside a localized region. We require very low electric and magnetic fields to prevent unwanted energy shifts. So there is a lot of electromagnetic shielding and sensors to monitor it."

Adrian then added, "We *also* use lasers to place electrons in those trapped ions into orbits that are sensitive to a changing charge. Then these ions are illuminated by yet another laser, shown in this picture."

Carl nodded pointing to the poster. "I get it. This laser is contained within a vacuum chamber to eliminate condensation."

"That's right," nodded Adrian. "It needs to be temperature controlled and vibration stabilized, so it gets its own optical table that has special thermal and vibration control systems. All that prevents variations due to effects other than a change in the charge. This probe laser must be extremely stable. If it varies, we might interpret that change as a variation in the charge."

Thomas waited for Adrian to conclude and then finished his overview, "Most of what you see of the apparatus in these photos is for monitoring various environmental or apparatus conditions to verify we aren't fooled by some spurious effect."

"We have ions in the trap and the probe lasers are on," Kathy announced from the control console. "The first data is now on disc and everything seems to be working just as we hoped."

The team joined her at the monitor to watch the data coming in. As the minutes ticked by, the team's euphoria grew. "All systems are performing as we expected," declared Kathy proudly.

"Yes, it's working," acknowledged Adrian enthusiastically. "This is probably the most exciting moment in my career. Soon, we will know something no one else does."

Thomas saw her eyes had teared up; he felt the same way and was smiling too hard to speak. He just stood there staring at the readout thinking about tenure. "The start to this school year has just been great," he thought.

"This is such an honor to witness this on my first day," said Carl. He shook Thomas' hand. "Congratulations, Professor Conrad."

Thomas grinned. "Team effort, Carl. Welcome to the Team!"

Mid afternoon, Thomas walked upstairs to his office on the second floor. He checked email and phone messages, feeling relieved that none required any immediate action on his part. He took a deep breath and started working on lectures for his class. His recent focus on the experiment left him a bit behind on class prep. This quarter he was teaching an introductory class in mechanics and kinematics. The freshman classes were always large, but the department would provide a fair amount of support. He had teaching assistants for grading, tutoring, and office hours. The three sections of the class were team-taught with two other faculty, and they agreed on the organization and material coverage. The University had a large engineering program and therefore a lot of students took physics as freshman. With three faculty teaching the class, the organization and material coverage was a team effort. All in all, it wasn't that onerous an assignment, although some of the students were not really ready for the material and some were a bit immature, a problem every year.

An email alert from Thomas' computer caught his attention. The subject line implied a speaking invitation, which intrigued him. "Dear Prof. Conrad," it began. "As organizers of The International Conference on Fundamental Symmetries, we invite you, or a member of your team, to attend and speak on your research during June of next year. The schedule will include only plenary talks with no parallel sessions. The conference will include an exciting scientific agenda but being in central Rome, the cultural opportunities are also rich. There will be an exhaustive companion program."

Thomas was surprised that they were inviting speakers nearly a year in advance, but he was really excited about the opportunity. A high profile talk just after his results will be ready and when he was in the middle of an upgrade to ET is just the sort of thing that tenure review committees would look for.

Thomas looked up from his computer upon hearing a knock. Adrian stepped through the doorway, "Do you have a moment, Thomas?" she asked.

She seemed excited and a bit breathless. "Certainly Adrian."

"I got this email from the fundamental symmetry conference this morning. I wanted to talk to you about going. This is just what I need; a high profile talk for my job search, especially if I want an academic position."

"I got a similar email, Adrian. I plan to go and speak on our experiment."

"Thomas, come on," Adrian said with exasperation. "You have given all the talks on ET. I need this opportunity."

"Adrian, I understand. Maybe we can find another meeting for you to speak at."

"This conference is the highest profile in our field. If I get a slot there, everyone will know who I am and what I've done."

"Yes, it is high profile," argued Thomas, "that is why we need to put our most senior person up front. This is my experiment and I should give the talk."

"Thomas, that isn't fair." Adrian was clearly angry and she raised her voice slightly. "I have been working fifty hours a week on this project for almost four years. ET is ready to run because of my efforts. Everyone in this field knows who you are. But I need to get some recognition."

"I'm sorry Adrian," Thomas stood firm. "I think I should give the talk."

Adrian glared at him for a long second. "Oh, screw this," she said while leaving the office quickly.

Thomas stared at the door for a time after she left. "She'll get over it," he reassured himself. "I'll work to find another conference where she can present." He turned his attention back to his class.

Celebration, No Unexpected Change

By mid October, Thomas was soaring high. With only four weeks of collection, the data were pouring in and the experiment was progressing as well as could be hoped. Theirs would be the most sensitive of any similar purposed project, and the physics community was full of anticipation for the result. In just eight more weeks, they would have their planned total of twelve and they would publish. They selected a specific length of time beforehand deliberately to control "researcher bias" - to eliminate the temptation to stop the experiment once they liked the result. Thomas knew that temptation had led to many biased results in scientific history. With that plan, Christmas couldn't come fast enough. They would have the data by then and the paper could be submitted soon after the New Year holiday.

Thomas felt his case for tenure was going great. He and Sam were doing great. The experiment was performing great. The team was happy and excited, albeit with some snark from Adrian. But physics dominated their lively discussions every day. It was all a dream come true for Thomas. He hadn't had that recurring nightmare since data taking started.

Like all scientists, Thomas knew that a working experiment was one of the best treatments for stress. His own team noticed his non-stop smiles and energy.

With everything so perfect, Thomas wanted to celebrate. He made reservations for dinner at one of the best restaurants in town, or least the best one within walking distance of the University and his house. The Cooked Goose was a great steak and seafood house. Thomas loved it, but so did everyone else. The food and ambiance were great, so even though the prices were outrageous, you had to plan a couple weeks ahead to get a reservation. The team members anticipated this night ever since Thomas let them in on his plans. "Dinner's on me. You've all worked so hard and I want to thank you in a tangible way," he had told them. The team left the lab early the day of the dinner with plans to meet at the seven o'clock seating.

Thomas made sure he arrived a few minutes early, but still Kathy and Carl had beat him there. Thomas added a tie and sport coat to his usual slacks and button down. Kathy and Carl, on the other hand, were quite the contrast to their usual attire. Kathy was wearing an elegant long dress, surprising Thomas that she even owned one. Carl was in slacks and turtleneck, a step up from the usual jeans and tee. Students usually only get to eat like this when their parents visit, so this night was special. After hellos and wardrobe compliments, Thomas informed the hostess. "Reservation for Conrad."

"Welcome, Mr. Conrad. Your table is ready, please follow me," she instructed.

Thomas didn't like the sound of mister, but it was his own fault for not making the reservation under his professor title. He waved to the students and they obediently joined him as they followed the hostess to a round table. The table was placed next to a window looking out on the restaurant's garden – an elegant setting. The three colleagues took seats, leaving the two next to Thomas empty. Kathy was looking forward to seeing Sam again and Carl couldn't wait to meet her. Although Thomas was rather private, Kathy and Adrian had offered some detail; the undergrad was curious to see the team leader's girlfriend. Kathy wanted to learn more about the woman who had distracted Thomas enough that he now had a life outside work.

When Adrian walked in, it wasn't just the Conrad table whose heads' turned. She was wearing high heels under a mid-length sleeveless dress that might be too cold for many to wear in October. The look was definitely stare-able and the restaurant clientele demonstrably concurred with that opinion.

"Hi, everyone," Adrian said as she approached the table, while the men rose slightly from their seats. Thomas had never thought of her as beautiful before, but now always would.

"Well, if I knew how good you three looked cleaned up," Thomas joked, "I would have offered to buy you dinner a long time ago."

"This restaurant is not casual dining," replied Adrian, "and we don't get to places like this very often. Such a dining experience obligates you to be part of the show."

"Right you are, Adrian," laughed Kathy. "This is very nice of you Thomas. What a great month this has been. ET running well. Weather has been great this fall. We have weekly entertainment on the quad. And Thomas has found himself a gal-pal. Definitely a time worth celebrating."

The waitress approached the table and asked, "What can I get everyone to drink?"

"I think we'd like to start with a bottle of Chardonnay," answered Thomas. "Glasses all around, but I'll need to look at your wine list for a minute."

She handed Thomas a menu booklet and after a few moments to inspect the group's drivers licenses, she turned her attention back to him. "Do you see something you like, or can I recommend an option or two?"

"No, I think I've got it. We'll try the Far Niente from Napa."

"Excellent choice. I will be back in a moment with the wine."

"Oh, we are expecting one more," added Thomas. The waitress nodded as she headed off to the wine rack.

Almost on cue, Thomas saw the hostess point out their table to Sam. As Sam saw the table, she exchanged smiles with him. She was wearing a mid length floral print; as always she attracted attention as she crossed the restaurant. Thomas' table seemed to be the center of attention tonight, an ego boosting experience he didn't have often. As Sam approached, Thomas stood, told her how good she looked, and gave her a gentle kiss on the cheek as they hugged hello. "Carl, this is Samantha, who goes by Sam," Thomas introduced. "Sam, this is Carl and you know Adrian and Kathy." Sam shook hands with Carl, gave Kathy a hung, gave Adrian a hug that almost seemed awkwardly long, then took the remaining empty seat.

"It is so good to see all of you," said Sam. "Thomas has told me so much, especially how great the experiment is going. It is a pleasure to meet you Carl. I hear you are upcoming star of physics."

"That was certainly nice of him to imply," Carl replied. "Thank you for the vote of confidence," he said with glance toward Thomas.

The moment was interrupted by the waitress returning with the wine. She poured a bit into Thomas' glass. He sipped it and nodded his approval. As glasses were filled, Kathy attempted to ask Sam where she bought the dress. Before she could answer, however, the waitress spoke up again. "May I quickly describe our special tonight and then I'll leave you to study the menu. We have a trout with garlic lemon butter herb sauce served with a side of butternut squash. Unless you need something else now, I will let you enjoy your wine and be back in a few moments to answer any questions regarding the menu and take your requests."

All six diners ordered a small salad to start, and as the waitress served them, they leaned back in their chairs to give her access to the table. Kathy's chair was situated such that she had the best view of the restaurant's garden. As she watched the salads being served, she scanned the attractive collection of plants through the window. There, walking from one of the outdoor tables toward the exit gate, was Harold Simpson and a young man Kathy didn't recognize. "My God," she exclaimed and pointed. "There goes that CUS guy whose been speaking on campus lately." Everyone turned to look where she indicated.

"Who is that with him?" asked Carl.

"That's his son, Jonathan," answered Sam. "I do the books for them. They are certainly an odd group, but they are nice."

"Odd?" asked Kathy. "I think they are a cult. They are way past odd."

"I don't know," began Sam's opinion. "They have some characteristics of a cult, but not some of the key negatives associated with that word. Although their views about Multi-Universe Travelers are crazy, I still think it's more of a new religious movement."

"You say crazy, but I think it's delusional. Their ideas are nuttier than the Church of the Flying Spaghetti Monster, and that's satirical," argued Kathy.

"Perhaps, but Pastafarianism has gotten some traction as a true religion. For that matter Scientology has been recognized by the IRS as a religion, and its views aren't exactly mainstream," countered Sam.

"You seem to know a lot about off-beat religions,

Sam," commented Carl.

"Of course I do," replied Sam. "I work for one. Once I heard their beliefs, I did some reading on cults and emerging religions. I wanted to make sure I understood what I was getting myself into."

The waitress brought by their entrees. The trout for Thomas, mushroom stuffed ravioli for Adrian, filets for Sam and Kathy, and a porterhouse for Carl. When the fourteen ounce steak was set in front of Carl, he was peppered with a number of appetite jokes. Thomas, noting that their toast had emptied the first bottle, ordered a second bottle of the Chardonnay, plus a hearty Chateau Pontet Canet to pair with the beef entrees. A second waitress helped serve the wine while their primary server set the plates and serrated knives. As the fresh glasses were served, Thomas raised his hands slightly, and said, "Bon Appetit!" After the brief intermission in the discussion, the topic returned to cult versus religion.

"Sam, the Changing Universe Society does have key cult-like qualities," lectured Kathy. "They have a lone primary leader who defines all they believe and is the only one who can communicate with their deity. He has no accountability to any higher authority and hence can dictate as he pleases. The members are very loyal, to a fault, and thus are very susceptible to exploitation."

"Boy Kathy," answered Sam. "You have done your homework also."

"Well the group is a big deal on campus and they have a sophisticated web page," said Kathy. "I'll admit I am assuming the loyalty thing, but heck they dress in a de facto uniform." Thomas thought Kathy was very animated by this discussion. He was a bit surprised how curious she was about them.

"OK, but there are many things that are not cult-like," replied Sam. "There is no evidence of any mind altering practices or control. All the members can leave anytime they want. There isn't any excessive monitoring or servitude of the membership. There is no requirement to cut any ties with outside friends and family. Simpson doesn't exploit the members for any sort of personal gain to the detriment of the members. He doesn't have a harem of wives, for example. Mostly it seems like a big happy club."

"Wait though," asked Kathy, "don't the members donate all their money? I heard a rumor to that effect."

"Yes, they do," answered Sam. "But they get a lot for that, so it's not obvious to me that it is exploitive. Here again, I think it's like a new religious movement. The donation is similar to a tithe. The money supports their commune, or church if you like. Each family gets a rather nice apartment and the facilities at the place are quality. They have long term facility planning and health care, which is definitely not cultish. It's almost like a quirky time-share. I work with many of the members but I'm not one. It's an interesting place, they let me come and go. Now, the members are so tied up in organization activities that they *are* effectively sequestered. Overall though, the living arrangements are good, people like it there."

"Well," quipped Carl, "whether they are a cult or not, their beliefs are out of this world. And that pun is intended."

"It doesn't really matter to me what you call their belief system," offered Thomas. "Their beliefs are just silly. How can they believe this stuff? And how did they just happen to settle on a belief system that parallels a science investigation in their own back yard?"

"The connection to your experiment is intriguing," commented Sam. "Perhaps, they did set up here due to the proximity to your work. The Simpsons moved here about three years ago, which is soon after you got funding and some publicity. Harold bought that complex soon after and then they started housing the following. I have to admit, in some ways the whole thing seems like a business adventure, however, I admit that it's their sincerity that keeps my cynicism at bay."

"But are we honor-bound to respect their beliefs?" asked Carl. "Can we ridicule them with impunity or is that inappropriate? I find it's fun to make fun of them."

"Boy, you are the embodiment of a gentleman, aren't you?" joked Kathy. The rapport between the two made Thomas wonder if there was more to their relationship than he was aware.

"I'm serious," Carl said emphatically. "The idea that some sort of entity creates and destroys Universes as a method of procreation just sounds ludicrous. It is very hard to resist the temptation to joke about it. So I want to know if it's OK, or is it just mean?"

"For me, I can't help making an occasional joke. The ideas are just too wacky," answered Thomas. "I agree we shouldn't go too far, but, come on, some of this stuff needs to be refuted. Appeal to ridicule is a logical fallacy, but it is effective in making a point. If such MUTs exist, why do they communicate with Simpson and only Simpson? How do they even communicate with him? Actually, the key question is, why did they pick him? Is he special?"

"And that's not all that's bizarre," added Carl. "How do MUTs cross universes? Why do they make and destroy them? Why do they only take a few people with them as they get ready to destroy the old one? It all seems so arbitrary. I don't see how Simpson has gotten so many followers."

"Don't judge them too harshly by their lack of science literacy," implored Sam. "They are a really just a nice group of people, who have a strange world view."

Throughout the evening's discussion, Thomas noticed that Adrian was very quiet, not her usual chatty demeanor. He leaned over and whispered, "anything wrong?"

"No, but I am feeling tired." she whispered in reply. She pushed back her chair and stood up and spoke to the table. "I think I will turn in early tonight. I am feeling a bit overwhelmed by ET. The experiment certainly is going well, but it's been quite a slog getting to this point. Now that things are stable, I think I'm having a bit of an energy crash. Thank you, Thomas for a great meal. It was very kind of you."

As Adrian stepped around her chair and began to replace it under the table, Thomas leaned in his chair to speak in a private voice, as the other guests voiced their good-byes, "Maybe you should take a day or two off, Adrian. You have been working very hard for an extended time. Maybe we'll have good news from the NSF the day after tomorrow and that will help replenish you."

"Yes, good luck on your visit," she said. "ET-2 is a good idea, I will be surprised if they don't fund it. Lunch, next week?" she asked Sam.

"Unfortunately, a lot of good ideas don't get funded these days," continued Thomas. "People have more good ideas than the NSF has money. So let's not count our Thanksgiving turkeys before they hatch."

"Lunch, next week?" Adrian repeated, keeping her gaze in Sam's direction.

"Certainly," Sam replied.

"You two are seeing each other?" Thomas asked.

"Yes on occasion," replied Sam as she watched Adrian leave.

Thomas was perplexed, though. Adrian was so down, he thought to himself. Even though she was excited about this dinner, she seemed disappointed. He wondered if something was wrong. She has been a bit off for a while. Maybe that conference talk was bothering her more than he had thought. Before he could think it fully through, the waitress appeared and asked about dessert. That topic got the group animated. It was clear they had all saved room.

The walk home was pleasant. Sam and Thomas walked slowly, hand in hand, enjoying each other's company. "I have to leave early in the morning for my trip to the NSF," Thomas started, "but it would be great to have you come in for a while."

"I wish I could, but I have an early appointment with a long drive. I should get to bed early," she answered. "But dinner was superb and I think it was great you did that for your team. I could see they appreciated it."

"I hope you're right," he said with a worry. "But I don't understand why Adrian was acting strangely. She seemed upset."

"Don't worry about it," Sam consoled. "I'm sure she had some personal thing come up that got to her. I doubt it has anything to do with you or the dinner."

"You are probably right," he conceded. "But it was out of character for her. Changing the topic, I was intrigued by your insights into CUS. You have thought deeply about them."

"Well yes," she admitted. "It's an unusual situation for me. I am still learning about who they are and what their goals are, but I want to make sure I know who I'm working with. When you handle the money, people assume you are responsible. In my line of work, you need a squeaky-clean reputation. I don't want to get tangled up in some sort of newsworthy event."

The couple arrived in front of Thomas' home. "I guess we didn't walk slow enough, we got here anyway and now the evening ends." Thomas pulled Sam to him and they shared a long, deep affectionate kiss enclosed in a comfortable embrace, rather different than the passion and urgency they usually experienced.

As Thomas entered his house alone, he thought back to that kiss. It clearly indicated a new phase of their relationship was beginning. He didn't know how to judge the development. He had spent so much of his life alone, he wasn't sure how to interpret these relationship signs. "Just enjoy the ride," he advised himself.

Funding Studies of Change

From his small college town, Thomas couldn't get a non-stop flight to DC. Feeling thankful that the mid-November weather was travel friendly, he changed planes in Chicago and then landed at Reagan National Airport in mid afternoon. Since this was just an overnight trip, he didn't have any luggage. Just a change of clothes and some toiletries in his work pack. He left the plane and walked through the terminal and took the pedestrian bridge to the Metro stop. The train arrived quickly and he took the short ride to the Eisenhower Avenue Metro stop in Alexandria. From there it was about a quarter mile walk to the Holiday Inn at Carlyle, where he would spend the night.

Just after Thanksgiving break the previous year, Thomas had visited the National Science Foundation program manager for Atomic, Molecular and Optical Physics when he had submitted his proposal for the upgrade to ET. The program manager implied he would likely support it, if the review panels were favorable. Over the course of the past year, the panels had met and his proposal was rated excellent by all the reviewers. Recently, the program manager told him NSF might be funding the effort and hence they'd like an update. They invited him to Arlington to discuss his plans.

Thomas spent the late afternoon and early evening in the hotel room going over the short talk he would give in the morning. He was satisfied with his Keynote slides, but did make a number of tweaks, mostly for clarity and sense. He knew the office staff would refer to his slides from time to time, when he wasn't available to explain details, and he wanted the document to be a useful reference. He removed jargon and acronyms replacing them with fully spelled-out phrases. He also made sure that the slides would stand on their own with full sentences and lots of embedded citations. All in all, he went through the slides several times making sure they told his story effectively.

After a few hours of the tedious and time-consuming work, the presentation was ready and he needed a break. He left the hotel and walked down Eisenhower Avenue to a sports bar. The baseball championship series was in full swing and he found a table with a comfortable view of one of the big screen TVs. He ordered a Maker's Mark, water, and a mushroom-smothered hamburger with an order of french fries. He then settled in for an evening of baseball.

The burger was excellent, but the game not so much. It dragged after the third inning, with one team making a never-ending string of errors. As he started his third Maker's Mark, he texted Sam. "Thinking of you," he wrote. "Anytime I watch baseball now, I can't help but think of when we met."

It was a fair while before she responded. "Too bad you're not here, Love. It'd be great to spin one."

Thomas smiled at that and sipped his drink, recalling the first time they spun one after the extra-innings game in The Gulpers' Guild. The game was getting more and more one-sided, so he left to return to the hotel before it ended. "Going to bed. See you tomorrow," he wrote back.

As he was walking along the sidewalk, his phone vibrated. "G'night."

Thomas woke at six without the need for his alarm to sound. That surprised him a bit given the time change for the East Coast. He had been sleeping really well lately. He wasn't waking to feelings of overwhelming dread. The nightmares had dissipated and he felt rested every morning. "How great success feels," he thought. He got out of bed and took a shower and dressed. He opened up his laptop to check for email. Nothing important this morning.

He headed downstairs to the hot breakfast the hotel provided. It wasn't spectacular, but it did satisfy. The coffee was better than he expected, but he always missed the Brewers Cup when he was on travel. After he ate, he went back to his room, brushed his teeth, packed, and then checked out of the hotel.

The NSF building was a few blocks back toward the metro stop along Eisenhower Avenue. Thomas was going to be a bit early, but that was OK. The security protocols would cause delay but there would be time for that. He had been here several times since becoming faculty, especially after getting his first NSF grant. Not only was there the occasional visit to inform the program manager about progress, like today's visit, but he had also served on review panels. He had been on two such panels in the last four years. He had a familiarity with the facility that came from those multiple visits. He pushed the elevator button for the floor that held the Office of Atomic, Molecular and Optical Physics - Experiment. He made his way to the office of the program manager, Fareed Raja.

"Good morning, Fareed," said Thomas as he knocked on the open office door.

"Hello Thomas," replied Fareed. "How was your trip?"

"Typical flight, no delays. So good I guess," quipped Thomas.

The office was fresh and spare, as if only occupied a short time since construction. Fastidiously organized, it was uncharacteristically devoid of books for a scientist. The shelves had a number of binders with label references to various project Fareed's office supported, but were otherwise empty. The desk had everything in its place and a coffee maker and demi-tasse set on the corner table looked pristine, as if they were only for decoration. Thomas was mildly surprised that the office hadn't filled up a bit more since his last visit.

"How is ET progressing?" Fareed asked. He was a slightly rotund but very well dressed man. In his late fifties, he had the body shape of one who spent too much time seated at a desk. His suits however were impeccable.

"It's going very well. We plan to stop the first data run around Christmas," answered Thomas. "We have looked at sensitivity trends and we get a weekly update as to the previous week's result. So we know how it's going. But we agreed to twelve weeks of running before our first public release."

"That is great to hear. I'm looking forward to hearing your upgrade plans." He then asked if Thomas would be open to sharing with colleagues from other NSF offices. Of course, Thomas agreed, and Fareed ushered him into a nearby conference room while he rounded up his peers. Once seated at the wood-grain laminated table, Thomas set up his laptop for the presentation. After a few minutes Fareed returned with two people in tow. He introduced Dr. Richard Kepler of the Office of Elementary Particle Physics and Dr. Joyce Carruthers from the Office of Nuclear Physics. With little to-do, Thomas began his presentation.

"Thank you for your interest in our research. Our present experiment, which we call ET, E for electron and T for time, can measure the transition wavelength to a precision of about about three parts per billion." Thomas clicked seamlessly from one slide to the next, and easily explained the project. "If we measure the wavelength to that precision over the course of a year, we will be sensitive to changes in the charge of about one part in twenty quadrillion per year. This precision is mostly set by how precisely we can tune our reference lasers to compare transitions in two different elements, cesium and mercury. A new development at the National Institute of Standards and Technology in Boulder, Colorado led us to realize that two transitions in ytterbium can be used to look for a change in the charge. This will eliminate some of the systematic uncertainties arising from normalizing measurements between two elements. We estimate we can get a factor of ten improvement in wavelength measurement resulting in a comparable improvement in the sensitivity of a changing charge. That is, we think we can get near one part in two hundred quadrillion per year."

"That was really clear, Thomas," complimented Joyce. "Thank you so much for that summary."

"Yes it was good," added Richard. "Although Fareed's office will be funding this, the results will be of interest to our fields. So we greatly appreciate you taking the time to come visit and describe your work."

"The funding decisions have all been made," said Fareed. "The support letters will be going out soon. I would assume you should see the funds early next year. We'll be in touch on that topic."

"Thank you all very much," Thomas said with some

relief. "It's been a very stressful year, but now that ET is running and with this great news about ET-2, it has been worth the struggle."

"Joyce and Richard have to go, but I'd like to discuss a sensitive topic with you, Thomas."

"Oh, OK. Sure Fareed," answered Thomas. Joyce and Richard departed and Thomas wondered what the sensitive topic could be - it sounded ominous.

"At the NSF, we are not sure what to make of the Changing Universe Society," begun Fareed. "It's unusual for a cult to build up around an experiment that we support. CUS has gotten a lot of press lately here at the NSF, especially because of the connection to your project. That is not the kind of press we want. If they are a harmless collection of science groupies, that's great. But this group has some sort of agenda and we worry it could end badly."

"I know all about CUS," responded Thomas. "I wish I could make them go away, but it seems they have developed a whole emergent religion based on the fundamental constants changing. They give speeches on the University campus frequently and we get calls and other inquiries from them. They seem harmless enough, but I admit they have a strange obsession."

"Whatever they are," warned Fareed, "cult or admirers, be careful with them. A good scientific effort can be ruined by the wrong kind of publicity. Remember how nuclear magnetic resonance imaging had to drop the word nuclear and become MRI. Even though it's obviously a nuclear physics process, the word nuclear just made people nervous and they didn't want the test. I don't want one of my better projects to get ruined by some side issue or bad press."

"I hear you," acknowledged Thomas. "We will be careful and not engage them. We can't control what CUS does, but we can control our own actions and responses to them."

"Thank you, Thomas," said Fareed. "I have a few minutes till my next meeting, let me walk you out."

As Thomas boarded his flight for home, he was flying high both literally and figuratively. His flight departed mid afternoon and he expected to arrive home mid evening local time. He couldn't wait. He was looking forward to seeing Sam. It had been a great trip to DC and the news about ET-2 couldn't have been better.

During his layover at O'Hare, Thomas took the chance to call Adrian. "We got the money for ET-2 Adrian," he said excitedly. "They tell me it will be in a financial plan during the first quarter of next year. We don't have to wait for the next fiscal year to start. We do need to do some paperwork, but we can start ordering parts by March or April, I bet. I can't get over how well this worked out."

"That is great news," she replied. "All the quotes are in and the longest lead item is ten to twelve weeks. We should receive all the equipment by about summer. It will only take a few months to assemble and test the upgraded systems. We'll be taking data during fall sometime. Good thing you hired Carl when you did. We'll need him."

"That's true, ET is going well so Kathy should have her dissertation data and be on her way." Thomas heard the boarding announcement. "Oh, I guess my plane is leaving, so I'll have to cut this short. I am so excited, I couldn't wait till tomorrow to tell you."

"Thanks for letting me know. It made my evening. Have a good flight."

"Bye," he said and hung up. He got in line to board his plane.

As Adrian hung up, a voice from her kitchen asked, "Who was that?"

"It was Thomas," Adrian replied. "We got the NSF funding. He's on his way home and will be here in couple hours."

"That is good news," was the reply. "It's good the NSF supports this line of research."

It was just about half past seven when Thomas arrived at his house, parking in the driveway. As he popped the trunk to get his pack out, he thought he saw something move along the side of his house. He took a walk across the lawn to get a good look down the suburban corridor between his and the neighbor's house. He didn't see anything out of the ordinary. Just the neighbor's unusually large cat jumping up on the wall between the two properties. Thomas grabbed his pack from the car and entered the house through the front door. The first thing he did after setting his pack on the table was to pop open a cold beer, a Mountain Standard IPA from Odell brewing. He took a big swig and then pulled out his phone to call Sam.

"Hi Sam, I'm back from DC."

"Welcome home, Love," She answered. "Did you get the news you wanted?"

"Yes! The NSF is going to fund ET-2. Its really exciting. ET is doing great and we will be able to start the follow-on soon after that experiment ends. A continuity in funding that will not be missed by the tenure review committee."

"Congratulations. That is really great. I'm proud of you Love," she effused. "You should do something to celebrate."

"Well that is why I called. I was hoping you would come over and celebrate with me. I have stuff for cosmopolitans," he prodded, almost pleading.

"Oh, Love. I can't tonight. I have an early morning meeting with a client and I still have some prep work to do. It's already getting a bit late. Can I take a rain check?"

Thomas sighed with disappointment. He knew how hard she worked, but he wanted to see her badly, to share his presentation play-by-play. "All the baseball playoff games have been tough on me."

"Oh, so your idea of celebrating is to spin one, is it?" she teased.

"Wait, it's not like that. I just really wanted to see you."

"Don't worry, Love," she consoled. "I was just messing with ya. Let's get together tomorrow. OK?"

"OK, see you tomorrow. Good night," he conceded.

"Good night, Love," she replied and hung up.

Thomas took a long sip of his IPA. He wondered if he heard relationship fatigue in her voice. They hadn't been together that long. If she was needing distance already, that didn't bode well. "I better ease up a bit," he thought. "I don't want to put too much pressure on her."

The Day Before Thanksgiving

Breakfast with Sam was always bittersweet, although today was a bit of a treat. Sam usually spent Thursday through Saturday nights at Thomas' place, insisting the other days had to be focused on work. She made an exception this week and spent Tuesday night, since they wouldn't see each other over the long Thanksgiving weekend. Thomas enjoyed the morning banter. But breakfast was also the symbolic finish to a very enjoyable evening. He hated to see it end. "My sister is having Thanksgiving dinner tomorrow. Sure you don't want to come? She's bummed that we have been seeing each other for five, six months now and she hasn't met you." He sliced avocado for Sam's whole wheat toast.

"Oh, that sounds great, but I've had long-standing plans for the weekend," she explained again. She was somewhat irritated that she had to explain again. "I am visiting some relatives up state and then visiting a couple of clients on Friday and Saturday. Sorry, Love."

"That's OK," Thomas replied. "But keep Christmas open. I bet that will be another opportunity to meet Tanya."

"You two must be very close."

He sipped his cappuccino and nodded. "Yes we are. My parents were killed in a car crash when I was seventeen. That was nearly twenty years ago, and she really helped me recover from that trauma. She is five years older than me, so she took over after the accident. She seemed to know when to be a sister and when to be a parent. I am very grateful that she was strong enough to see the two of us through that rough stretch. We still spend a good deal of time together. Though that usually consists of her, and her husband Mark, cooking me dinner. The relationship is still a bit one-sided, even at my age. A bit embarrassing, actually."

"I look forward to meeting her." Sam smiled, leaned over behind him and gave Thomas a kiss on his neck. It was the kind of kiss that made one consider skipping a morning of work. He watched disappointingly as she gathered her things. As she opened the door to leave, she gave him a quick wave, adding, "I'll be back Sunday, Love."

Thomas finished his yogurt and put the dishes in the dishwasher. He made himself a tuna sandwich, grabbed a pear and filled a small tupperware with vegies for lunch. He put his laptop, lab notebook and lunch in his backpack then headed out the door.

The weather was balmy for late November; the Brewers Cup had his order waiting for him soon after he walked in. As he walked across campus toward Grunderson Hall, CUS was holding another rally. "Seems like they do this a couple times of week," Thomas thought. "The crowds are still growing, though. This man must really have some appeal."

Thomas wasn't paying much attention, but, as he walked by, he heard Howard refer to *Oumuamua*. He couldn't resist stopping to listen in. Howard was recounting the story of Oumuamua, an asteroid that originated from somewhere outside the solar system and was observed traversing our neighborhood. A few scientists thought the object might be artificial; these were few, but their suggestions were thought provoking. Thomas found this asteroid fascinating and it intrigued him that Howard had latched onto it. Howard's claim of the day was that the MUTs were keeping on eye on us and Oumuamua was one of the tools they used. Thomas emitted an audible sigh when he heard that.

"Oumuamua is an object that was observed in October 2017 by a telescope in Hawaii called Pan-STARRS," stated Howard. "That telescope is designed to look for objects in the sky that are changing with time. It finds objects with brightness changes, or objects that move relative to other stars. Pan-STARRS has been very successful finding asteroids, comets and supernovae, for example. Presently, its focus is the search for near-Earth objects. NASA wants to identify any that might risk collision with our planet. They hope to identify such things a few years before they might collide with the Earth. That might provide enough time to react if necessary."

Thomas was impressed with Howard's command of the technical issues. "He must have some educational background in the sciences," Thomas concluded.

"Oumuamua is estimated to be about five football fields long. But the strange thing is, its width is only similar to the width of one football field. This dramatic oblong shape is very unusual for a large object. It is by far much more oblong than the most extreme examples found previously." Harold used animated hand gestures to emphasize the asymmetry in the object's shape. "It's shaped like a cigar!"

"The object is speeding and its orbit indicates it is not bound to our Sun. This object came from outside our solar system. Given our understanding of asteroids,

Pan-STARRS should not have been able to find such an object. They would be much too rare. Our understanding of how such objects might be created also can't explain the speed. You might say 'We just don't have a good understanding.' But that isn't reasonable. The dynamics of the creation is all determined by gravity, a very well understood process. What was seen was statistically very improbable. The observation of this object implies there should be a million more such objects than we would estimate." Harold stopped for a dramatic pause, shaking his head to make it clear that something was wrong with the accepted science of this object.

"If Oumuamua came from a star, it would have to have been ejected with an exceptionally large velocity. Again, this is statistically strange. This object is very shiny, ten times that of a typical asteroid. We would have expected our first observation to be a typical extra-solar object, not something strange. Why would the first interstellar object we see be such an outlier?"

Thomas wondered if the outlier characteristics made it easier to observe? "If this scenario wasn't so crazy, I might look into that," he thought.

Harold continued on. "But there is one additional mystery of Oumuamua that is really telling. This object had a small acceleration that deviated from what would be expected from gravity alone. It appears that it gave itself a thrust, somehow. Some claim that could be due to a gas pocket releasing after warming by the Sun. But no such *comet tail* feature was ever seen. That certainly is outside natural behavior."

Thomas was actually enjoying this. The technical discussion was clear and the conclusion that was coming was being well laid. Thomas did think that Howard was overplaying the probability card a bit, but he was making an interesting case.

"In fact some serious scientists, from Harvard no less, wrote a piece for Scientific American, a reputable publication, that this could be an alien probe. If so, it resolves all the oddities. If some far-away civilization sent the probe to us, it explains why such a rare event happened on our watch. It also explains the course correction that it underwent. Those of you who have been following my teachings know who would send such a probe. The MUTs are keeping an eye on us because they know the time is coming. The charge will begin to change and life will become impossible. The MUTs need to keep abreast of who their followers are. Oumuamua was one of their ways to watch us."

Thomas thought that went off the rails pretty fast. Great discussion of asteroid science that descended into extra-terrestrial science fiction.

As Thomas continued his stroll to the lab, his thoughts drifted to Adrian, his able post-doc assistant. She was an excellent scientist and Thomas was lucky to have her as a postdoc. She had been with Thomas almost since he was hired four years ago, a long time to serve as a postdoc. She had proved her worth in those years. She had the ambition of a person who was aware of her own talents. She had assembled and tested most of the apparatus. She was also an effective mentor to Kathy and a track record of mentoring students was a strong CV item for aspiring professors. Although the University allowed postdoc stays for up to five years, Adrian was ready to move on. Thomas knew she had been looking for a new position and was encouraged by the progress on ET. They had been taking data now for over two months and she could see the reward for her efforts coming into view. With anticipation of the impending paper, she had begun to put in additional effort on her job hunt. Thomas expected that she would confer with him over the job hunt. He knew that the presentation in Rome would have been a boost to her search, but he did not regret the decision.

In a moment of frivolity back when they had started the lab set up, Adrian had invented the name for the experiment, ET. She choose it not only because she loved the movie, but because the experiment was designed to search for a change in the electron charge over time; E for electron, T for time. The moniker had evoked eye rolling smiles among the nerd-appreciative science crowd, but it was successful. The scientific community competed in an unofficial contest to invent the most memorable mnemonic for a collaboration. The name could be clever or humorous or even an honorific. But it needed to evoke a particular team and effort to be effective. You wanted an audience to nod their recognition whenever your experiment was mentioned. A clever name could help with that. ET was a bit silly, but everyone knew you were referring to the experiment in Thomas Conrad's lab when it was spoken. The whole team, Thomas in particular, were happy with their label.

Adrian tended to work late into the evening and rarely beat Thomas to the lab. But lately, it seemed to happen a bit more often and she was already deep into her work when he arrived recent mornings.

As Thomas came into the lab, Kathy was reviewing the latest data from ET with Adrian looking over her shoulder and Carl studying the electronic log book for the past week. They looked up when he entered.

"Thomas," Kathy said with concern. "The last week of data shows a change. According to this, the electric charge is slightly stronger than it was a week ago."

"How far back do you see this?" Thomas asked as he put his lunch in the fridge.

"We have been taking data since the end of September, which is nine weeks. The first eight weeks were flat as a board. So now we have a hockey stick curve. It just started increasing over the last week." Kathy was speaking fast and nervously. She did not want anyone to suspect that the analysis was flawed That was Kathy's task and she was worried.

"How significant is the change?" asked Thomas.

"It is consistent with no change, but at a small probability," answered Kathy. "If it really is changing, the statistics will be clear in a week or so."

"It must be some sort of hardware problem," Thomas said to Kathy's relief. "Let's check the calibration and the laser performance over the past week," he instructed.

Adrian checked the calibration and found no problem. Kathy verified that laser power was constant as expected. Thomas looked at the extensive data records that continuously check the status of the apparatus and found nothing anomalous. Carl made graphs of all the environmental parameters of the dark room for the nine weeks of data. Nothing seemed amiss. The electric charge value found by the experiment was constant from the end of September until just a few days ago and then started to change. The day passed quickly as they performed the various tests.

"This has to be an experimental problem," Thomas said. "The change is not only fast and large, but it just turned on. Physics doesn't do that. The laws don't

91

just change one day." Thomas was perplexed. If the charge did change, it should have always been changing. It shouldn't just start.

He knew some theories saying that change happened in the past and then stopped. But nothing indicated that such an effect might just turn on some day. "Why would we just happen to be looking during the one day the change started when the Universe is a four trillion days old? We have only been watching for about sixty of those days. That is really improbable and just doesn't make sense. We will need to go over everything in great detail."

The room was very quiet, which was strange for this group. Usually, you had to interrupt to contribute.

After a substantial pause, Thomas finally spoke again. "This is very worrisome and disturbing, but it is getting late in the afternoon and I need to hit the road. I promised my sister I would come up for Thanksgiving dinner tomorrow with her family and some of their friends. I'm supposed to be there by mid evening tonight. I don't want to leave too late. I plan to drive back on Friday, so I guess we'll have to work on this more later. I will come in on Saturday and get started."

"I plan to have dinner tomorrow with friends and then a short road trip," replied Adrian. "But this is just too weird, I plan to come in over the weekend and look into things some more."

"I think I'll join you. Will you be coming in on Friday?" asked Kathy.

"No, I'll be in on Sunday, since I get back late Saturday," answered Adrian. "This is intriguing. It's probably some instrumental mishap, but it is also exciting. What if it is correct? Could be the scientific discovery of the century. We need to let people know about this ASAP."

"Don't get carried away with this, Adrian," lectured

Thomas. "Some component probably went south leading to a shift in some voltage offset somewhere. We're not booking flights to Stockholm any time soon." Turning his head toward Kathy, he added. "If you are available, I suggest we turn things off Saturday morning, remeasure all the offsets and baselines, do some cleaning and maintenance and then restart. We should have the system running again by Sunday evening sometime."

"Sure," Kathy replied, "but it still is exciting. I guess if we do find a problem it will be frustrating. But this really heats things up. Anyway, I'll make sure all the analysis is posted to our electronic logbook."

"Sure it's exciting, unless you were hoping for a quick result to publish for a tenure review." Thomas said while moving his gaze to Adrian, "or a job hunt talk." He diverted his glance to Kathy, "or a dissertation. I fear this could really slow us down." Everyone felt the foreboding fill the room as Thomas laid bare the career implications.

"I can come in on Friday," said Carl hopefully. "Is that OK, I really want to see how this gets resolved."

Thomas looked at Carl with a hint of annoyance and snapped. "Of course you can come in. In fact I would expect it. You are part of our team now, right? If you don't see yourself as such by now, you won't make it as a scientist."

Carl nodded, but didn't respond.

Kathy was struck by the acerbic tone in Thomas' voice. "That really seemed inappropriate," she thought. Adrian noticed the look on Kathy's face. When they made eye contact, there was an unspoken expression of disapproval.

The atmosphere of unease, with a touch of excitement, felt tangible in the room. All the researchers were fascinated by the result but they worried about what it meant for their careers. All four scientists were silent with their personal concerns for a moment. The second unusual silence in the afternoon spoke to the emotional toll the situation was extracting. Thomas glanced at the clock and gathered his work pack and papers; wishing his team a good holiday, he left the room with a grimace.

Conversation, Might Rules Change

Thomas was distracted on the long drive across the state. He was obsessed with the project and the aberrant result. The time passed quickly and it seemed only an instant passed before his arrival. He parked on the street in front of the familiar house, now lovely with mature landscaping. Large flowering trees were spaced across the lot, although their leaves were dropped this time of year. Tall evergreen hedges lined the driveway and property line, making a decorative border; Thomas meant to ask what they were, but never remembered once the conversation started. A large planter under the living room window held an arrangement of small pumpkins and vibrant mums. It was dark when he arrived and the backlighting made it easy to see Mark through the glass. He was fussing with some fall decorations on the coffee table. "This couple sure knows pretty", he said out loud to himself.

Just as Thomas was about to knock on the door, Mark opened it. "Hey there brother-in-law. Come on in," Mark cheerfully greeted. "How are you doing? We haven't seen you since your public lecture. It was great by the way. Sorry we didn't get a chance to talk afterwards, but you looked rather busy."

As usual with Mark, it was sometimes hard to contribute much to the conversation. Thomas wondered how long the man could go without a breath. "No worries

95

and thanks. I'm glad you enjoyed the talk," Thomas responded as they shook hands.

"Hi Thomas," Tanya called as she came into the room from the kitchen. She walked up quickly and threw her arms around him. "It's so good to see you."

"Yes, it's good to see you too. Been an odd week and it's nice to get away. Thanks for hosting this dinner."

"Come into the kitchen and have a beer. I have to finish up preparing some things for tomorrow. I'm trying to do what I can tonight. You know how busy Thanksgiving morning is for the cook."

Thomas struggled to fall asleep and it was two a.m. when he finally succumbed. As a result he slept in later than he had planned. Even worse, his nightmare, returning with a vengeance, was more vivid than before. Thomas didn't require expert advice to realize that the recent ET results revived his stress regarding tenure. Waking, he laid in the sweat-moistened bed and studied his surroundings. Tanya's guest room was furnished in a country style that did not provide the same comfort as his home's classic-modern style. His mind drifted to his last evening with Sam. The images were powerful, easy to hold his concentration. He could almost hear her say, "Do you want to spin one, Love?" He took several deep breaths as he gradually relaxed.

After twenty minutes of mental yoga to steady himself, he stood and entered the bathroom. Looking at himself in the mirror, he was a bit surprised to like what he saw. Even after the nightmare, he felt strong and alert. He thought about all the ways Sam had changed his life for the better. Certainly, he felt mentally more stable with her in his life. He hadn't had the nightmare in weeks and he concluded that sleeping un-alone had much to do with that.

Meeting Sam was a stroke of luck. He needed her support to get through this frustrating period in his life. She was so beautiful and smart, it was easy to want her. But he now realized that he needed her too. They hadn't been together long, but he began to consider that he was in love with her. Thinking of Sam, he recovered from the nightmare much faster than focusing on furniture. Not really surprising, he admitted to himself, but very helpful.

The shower in Tanya's guest bath was a delight; the water was both refreshing and soothing. He chuckled as he only now, this late in life, realized water possessed this duality. After stepping out of the shower and drying off, Thomas put on the slacks and seasonal shirt he bought just for this occasion. Tanya took holidays very seriously and put in an enormous effort. In response, Thomas always bought a new outfit for these parties. He loved his sister and this was one way he showed his respect and appreciation for her kindness.

The turkey was already in the oven and Thomas followed the Thanksgiving aromas to the kitchen. The day's dinner preparation had all the makings of a great dining experience. Tanya, was a great cook but she was outdoing herself this year with a display of culinary prowess. The kitchen was awash in partially prepared dishes; sweet potatoes and marshmallows ready to bake, asparagus coated in salt and olive oil ready to broil, bread homemade from scratch yesterday, cranberries boiling on the stove, pealed and quartered potatoes ready to boil and mash, spinach salad ready for wilting bacon grease, two pumpkin pies cooling on the counter.

"Good morning, Thomas," Tanya welcomed in a voice that almost sang. She was clearly in a good mood and her disposition was catching. "Boy, you must have been exhausted. I haven't seen you sleep this late since you were a teenager. But you do look festive. I am better prepared this year, though. I bought you an apron so you can't use new clothes as an excuse not to help." She smiled at him.

"Good morning to you, too," he replied. "This all looks amazing. How long have you been at it?" Thomas prepared a simple bowl of cereal for breakfast. He didn't want to feel hungry all day waiting for the feast, but he also didn't want to spoil his appetite before the main event.

"I got up at six. Cole and Kelly don't show up until one. So I have two more hours to finish. I hope to have much of this done before they arrive so I can enjoy the party. Mark cleaned the house all day yesterday and has been decorating this morning. He could use some help setting the table, I think. You remember where the china and Mom's old silver is kept in the dining room, don't you?"

"Of course, I'm on it. Place settings for five. Do you want me to get out the service ware too?"

"Please," Tanya responded.

Thomas walked into the dining room and began removing china from the cabinet. Mark walked by carrying a large paper turkey in a pilgrim hat. "Hey guy. Looking to be quite the feed-bag, huh?"

"It certainly is," answered Thomas. "Tanya really puts on a show. I can hardly wait for dinner. The trick is: don't eat too many snacks beforehand."

"But don't eat too little and get overly drunk beforehand either," added Mark as he headed off to find the turkey a roosting spot, "Either way, it should be a great day."

Dinner was living up to expectations and the company was excellent. Tanya invited Coleman, aka Cole, and Kelly. Thomas had dined with these friends with many times at his sister's home. It was a fun-loving crew and Tanya made sure there was plenty of wine for the day.

"I picked out this bird a week ago and the farmer butchered it yesterday. Never been frozen," bragged Tanya. "Its locally raised and never caged. I hope its good. I usually have one of those large factory raised birds." Mark carved the bird at the table and each slice off the breast was golden brown and juicy. Kelly refilled wine glasses as Tanya set the spinach salad on the table. Cole and Thomas made the final trip to the kitchen for the remaining side dishes.

With everyone still standing around the table and enough turkey servings cut and ready to eat, Mark set the carving tools aside and raised his wine glass in toast. "I want to thank you all for coming. We love this holiday and are grateful that you are sharing it with us. Tanya, my lovely wife, you have done a great job again. I love you, even if you are rooting for the Lions today." As the friends gave a polite laugh at the weak joke, Mark added, "Please sit down and start passing food. I'm hungry."

Mark served himself some turkey and requested plates to fill. As Cole took the dish, Mark added, "Thank you dear bird for giving your life for our dinner."

Tanya gave him a sneer and reminded him, "The turkey didn't have much of a say in the matter, Mark."

Everyone laughed, and started passing their plates for Mark to fill their requests for dark or white meat, as the side dishes passed around the table. Tanya made much more food than five people required for one meal, even after fasting most of the day in preparation of gorging themselves. The plates filled quickly and the consumption began.

"Interesting world, turkeys live in," Cole offered while looking at a bite size portion of the bird on his fork. Cole was an amateur philosopher and his speaking style could easily be mistaken for that of a preacher. He had a skill for making a dramatic point through parable and today he had quite a holiday story to tell. "Every day as they grow up, the farmer comes to them and feeds them. He takes care of them and protects them from predators. He makes sure they are healthy and their offspring do well. As they grow, they come to associate the farmer with good things. Then the day before Thanksgiving arrives and their world changes suddenly. They see the farmer coming and they start thinking about being fed. But then the farmer grabs one and wrings its neck. The other turkeys must be shocked by the violence. They can't fathom that the rules of their existence changed with the rise of the new day sun. Some philosophers think man may be in for a similar fate. One day the conditions of our Universe might just change. We'll be as lost and confused as the turkey who witnessed his friend become our entrée."

Thomas wondered if Cole had prepared this thesis specifically for Thanksgiving. Regardless, he was disturbed by the metaphor. He couldn't stop thinking about ET. Mark entered the conversation with a question. "But what in our experience is represented by the farmer?"

"Ah," started Cole. "Consider Europe in the mid-fourteenth century. The Catholic church was effectively a branch of government. Then the Black Death hits. People were dying in huge numbers and nothing they tried seemed to help. The Church indicated that God was displeased and brought this scourge down on humanity, telling their flocks to atone for their sins. But before long, people noticed that those of the Church were dying in equal numbers to the populace. This created an awakening in folks and a loss of confidence in the Church. The Church lost a great deal of power. Many historians claim this gave rise to the conditions that led to the Reformation. I would claim that this calamity was akin to the farmer and the Church a bit like the turkey."

"I don't know, Cole," commented Mark. "That seems like a very slow unravelling. Not like the turkey metaphor at all. The Church had time to react and if they had adjusted properly, the impact would have been diminished. Furthermore, the turkey dies in your defining example. The Church is still strong today."

"I could reference numerous natural disasters that you might find more pertinent," replied Cole. "Pompeii has a trajectory that might better fit your requirement of speedy demise. But I like to take a broader view. Take the 1929 crash, for example. The lives of many people were summarily uprooted and drastically changed as a result of an economic cataclysm. The main effect unfolded over a few years, but very dramatic."

"All right, I get you," accepted Mark. "The turkey example is rather stark and simplistic compared to the human experience. I'm not a fan of your Black Death example, but other natural disasters might fit the bill."

"Well, I think you should take the Black Death example but don't assign the turkey role to the church," Tanya interjected. "Half the population of Europe died. Before the plague, the people had a particular lifestyle and comfort level with fellow citizens and travelers. Once

101

that plague arrived, it hung around for couple centuries, resurging every twenty, twenty-five years. Labor was in short supply due to the deaths. Everyday life was very different after the arrival of the plague. I think it fits your turkey story well."

Thomas' mind was racing again, he could feel he was losing the sense of calm that began his morning. The frustration was so painful, it hurt. He stopped eating, tried to steady his breathing, and was simply staring into his food. Tanya brought him back, getting his attention, "Thomas?"

"Huh?" Thomas responded.

"You were somewhere else. Are you OK?" She asked.

"Oh yes," he replied. "We had some problems in the lab yesterday and I am afraid it is distracting me. I'm sorry. I guess I am not very good company today. May I have some more turkey, please." He handed his plate over to Mark, who served him his third helping.

"And some more wine," as he handed his glass to Kelly, who had become the day's unofficial bartender.

"Good idea," Mark clapped. "Kelly, please fill all our glasses. I'd like to make a toast."

Kelly opened yet another bottle of Rombauer Chardonnay and circled the table topping off glasses. "I'm beginning to appreciate the wisdom of my husband ordering an Uber to come over. We clearly are enjoying ourselves too much to get behind a wheel."

"True that," said Tanya. "Of course, you are welcome to stay here tonight if you'd like. Of our three bedrooms, only two are taken."

"Thank you, but it's still early. We'll see how we feel after pie and coffee and then port and cigars." Tanya laughed at the cigar reference. Nobody in the party smoked cigars, but Tanya was sure she could scare up a bottle of port from the liquor cabinet.

Mark stood and tilted his wine glass toward Tanya, "I want to toast my beautiful wife and her efforts on this fabulous meal."

Members of the group raised their glasses and said either, "Here here," or "Thank-you, Tanya."

As the evening grew old and Cole and Kelly left, Tanya sat next to her brother and took his hand. "I'm sure those two are the lion's share of the local Uber revenue."

Thomas smiled but didn't respond. He was getting tired.

"Are you doing OK, Thomas," she asked. "I am certainly glad you came today and I wish you wouldn't leave tomorrow. I am worried about you. This tenure decision has you tied up in knots."

"I know, I know," he answered. "If I can just get through this phase of our experiment and get it published, I think the stress will go away."

"I don't understand. You have the data. Why can't you publish?" she asked.

He looked at her with pleading eyes. "We discovered a hitch in the data. I'm worried it means that something is wrong. The team will need to make a huge effort to understand it and I'm not sure we will resolve it quickly. We are so close to completion, we can smell it, and this hitch could mean a serious setback. We are all concerned about the consequences."

"Thomas, you have always been able to work through these hard problems. You are always telling me, just divide it into manageable parts and solve each part. Follow your own advice and it will come together."

"Thank you, Tanya. If you don't mind, I think I will head up to bed. Dinner was great."

Thomas Conrad was sitting at his office desk, wearing a feathered turkey costume, trying to estimate the laser power required for his proposed next experiment. The door to his office burst open, shattering his concentration. His department chair, DeeDee Champton, stormed in wearing denim overalls and a wide brimmed hat. She was carrying a pitch-fork, tines up. She was attended by three senior faculty members wearing jeans and flannel, leaving two security guards standing just outside in the hall.

"Thomas, your work has been awful. Not just sub-par but awful." She pounded the floor with the pitch-fork handle and his desk, along with everything on it, disappeared. "We have decided to take early action to rid our department of your unsuccessful program."

She pounded the floor again and all the other furnishings, books, and Thomas' backpack disappeared. Even the chair was gone. Thomas was now standing in front of her, stiff with fright. "We have talked to the bank and your house and its furnishings have been repossessed. Your car has been towed."

She pounded the floor one last time and the turkey outfit lost all its feathers. He desperately tried to cover himself with his unwilling hands. "This academic life you have taken for granted is over. Good luck in your future endeavors, as if you have any future. Security, escort Dr. Conrad off campus. You are no longer welcome here."

As DeeDee turned, she disappeared along with the other faculty members. Handcuffs appeared on Thomas' wrists and the security guards were instantly next to him. Each took an elbow and they began pushing him out the door.

Thomas jolted up and stood next to the bed in the dark. He was panting so heavily he was on the verge of hyperventilating. His heart was pounding and he felt light headed, as if he was going to faint. He sat on the edge of the bed as he settled down. "That damn dream keeps getting worse," he said quietly.

Evidence for Change

Kathy celebrated Thanksgiving with a few other holiday-orphan graduate students who were studying too far from home to make the trip to visit family. She was an intense and athletic woman with slight workaholic tendencies. On Friday, she rose early, despite a slight hangover. Her obsession in solving the anomaly had grown in the past thirty-six hours. All she could think about was ET, but the lab's closure over the holiday frustrated her. She was fearful that this damn anomaly would screw with her dissertation, graduation and all her future plans.

Kathy loved being a scientist and she engineered her academic career to support her strengths. She double majored as an undergrad in physics and computer science and aimed for a graduate program that would support and challenge her. She knew she was evolving as a student, from one focused on homework and tests with answers, to an independent researcher who could justify her conclusions. Her peers often remarked on her analytical skills - she seemed to possess an unnatural ability to focus on a problem and create solutions. She actually enjoyed writing code. She took her first formal software courses in a summer program in grade school, discovered she was good at it and continued those studies in high school. She knew computer languages inside and out, enabling her to focus on the algorithm.

Kathy started doing research in Thomas' group soon

after finishing her coursework. She was thrilled when she got the job. She was fascinated with Professor Conrad's work and had angled for the position, soliciting her professors for recommendations. She seemed to always be in front a computer, whether in the lab or elsewhere. Especially over the past year, she was singularly focused on getting the result, writing it up, and graduating. With the steady progress of the ET project, she'd been very optimistic and energized, and even started outlining and organizing her dissertation.

Writing the dissertation brought on monumental dread; the mere mention of the word made her stomach clench. Kathy hated writing and she knew her dissertation was basically a book describing her measurements and deductions. Experienced students had advised her that it would take six months to write this book - another reason to dread it. Writing was not an interest for many science students, herself included. She actively avoided writing classes as an undergrad. Her dissertation was going to be a slog. "Get started early," or "just do it," were the admonishments she gave herself. Scribbling these and similar encouragements on sticky notes that she determinedly attached to the edges of her monitor where, ignored and forgotten, they lost their stickiness and fluttered unnoticed to the detritus on her desk.

On Friday after Thanksgiving, however, Kathy did not need sticky notes to motivate her. She arrived at the lab before eight and got started sorting through the data.

At about half past nine, Carl opened the lab door. "Good morning, Kathy." He put his bag lunch in the fridge.

"Good morning, Carl. I made coffee if you want some."

"Great! Thanks," he replied. While pouring himself a cup, he asked, "What do you want to do first?"

Kathy quickly outlined her plan. "My goal for today is to do a good study of all the environmental and slow-control parameters. We did some quick checks on Wednesday, but I want to go through each with a fine-toothed comb today. Tomorrow, I think Thomas will want to turn everything off and then we'll restart on Sunday."

"OK, tell me what you want me to start on," Carl said enthusiastically. He did not seem to hold any sensitivity from Thomas' admonishment on Wednesday but instead grabbed a legal pad and took notes on Kathy's instructions.

"Make a plot of the temperature reading within the optical resonator enclosure. Do a correlation analysis with electric charge value. Let's see if they are correlated. The statistical packages included with our analysis software will have a tool that will do the correlation. The temperature data is kept within our database. Export those values and their time stamp along with the charge values at times since we started taking data. Shouldn't be too difficult a calculation but a bit tedious moving the data around."

"I'm on it," said Carl as he refilled his coffee cup and moved over to one of the workstations near the door.

Carl took a couple of hours to get the code to access the database correctly and then calculate the correlation between the temperature and charge. During that time, he had to ask Kathy a number of questions, since his software experience was limited. But by noon, he had the answer. "Kathy, there is no correlation. I mean, I see *no* correlation. The probability that a temperature change caused a measurement error in the charge is infinitesimal. The temperature held steady as a rock before and after the change turned on."

"Thank you, Carl," she replied. "Good job, we'll

make you a programmer yet. Maybe we should break for lunch before we start the next analysis."

The two students grabbed their lunches from the lab fridge and sat down to eat. Through the mild autumn, the team usually sat in the quad to eat, but today the weather was cold and damp, and Kathy did not want to take the time. They exchanged a few pleasantries about how they spent their holiday. Carl had a brought a turkey sandwich with a layer of cranberry sauce - a family tradition he said. "Kathy, what do you think of Thomas as a mentor?" asked Carl.

Kathy nodded and frowned as she snapped the lid on her plastic container, now empty of the leftover salad from yesterday's dinner. "I've been very happy so far, although I think I'm ready to graduate and I'm not sure Thomas will see it that way. I've been a bit afraid to talk to him about it, actually. Why do you ask?"

Carl nodded and sighed, and then offered her a slice of sweet potato pie - he had brought two generous portions to share. Kathy accepted and offered him the gluten-free pumpkin muffin one of the grad students contributed, a sad undersized misshapen lump of a thing. "I don't know. I just get a strange vibe from him. Like he doesn't think I can really handle the job."

"Thomas pushes himself and everyone who works for him hard. But I've never seen him be unfair. Plus I think you have joined at a good time. The NSF funded ET-2 and you will be able to help assemble it and then get data very promptly. You should be on a fast track to graduate."

"Thanks, it's good to hear that. I was a bit put off by his attitude on Wednesday," admitted Carl.

"I agree that was not right. But I think Thomas let the stress get to him. He is really worried about tenure. I'd give him a pass at least this once."

Over the course of the afternoon, they conducted comparisons to the charge value, verifying the integrity of all the equipment. They checked the pressure monitor of the optical resonator in the vacuum chamber. The data acquisition system's electronic offsets were routinely measured and stored, and they checked the electric and magnetic field monitors providing those values; they checked the accelerometers which measure the vibrations of the various optical tables - all systems appeared normal. Next, they checked the laser polarization measurements and the particle count levels in the clean lab room. They verified the humidity levels and atmospheric pressure. Nothing correlated to the anomaly. They took a breather before confirming the stabilities of the clocks, their last task of the day.

As evening rolled around, the two students completed their goal for the day. "Wanna get something to eat," asked Kathy. "Black Friday is traditionally pizza night around campus and The Gulpers' Guild always runs half-price on brews."

"Yes, that would be good. I didn't realize how hungry I was, but now that you mention food," Carl let his comment trail off.

They locked up the lab and headed toward hallway to the stairs. As they started down the hallway, they saw someone dash up the stairwell, as if startled by the students' unexpected presence.

"Who was that?" asked Kathy. "They seemed to move awfully fast once they saw us. Like they didn't want to be seen."

He shrugged. "I didn't get a good look," answered Carl. "A lot of people have labs in this basement, and maybe seeing us reminded them of something. I wouldn't worry about it. We keep the lab locked, anyway.

Saturday morning was cold and drizzly, matching Thomas' dour mood. He was hunched against the light rain; a loose rain jacket protected both him and his backpack holding his laptop. But the treats in the paper sack were not as well covered. With the team coming in over the holiday weekend and the confusion with the data, Thomas figured he needed to do at least a little something to help morale, so he picked up a dozen scones at the Brewers Cup, four each of blueberry, Dutch apple, and raisin-pecan. The bakery bag was getting damp and he quickened his pace crossing the campus to Grunderson Hall hardly noticing anyone or anything around him. He had spent much of the last forty-eight hours considering what he wanted to do in the lab and it killed him that he couldn't do any of it. The more he thought about that, the faster he walked.

Kathy had already started a pot of coffee and by nine a.m. that morning, Kathy, Carl, and Thomas were all in the lab, drinking coffee and eating scones. Kathy quickly recapped the progress that she and Carl made yesterday. Thomas smiled his approval.

"OK," Thomas said, "today we're going to turn everything off. While we do that, we are going to systematically check the magnetic and electric field monitors and compensators along with their response with each switch we flip. Finally, we'll shut down the atomic beam that fills the trap then the lasers that create the atom trap. Any questions?"

"Thomas," asked Carl, "why do we worry about stray fields so much?"

"Christ Carl," answered Thomas impatiently. "That's a very fundamental aspect of this experiment that you should understand by now." Thomas didn't notice Carl's cringe. He just kept lecturing. "Basically electric and magnetic fields can slightly distort the atomic orbits giving rise to small shifts in the orbit binding energy. If the fields never change, this effect will be constant and won't result in an error in our search for a change. However, it's hard to keep the fields so small and constant. Even moving a piece of equipment can change the magnetic field at some location. So all our equipment is isolated and we avoid entering the laser lab while it's running. We don't move anything in the dark room and we have a lot of compensation systems to cancel out magnetic and electric fields. We want the stray fields to be small and constant."

Carl nodded and started the day's tasks.

Thomas wanted some time for the field monitors to settle after each component was switched off. He decided that five minutes should be more than enough time, but that meant they averaged about only twelve shutdowns in an hour; the day was consumed by switching switches and reading output from sensors.

As the day came to a close, Thomas was clearly frustrated. All the values matched what they had measured back in August and September as they assembled and tested the apparatus. All that testing and verification did not reveal the cause of the anomaly. At one point he had even tried rolling a large metal cart up near the atom trap. Sure enough, he saw an effect that went away when he moved it back.

By early evening every piece of equipment in the lab had been systematically turned off. Thomas sighed and ran his fingers through his hair. "I'm going home. We'll see how it goes turning things back on tomorrow," he declared. "No clues yet as to why things have been different over the past week." As the three scientists left Grunderson Hall, the sidewalks were flowing with water from the all-day rain.

Thomas walked home from the lab a bit faster than usual, frustration clear with each step. As he approached, he saw movement near the side of the house. The dusk of late November and the heavy cloud cover made it hard to see clearly, but he was sure he saw something. He picked up his pace and nearly ran to the driveway that passed along the house to the garage in the back. As he got to the point where he could see its whole length, he saw Sam, in an oversized hoodie, watering a potted plant in a window box. "Hello Sam," he called with relief.

"Hi Love," she responded. "I thought I would surprise you, but you weren't home. I tried to call but you didn't answer your cell. As I was wondering whether to stay or not, I noticed this plant looked wilted."

"Thanks for watering it, but I think it's basically gone dormant for the winter. I fear that my cell reception is very poor in the basement of Grunderson Hall and I was down there all day. Come in and get warm."

Sam poured them each a glass of wine, while Thomas set his stuff down and slipped out of his slicker. He hung it in the bathroom to dry and lined up his wet shoes beside the door. He gratefully accepted the glass of the hearty Zinfandel that Sam offered as he sat on the couch beside her. Sam placed her hand behind Thomas' head and pulled him into a kiss. Sam let go and leaned back. "Well that was unremarkable. Something bothering you?"

Thomas grimaced and sipped the wine. He didn't want to complain, but he was so frustrated he had to tell Sam about the problem in the lab. "Yes. Our experiment is seeing a change in the charge value. I can't believe it's correct, but our efforts to find something wrong are coming up empty. I am really bummed out. Things were going so well and now we have this anomaly that will sidetrack our plan to publish quickly. I can't see a path forward to tenure with this. Unless we find an explanation, ET is just an unidentified systematic error."

"Why can't the result be correct? Perhaps, you can't explain it away because it's real." Sam was trying to be comforting, but Thomas was very tense.

"Physics laws don't just change one day. There are good reasons to think the charge might be changing, but it should always be changing. I don't see how this can be true." He heard his voice getting louder and more emphatic.

Sam decided to take another approach. She scooted back close to him and put set her hand gently on his groin. She whispered in his ear. "I think you need to focus on something else for an hour or so. You can go back to work in the morning. But tonight, you're mine. Let's spin one and then have a pizza delivered. We can drink what's left of the beer you have with the pizza and by then, I think we'll be ready to spin one again. If my plan works you'll be much more relaxed when you hit this tomorrow." She smiled at him. When he smiled back, her hand gave him a firm squeeze.

Sunday morning, Carl was in the lab first. He prepared the coffeemaker for the first pot – that was the extent of his confidence with the equipment in the lab. He knew that the plan for the day was to turn all the equipment back on, but he hadn't clue where to begin.

He munched on a breakfast burrito that he bought on the way in and listened to the coffee squirt into the carafe.

Carl grew up in Boston and did his undergraduate study at the University of Chicago, learning he could cheer both the Red Sox and the White Sox with no conflict of conscience. Kathy was a good mentor and with her enthusiasm, he found he liked the process; he was a natural problem-solver. He had an excellent understanding of the physics, but was new to the hands-on work and he knew he had to work hard to catch up on that front, as well as getting comfortable with the software that accumulated the data. He was picking up the programming quickly and he liked that. He enjoyed problem solving and using a computer just seemed fun to him.

The coffee was ready and he poured a half cup. He didn't actually enjoy coffee without plenty of real cream and turbinado sugar, and the lab did not have those. He wanted to appear to be a team player and sipped the bitter brew black. He drank his coffee and ate a pastry he bought on the way in, while he waited for the others.

Carl felt great pressure to succeed. His parents were the first in their families to be university students and both were highly accomplished. His mother was a history professor at Boston University and his father was a chemist at Harvard. Quite a legacy to live up to. He was an only child and his parents were always giving him advice about his career, his love life, how to manage his money, how to pick his friends. He loved his parents, but they were overwhelming. Thomas' demanding style echoed his father. Carl feared that it would take longer than Kathy predicted for him to understand all the systems well enough to write a dissertation.

Within the hour, all four of the scientists were in the lab. It was eerily quiet with everything off. Thomas brought scones again and they enjoyed the light breakfast while planning the order to turn things back on. Like yesterday, this was not difficult, just time consuming. Thomas' goal was to confirm that today's readings tracked with yesterday's observations. Even while they were talking, Adrian was busy at work on her laptop.

As the systems were turned on every five minutes, the team multi-tasked to avoid the boredom. Kathy and Thomas reviewed the date in close detail. The electric charge had indeed changed. It had been constant for the ten weeks up to the previous Friday, six days before they discovered it the day before Thanksgiving.

Thomas felt his chest constrict and his breath quicken and he fought for a calm voice. "Double check the blinded offset," Thomas instructed Adrian.

"How does the blindness work?" asked Carl, who looked up from his efforts verifying the position of all the optical elements. He had studied the idea of blind data acquisition and double blind experiments, but he wasn't clear on how ET implemented it.

"The data result is blind to us," explained Thomas. "We don't want to bias ourselves by knowing the answer before we have done all the cross checks that confirm the result. Otherwise we run the risk of stopping our tests once the answer agrees with our expectations. We might not check everything as carefully as we should or miss something.

Carl nodded his understanding and Thomas continued, "The rate of change of the electric charge is actually reported by the computer as the true measured value plus a random offset that is unknown to us. Once all the data have been confirmed to be valid and all the systematic studies check out, and only then, the offset is revealed. We then correct the reported value by that offset. Since project start-up in September, we conducted the offset correction weekly; consistently after the correction, we observed no change in the charge. So I'm worried that maybe something went wrong with that."

"That was one of the first things I looked at on Wednesday," added Adrian. "And I've been looking at it again this morning. It all checks out. Of course to verify it, I revealed the list of offsets going into the future. That is I was able to verify ahead of time that last week's offset was indeed what was used when the computer reported the result. This morning I also checked the offset that was going to be used for this week's result. If we want to extend a blindness process into the future, we'll have to reset that system."

"But wait," said Carl. "If you can expose the offsets, doesn't that mean you can see what they are ahead of time and know what the answer is while you are analyzing? How is that blind?"

"That's true," replied Thomas, going into professorial lecture mode had calmed him in the moment, but Carl's question irked him, and it showed in his voice. "There is an honor system in our blindness technique. We are a small team and know each other well. Certainly we trust each other to respect our agreements for the blindness scheme we have chosen, but it is also true that the logs would indicate if the offset list file was accessed. Those logs cannot be edited because they are write-locked with a password none of us have."

Thomas turned his attention to Adrian. "Yes, please reset the offset generation so that when we start taking data later today, it will be good to go."

Looking back and pointing a finger at Carl, he sternly lectured, "Carl, you should study how blindness schemes are implemented in various experiments. It's a fundamental scientific technique that you should be familiar with."

Carl shook his head and went over to see what Kathy

was up to.

A few days later the next installment of data was available and it was clear that ET indicated that the change in the electric charge was accelerating, even with the limited additional run time.

"This is really perplexing," sighed Kathy. "Even with only three days of data, we see an effect. The equivalent charge change, if that is what is happening, is about one-half part per quadrillion in just one week. I guess one disadvantage to having the world's most sensitive experiment is that we can't call to see if anyone else is seeing the same thing we are."

Thomas was just about to reply, when the lab's phone rang. Thomas heaved a sigh of frustration and answered.

"Professor Conrad, this is Harold Simpson. I represent the Changing Universe Society. You may have seen our rallies on your department's square."

He could not restrain the unseen eyeroll that the announcement inspired. "Yes, I am familiar with your group," replied Thomas.

"Good. I'm sure you understand that we have a keen interest in your ET experiment. I know that you have been collecting data for a few months now and I was hoping you would let us know what you have found so far. We'd love it if you would come speak at one of our meetings."

"We are not ready to publicly release any results yet. We haven't finished our analysis." Thomas distractedly picked up a pen and began quickly clicking its retraction button.

"All right. We will be patient a bit longer. But as taxpayers who support your research, we feel we have a right to know what you have learned. Especially on a topic this important. We will be watching."

The reference to 'watching' recalled his sense that someone had been casing his house. "Is that an implied threat?" Thomas asked.

"No, I'm not threatening you," responded Harold. "I am just letting you know that we are very interested and will keep our eyes open for developments."

"That sounds like a threat to me," countered Thomas.

"Well, anyway, good day to you," said Harold.

"Good day to you also." Thomas was glad he was able to remain mostly composed and didn't snap at the man. He just grunted and hung up the phone.

"Who was that?" asked Adrian.

"That cult leader Simpson."

"Did you hear that all his cult members liquidate all their assets and donate them to the cult," commented Carl. "Or should I say emerging religion. They all live in his compound near downtown. It just seems bizarre to me."

"It is amazing. Some people must really be lost and will believe anything and follow anyone," commented Kathy. "Last week when I walked in, I saw at least 40 people wearing that blue arm band. I must say, however, that spaceship logo is rather well done, even if they are nuts."

119

Consequences of Change

Thomas left the lab at quarter to four, much earlier than usual, because the conversation with Harold had disturbed him. During the walk home Thomas started talking to himself, albeit quietly, "What would CUS be willing to do? What could they do? It's a science experiment, for Christ's sake. We can't force a result."

He entered the house and hung up his coat. He set his pack on his desk and, needing an energetic atmosphere, turned on a reggae Tidal playlist. As the syncopated beat vibrated the walls, he snagged a Mountain Standard IPA from the fridge and settled at his desk. From his covered bookshelf, he pulled out a private notebook. He used this notebook to flush out ideas that were still too speculative to discuss with other scientists. Some things you needed to think through before you told somebody.

What if the change in the charge was real?

The thought disturbed him and he wanted to fully understand the consequences if the change was real. He posed himself a question, He wrote that question in the notebook. "How large can the electron charge get before it manifests in other ways?" He remembered Cole's Thanksgiving homily and it frightened him. "Did the Universe really just transform one day?" he asked. The thought chilled him and he admonished himself, "This result couldn't possibly be true, so stay focused on checking the experiment," he tried to tell himself. But his curiosity kept bringing him back to possible consequences.

"If there are implied impacts or restrictions from other measurements on the ET result, I better know what they are," he told himself. His work required he should do this study and that comforted him, or maybe more accurately, gave him permission to consider these lines of thought.

After dating the first blank page in the notebook, Thomas first described the ET result and quantified what they had seen in a few different ways for reference. Then he made a list of some potential consequences of a changing charge. He also added some first notes by each. Although Thomas' notebooks contained lots of calculations and formulas, they also included narratives describing his thoughts. In particular, this private notebook read more like a journal or diary. The text could be read and understood by almost anyone. The book nearly recited itself to him. He had heard about the impact of charge on solar burning before, so it was the first entry.

The Sun produces its energy through proton-proton fusion. The rate of this fusion process is determined by a competition between two natural forces; the strong nuclear force and the electric force. In the hot center of the Sun where this fusion takes place, all the hydrogen atoms have lost their electrons due to the high temperature. For two protons to fuse and release energy, they must get close enough for the nuclear strong force to join them. But the strong force only exerts its influence over a short distance, so the protons must get very close for fusion to occur. However, the protons repel each other due to their like-signed electric charges, so a proton must have a high energy to overcome that repulsion and get close enough for fusion. The bare protons in the Sun have a spread in energies determined by the tem-

perature. Even though the temperature is hot, only a very small fraction of the protons in the hot Sun's center have enough thermal energy to overcome the repulsive electrical force and achieve fusion. This delicate balance depends on the relative strengths of these two forces. That balance will be altered if the charge changes. If it increases, fewer protons will get close enough to fuse and the Sun's energy output will decrease.

The nuclear energy levels in carbon are sensitive to the value of the electric charge. If the charge changed by just two percent, the production of carbon in stars would stop. That would have been bad for us if it happened a couple billion years ago, but now we already have our carbon. Anyway, two per cent is a very big number, way beyond what ET sees.

The power grid effectively moves electrons around the world and it is the charge of the electron that defines the power transferred. If the electric charge increases, then the effective current moving through a circuit will also increase. But it is a direct proportional relationship. The observed small changes will be negligible for any time to come. The power companies would not see anything unusual.

If the charge gets too big, the strong nuclear forces that holds nuclei together would be overwhelmed by the electric repulsion of the nuclear protons. A quick estimate found that if the charge was about four times larger, carbon would fall apart. This is very large compared to the ET data.

The color of stars would be changed as the luminosity is altered. The most intense emitted *wavelength from a star would change as the square root of the charge. That is, a star would redden if the charge increased. But the difference in color due to the results of ET would be too small to see, literally in this case.*

Chemical bonds typically weaken and molecules become less stable as the charge increases. This paper reference calculates the impact of the charge value on the energy of the critical carbon bonds that determines the stability of DNA base pairs. If those pairs became less stable, that would be a problem. The paper implied that large changes in the charge would have an impact. The estimates for a hydrogen bond found that a one percent increase in the charge would decrease the reaction energy by a bit less than one percent.

Thomas began to reread this recent passage. After many pages of notes and calculations, He did not find anything that would cause an observable effect given the size of the ET result. Some process needs to greatly amplify the effect somehow. He considered this out loud, "I wonder if there is there some collective effect that would increase the impact? Otherwise, there is unlikely to be any observation that precludes that ET is due to an actual variation in the electric charge."

He considered this amplification possibility for a while and realized that a macroscopic object has a lot of atoms. He had one idea that he added to his list.

A collective effect may result from the sum of a large number of small effects, such as might happen in a macroscopic object due to changes in its makeup of atoms. For example, a fast change in the charge would create a sudden force between atoms in a solid. Even though the force induced between two individual atoms might be small, there are a lot of atoms in a person, for example. An instantaneous change of one part per million would cause a total force on the body that would be fatal. The required change is still very large compared to what we see in the lab, but we're getting closer. But the rate of change for this example would have to be very fast, faster than the change ET sees. There might be observable consequences, but the rate of change ET sees is much too slow for this scenario. In any case, it's intriguing that the collective effect due to a large number of constituents amplified the observable effect.

The effect the team saw was much too small for any observable consequence that Thomas could come up with. In that regard, although a change of a few per cent would be very large, their experiment just didn't see anything at that scale. In another view, however, it did surprise Thomas that if the charge changed by only a factor of a few, or even a small percentage, it would have dramatic consequences for the Universe. Others had made this point previously, but now Thomas had an appreciation for their arguments.

He looked up at the clock, saw it was well after midnight, and realized how tired he was. He put the notebook back in the covered bookshelf and then tried to call Sam. She didn't pick up, but that didn't surprise him. After all, Wednesday was one of her *working* nights and she probably turned off her phone before going to bed.

Thomas woke up early, a late bedtime and a nightmare notwithstanding. He took a quick shower, and ate plain yogurt for breakfast. He walked gingerly to Brewers Cup, got his drink and headed toward campus. He was feeling beaten and the excitement he felt just a few weeks ago was gone.

As he walked through the quad, Harold was speaking again to several dozen acolytes. Although Thomas noticed the engaged crowd, he didn't stop to listen. He was too distracted to hear anything without an effort.

Entering Grunderson Hall, he headed directly upstairs to his office. Ordinarily, he would drop by the lab first, but he was very behind on teaching preparation. He had class at eleven today had no lecture planned. He needed to focus on that, at least for the morning.

After class, the afternoon began to slip away; Thomas stopped by the lab before heading home. Carl was the only one there.

"Hi Thomas," Carl said cheerfully. "I didn't expect to see you. I thought you had classes this afternoon?"

"Hi Carl," Thomas replied unenthusiastically. "How are things going here. Well I'd guess they must be doing OK since Adrian and Kathy aren't around."

"That's true. Everything is running well. In a few days the next data set will be ready."

"Great and thanks. I guess I'll head home," said Thomas.

"Thomas," Carl shifted in his chair and diverted his eyes for a moment.

"What is it, Carl?" Thomas worked to keep his impatience out of his voice.

"I do want to mention another incident of someone in the hall. They were acting very suspicious. You know, furtive, like they didn't want to be seen. I got a better look this time and I think they were wearing the CUS tan shirt and arm band."

Thomas sighed. "We can't keep them out of the building. But we can keep the lab doors locked and computers password protected. Don't worry, I think we're safe."

As Thomas left, that bit of news didn't help with his nerves. "What are they up to?" he asked himself.

As Thomas walked up his driveway, the lights were on in his house, and he saw a man just inside his living room. He was shocked and jogged to the front door. He dropped his pack on a porch chair, unlocked the front door and sprinted into the room, but the intruder, alerted by the sound of the door, was dashing to the back of the house. He stumbled into a kitchen chair that slid across the floor and hit the wall. He grabbed another chair and threw it behind him and into Thomas' path. Thomas leapt over the chair and gave chase, but the invader was fast, ran out the back door, and across the yard. As Thomas pushed his way out the back door and into the yard, he was sure he would catch the man at the fence. But the man jumped up, grabbed the top and pulling himself up, scaled the six-foot privacy fence with ease. Thomas tried the same stunt, but wasn't agile enough to pull it off. He fell backward, landing on his backside on the unraked wet leaves. Thomas had no hope of catching the escapee and stood up, winded, in the grass catching his breath. It was probably a good thing, thought Thomas. He had no idea what would have happened if he had caught the guy.

He brushed the leaves from his jacket and returned to the house. Clearly the house had been searched. Household items were scattered throughout the living room and kitchen. The bedrooms seemed mostly untouched, but someone certainly went through the drawers. He looked around at the mess with a sense of hopeless fatigue. He decided he should let the police look at things before he cleaned up. He went back outside, called the police, and waited, for what seemed an eternal thirty minutes on his porch for their arrival. Thomas' mind was racing trying to understand why his house would be searched. Were they looking for something or just trying to intimidate him?

The police inspected the house and took Thomas' statement about the evening's events. The police weren't very encouraging about apprehending the culprit. The description Thomas gave wasn't very detailed and it would be hard to connect anyone to the break-in. For insurance purposes and their report, they said, Thomas escorted them around the house to see if anything was missing. All his belongings appeared accounted for. The only real loss was the damage to the back door lock.

"Do you have any idea what they might have been looking for?" asked Officer Daniels, a large imposing man with unblinking eyes.

"No, I don't," answered Thomas. "If they weren't here to steal something, I don't get it. It's not like I have a treasure trove of government secrets hidden here or drug money stashed in the cupboard."

"Do you have any enemies that might want to hurt you?"

"No. I have had some uncomfortable encounters with that new group, CUS. I wouldn't have predicted they might do something like this, but they are a very odd organization. Harold Simpson called me and said something that might have been a threat, but it would be open to interpretation. They are interested in the results of the experiment I am conducting and they're a bit pushy about it."

"Yes, we are familiar with them," answered the policeman. "But we have not had any trouble with them. I'll make a note of your concern in the report. If you find that something is missing while cleaning up, let me know. Otherwise, all I can suggest is that you get better locks and maybe an alarm system."

After the police left, Thomas started preparing to clean up and put things away. When he got to his covered bookshelf, he noticed that his private log book was not in its usual place. "Would someone want to look at that?" he asked himself. He wondered how they would even know it existed? The notebook is almost a diary. There isn't anything valuable in there, but if it gets out, it would be embarrassing. He picked up the notebook and stared at it. Suddenly a deep feeling of dread came over him. "Oh no, the details of the recent ET result are in there. Damn, I don't need this if I want tenure."

Thomas felt rather shook. He made himself a cup of chamomile and sat on the couch to try and relax. After a moment of quiet, he called Sam. After an exchange of greetings, Sam asked, "What's up, Love? You sound shaken."

"Someone just broke into my house. They didn't take anything but they made quite a mess. When I'm done with my tea, I plan to clean up."

"My god," she gasped. "That's horrible, are you OK?"

"Yes, although I am a bit scared by it. I think those CUS people are getting out of hand so I wanted to warn you as soon as possible. Be careful when you're here."

"I will, Love," she replied. "Let me come over and help you clean up. I bet you could use some company."

Finances, Preparing for Change

Jonathon tapped the steering wheel of his rental impatiently; it was a Corolla, light grey and nondescript, a few rungs below his usual standards, but it did come with satellite radio. While stopped in the vehicle line, he cast a worried eye at the lowering clouds and turned down the volume on the eighties classic station to open a weather app on his phone, to see if the forecast was shifting. He had picked up the rental in Pierre, and the conditions had been mild, at least for North Dakota in mid-December, which meant that only a grey mist blew in shivering gusts. The app indicated the seasonable weather would hold; Jonathan sighed and fumbled at the radio, which suddenly blared saccharine holiday tunes.

He swore colorfully and profusely; he hated the holidays. He slammed his fingers onto the radio display until an acceptable station played. The holidays weren't the problem, he admitted, it was this queue. He had been creeping along for at least an hour, with twenty cars still ahead of him. He had chosen Portal as an auspicious place to cross the border; he had always crossed easily before. Some easy banter with the Canucks in the Mountie hats, flash the US passport, and he was in. He did not believe in any god, but he muttered a prayer for intercession. He prayed that the Canadian Border Services weren't conducting searches of the vehicles. His mind flashed to the contents of the Corolla's trunk, and he visualized the two carryon roller bags and their precious cargo, bundles of neatly stacked bills. These two bags were the last of the cash reserves that had accumulated over the past few months. Carrying the cash over the border was a risk, but he wanted to be rid of the albatross, and prepare for the next phase of his plans. He knew getting the cash deposited into accounts here would be easier than trying to transport it by air during his later trips.

The thought of first-class travel to exotic balmy beaches distracted him, so when he finally rolled up to the checkpoint he was calm and confidently showed his passport. A few jovial words back and forth and he was clear. They told him that a crime was committed down in Vanville and the US Homeland Security expected the gang to cross the border.

"Damn shame," said Jonathon, tucking the passport into his breast pocket.

"You're not wrong," said the Mountie. "Now you just have a pleasant visit up in Regina, Mr. Dobbins. Saskatchewan welcomes you."

The delay at the border set him back an hour or so, but he had made a reservation at the Delta Hotels by Marriott in Regina, so he was not worried about losing time. He checked into the hotel at seven, with plenty of time for a soak in the hot tub and a stiff drink or two at the bar. He ate steak. After dinner, he transferred some of the neat cash bundles into a briefcase he picked out at the thrift store back home, choosing one that looked worn, and nondescript.

The following morning, he dressed in baggy and boring clothes, somewhat new jeans and a plain blue pullover shirt with no labels or patterns. He ate breakfast while studying a map of the small city. He had laid out an easy walking loop that would pass by all the banks he planned to visit. Once he was ready, he checked out, put his bag in the car, put on a warm jacket, his cheap glasses and, grabbing his briefcase, headed out to his first destination. He locked the roller bags in the trunk of the Corolla, parked in a secure place in the hotel garage.

The mist and heavy clouds had dissipated in the night and a pale winter sun shone ineffectually against the brisk wind. He walked by a Tim Hortons and decided to get another cup of coffee for the trek west to the RBC Royal Bank.

The shortest line was at the left-most teller. He queued up. After only a few minute wait, he approached the young man behind the counter glass. He wore a name tag with Robert engraved. "I'd like to withdraw nine thousand, four hundred and twenty six dollars, please Robert." He always kept it below the all important ten thousand threshold and he always chose seemingly random values.

"May I have your account number and see your ID, sir?" replied Robert.

"Certainly," answered Jonathan as he passed his passport through the slot in the partition. He pulled a note pad from his briefcase and read the number to the teller.

"This all looks to be in order Mr. Dobbins. Brand new passport I see. Hardly any transit stamps yet."

"Yes, I had to renew my old one a few months ago."

"How would like your cash?"

"Hundreds, please."

As Robert counted out the money, Jonathan was making a mental list of the other cities and towns he wanted to visit over the next couple days. The various institutions weren't all that far apart, but it would require a number of drives.

Jonathan placed the cash in the brief case, and left the bank. He walked further west to a branch of BMO bank of Montreal. He entered and walked up to an idle teller. "I'd like to deposit some cash, please. Some of it is in US dollars, and the rest is Canadian dollars."

"Good to see you again Arthur," the teller responded cheerfully. She spoke with a local twang.

"Thank you Sandra." He was really surprised she remembered him. Certainly dealing with small bank branches in small towns had their disadvantages. He felt a twinge of alarm, but assured himself that it was typical Canadian friendliness. He figured he had been here too many times in the recent past. But he didn't have any plans to return to Canada for a while, so perhaps it didn't matter. Also, she didn't know his real name and he planned to close the accounts at this bank in a few months anyway.

As Sandra diligently counted the tidy stacks of hundreds, Jonathan ruminated on how association with CUS had provided him with assets in addition to the vast amounts of cash. The CUS gig produced interesting connections, like the fellow who fabricated fake IDs. He must have a curious past to have developed that talent. I wonder if he has an insider at the State Department. He even got the biometric chip working properly."

After the deposit was completed, Jonathan went outside and found a discreet place to sit in front of a nail salon, sheltered from the insistent north wind. He pulled out his iPad and logged on to one of his favorite cryptocurrency sites and placed an order using the cash he had just deposited. He didn't always purchase cryptocurrency so soon after the deposit, but he varied the timing to deflect patterns. He knew this system wasn't perfect. But he also knew it was complicated. The money followed many trails in small amounts. He never kept large amounts in any one account; that was key. When CUS got the donations, Jonathan kept it spread around and moving. In fact, he had avoided a paper trail, or at least a consistent one, for most of the money the new members contributed. Moving the assets around effectively was tedious and time-consuming, but he was meeting his goals. All the money was accumulating in those island banks that ensured privacy. Once the transaction was complete, he put everything away in his briefcase and started the walk southwest to the next bank, BDC Business Development Bank of Canada.

After another deposit, he headed east to HSBC bank and then to Canadian Western Bank. By now, it was a bit after noon, so he bought a sandwich and iced tea but the wind tore at the wrappings making it difficult to eat. The iced tea chilled him and he wished he had ordered a coffee. He sat on a bench in Victoria Park to eat, then took his time walking around the park, persuading himself that he was enjoying himself. He then headed back north to the hotel to pick up his car and start the drive onto Saskatoon.

The drive was just under three hours, a straight shot across the open prairies. He couldn't imagine who would choose to live in the forsaken landscape, although the unending plains were good for planning. He played his satellite radio and once more reviewed his itinerary. He would arrive in the town just before the banks closed. He planned to duplicate the process he used in Regina: go to a bank to withdraw an amount, go to another and make a deposit, then pause to place an order for the cryptocurrency, and repeat until the banks closed for the day. He always chose a low amount to avoid drawing attention to his activities. He used several cryptocurrencies and avoided the money trails crossing. He was taking a hit on the currency exchange, but knew that the minor transactions were key to anonymity.

By the time he left Saskatoon it was dark, as the

nights came early this far north this near to solstice, so he found a roadside motel and pulled in. He was wiped out - he had to keep alert every step of the way. No hot tub, no steak in this Podunk joint, but it looked clean enough. He requested a quiet room and got one facing away from the highway. He brought his roller bags and unzipped them to assess his progress. Through his meticulous efforts, he had reduced his cash bundles by a third. He condensed the cash to one bag and loaded the briefcase with bundles of cash for tomorrow's transactions.

He brought an extra sandwich from Saskatoon for his dinner, knowing from experience that he had few options for a decent dinner in the wasteland outside town. The wilted sandwich was not adequate, but he didn't want to leave the room. He would make up for it with a hearty breakfast in the morning.

As he ate, he reviewed his map and routes. The cost of this three-day excursion was not high, but he was careful to put all the expenses on one account. He set up the discrete account for these financial transaction trips. The billing address was a post office box, he paid the bill by electronic transfer from a linked checking account, and the card was set up as a business account with only a company name. As soon as the trip was over, he would cancel the card, close the account and change the name of the shell company. He had already set up another expense system for his next trip. It was planned for February, leaving him plenty of time for the arrangements for any trip after that.

Jonathan spent the next three days moving between banks and hotels. On the third day, he drove back across the border, returned the rental car and made his way home.

Kathy snapped the lid on her empty salad box. She was alone in the lab and hoped that a short lunch break would help clear her brain. Something was bothering her about the data. She couldn't quite put her finger on the cause, but there seemed to be a strange pattern in the calibration figures. The deduced offsets seemed to have a discrete step pattern that would indicate some sort of computational issue somewhere in the system. The effect was small, however, and she couldn't be sure she wasn't just seeing a pattern in the random noise fluctuations of the measurements. After spending over two hours staring at code and data numbers, she decided it must be noise and that it was time for some exercise. She had been sitting for hours and felt stiff. She got ready to go for a run.

Grunderson Hall had locker rooms in basement, just down the hall from the lab. Kathy took her pack, locked the lab door, and went to the shower room. She changed into her running clothes, a warm dark pair of running tights and long sleeved tee. She pulled a fleece over the tee, grabbed her gloves and cap, then locked her locker.

Her route took her in a grand sweep around the sprawling campus. The ivy on the oldest buildings was dramatic against the damp brisk winter sky. The glee club was singing carols in the quad, and she smiled at their antics as she settled her earbuds under her pompom hat. She ran past the botanical garden, the intramural fields and the immense football stadium complex. She skirted Greek row, and came back toward the quad through the covered walkway of the history department building.

A small group had gathered near the glee club who were packing their gear. Kathy saw Adrian and Sam talking. That struck her as curious. She stopped her run and stretched her abductors at a table far enough away to be discreet. She observed the two, trying to glean from their body language, the content of their discussion. They appeared more animated than a casual 'hello' in an accidental encounter. Adrian was making a point with lots of handwaving and head nods. Sam had her arms crossed and was shaking her head. Kathy thought it looked like an argument, but couldn't fathom what they could be discussing.

After a short time, the two shared a hug and went their separate ways. It was clear to Kathy that Adrian was making her way toward the lab, so she ran over to her, as if she was just finishing her workout.

"Oh hi Kathy," Adrian said when she recognized her approach.

"Hi Adrian," Kathy panted. "Did I just see you with Thomas' girlfriend?"

"Yes. I ran into her on University Avenue and we started talking. We were headed the same way so we walked together for a while."

"But you seemed upset," probed Kathy. "Angry."

"Angry is the wrong word," replied Adrian. "I would say more frustrated. We were talking about CUS. I can't believe she works for them. We had a disagreement about whether it's a cult or not."

Kathy didn't pursue it any further. The story sounded plausible but it was strange. She didn't think these two knew each other well enough to debate so passionately. It seemed odd. They walked back to Grunderson Hall, where Adrian went straight to the lab and Kathy went to take a shower.

Transparency Brings Change

Harold Simpson increased his campus exhortations in the quad to at least twice weekly. Often they were early in the morning as Thomas arrived, and he would stop to listen, choosing an unobtrusive spot in the back. He usually sat on a concrete planter wall, to sip his Brewers Cup and nibble at the scone of the day. Today, Thomas sat on a concrete planter wall to listen to Harold's latest missive. This spot allowed him to beat a quick exit and had the advantage of the morning sun; the mid-December days were chilly, and the sun was always welcome.

The last days before the holiday break were festive and Thomas enjoyed seeing the students let loose. He didn't want to fight the sizable crowd when he departed and Harold always talked longer than Thomas was willing to stay. The spot allowed him to hear Harold's latest message and observe the crowd without being a member of it. The crowd had grown lately and Thomas was surprised to see a news camera crew covering today's event.

Certainly, many in the audience were students who were looking for entertainment. Some of them wore Santa hats and festive scarves. Even though the morning temperatures were below freezing most days, many people were wearing the tan shirts and blue armbands, without jackets. Thomas removed his leather gloves before unwrapping the scone. He sipped his coffee while Harold spoke.

This morning, Harold stood on a concrete planter on the eastern side of the quad, where he and his followers usually gathered. He was already going full steam and the arm-banded attendees punctuated his speech with cheers and exclamations of support.

"This University has concrete evidence that the electric charge is getting larger, and quickly. The charge is changing at a rate of about a part per quadrillion per week, presently. But it will accelerate. Within five years, molecular stability will begin to fail and that will wreck havoc on our lives. Why won't the University release these results? Soon we will see the consequences. Cancer clusters will abound. We will see climate effects. People need to prepare and the Changing Universe Society has the solution. Those who join us will be saved. Actually more than saved, you will be transported to new realm, a new universe. You will witness a reality you cannot imagine. The joy and purpose will be absolute. If you don't follow us, you will succumb to this universe's demise."

Thomas was aghast. How could anyone know the details of the project? Thomas knew only one place outside the lab that recorded the possible consequences of a changing charge - his private notebook. It must have been those CUS kooks who broke into his house. The thought both chilled him and infuriated him. Whether the change was increasing was still an open question, however, and Thomas hadn't described that in his notebook. They must have gotten details from someone in the lab. How else could he know that? Slowly, Thomas' shock was evolving into anger. "How did Simpson know we see a change in the charge?" He asked himself, actually aloud.

As Harold continued to speak, his eyes scanned the crowd and he saw Thomas. "Look there, sitting on that planter in the back. That is the man who heads the research team that has seen the charge change. Thomas

Conrad, why won't you tell us what you know?" He called out to Thomas while pointing directly at him.

Thomas almost went into a panic. A half dozen acolytes split off from Harold's crowd and swiftly walked towards Thomas. He stood up, uncharacteristically leaving his coffee cup on the planter. The number of people coming toward him grew to about ten, and Thomas began to feel real fear.

He put up his hand. "Stay back. I don't want any trouble," he exclaimed.

But they kept approaching. He started backing away, slowly at first, but the small crowd was closing. One of the CUS members said "We just want to talk."

"Yes, we just want to talk," said another.

Thomas turned and began to walk briskly, looking over his shoulder often. The crowd also started walking faster. "What will they do when they catch me?" he thought to himself. He decided he didn't want to know the answer and started running toward Grunderson Hall. The group started running also, but as Thomas checked back, he realized that they didn't intend to catch him. "Were they just sending a message? he asked himself. He stopped looking back and just ran as quickly as he was able until he was inside Grunderson Hall.

Thomas caught his breath in the hall way, while making sure the pursuers had desisted. No one followed. He guessed Harold had called them back. Once he was sure the chase was over, he went straight to the lab. Now that his panic had calmed, his anger returned.

As Thomas burst into the lab, the other team members were already there. "Who told him?" he demanded loudly.

"Who told who what?" asked Adrian.

"Who told Harold our results? He just gave a summary of them outside. He knew we saw a change and he knew the magnitude. That information could only come from this laboratory."

"I haven't talked to anyone from CUS," Adrian stated very firmly.

"Neither have I," Kathy answered. "Actually, I'm rather offended by the accusation. I've dedicated several years of my life to this project. Why would I jeopardize it?"

"I haven't talked to anyone, let alone CUS," Carl added.

"Well, somehow Harold got information we planned to keep to ourselves. Any ideas how that happened?" Finding the denials convincing, Thomas' anger was transitioning to frustration and stress. Two feelings he knew well.

As Kathy started to speak, the lab phone rang. Carl picked up, "Hello."

"Hello. This is Cindy Freedman from the City Tribune. May I speak to Thomas Conrad, please?"

"Thomas," Carl whispered even though he had his hand over the speaker, "It's Cindy Freedman, a reporter from the Tribune."

"What!?" Thomas asked in shock. "How did she even get this number?" He took the phone from Carl and addressed the caller, "This is Thomas. How may I help you?" He tried to be calm, but he was becoming overwhelmed.

"Hello Professor Conrad," Cindy began. "I was at the gathering outside, when Harold Simpson made the claim about your data. I also saw you run from the crowd. I hope you are OK."

"Yes, I'm fine. Thank you for asking," answered Thomas nervously.

"I would like to ask you a few questions about your research and I was hoping we could meet. I can buy you lunch if you are free around that time?" She had a friendly, enticing voice that made Thomas want to trust her. But he was very uncomfortable with this situation. Even if he wanted to talk, he would need time to consider what he should say.

"I have no comment at this time," Thomas said while hanging up the phone. He turned to his co-workers. "This is bad. Really, really bad," he sighed.

Kathy had been sitting at the computer ever since Thomas had arrived. "Something else happened, Thomas, and I think you should know. Last night I noticed a login on our data cluster that seemed out of place. I just assumed that one of you must have logged in from an unusual device. But looking at the log files now, it's clear that the login came from a location that has not been logged before. If none of you used a new device to log in at about one a.m., I think we were hacked. If the hacker looked at our electronic log books and analysis notes, none of which are secure once you are logged into our cluster, he or she would know everything we have found."

"Change all the passwords and disconnect the damn cluster from the internet," Thomas barked. "For the foreseeable future everyone comes to the lab to log on."

A couple hours of studying computer logs with Kathy didn't help identify the hacker. Frustrated, he needed a quiet place to think this through and he headed for his office. As he walked slowly down the halfway and up the stairs, he kept going over things. "The guy who broke into my house didn't take my notebook," he thought. "Did he read it or maybe photograph it? I have not put any of those notes into our electronic log book, but how did Harold know about those effects? I guess he could have done his own estimates. The guy does seem tech savvy, even if he is crazy."

Once Thomas arrived at this office and sat at his desk, he realized he had a large amount of voicemail. Twelve messages in just over an hour. He slumped as he started to play them. A couple calls were from Harold, to which he had no intention of responding. His sister called. She heard a news report and was worried about him. He'd call her later, but the realization of a news report made him cringe. News report. Already? Two local news stations called and a national news outlet wanted comment. He just rubbed his eyes while listening to those. One from a student who had a question about his final exam grading. Finally there was a short message from his Department Chair requesting that Thomas come see her as soon as he got to his office. Thomas did a mock knocking of his head on his desk a few times, took a deep breath and then headed down the hall to the DeeDee's office.

"I want you to give a colloquium on your results as soon as you can get one together," dictated Prof. Champton. Deborah Dana Champton, or DeeDee to her friends, had been Chair for six years now and she had been really good at the job. Thomas knew that his start-up package and several institutional grants were a direct result of her efforts. He was indebted to her and couldn't say no to anything she requested.

"DeeDee, we haven't completed the collection of data. I certainly don't want to present anything until we have had a chance to analyze what we are observing," Thomas pleaded.

"I understand your reticence Thomas, but this is not a normal situation," DeeDee explained. "My office is being inundated with inquiries. That film clip of you running away from CUS members is on the local news channels. The incident is already on cable news for Christ's sake. If you stand up and give a status report emphasizing that people shouldn't read too much into the result, that's fine. But you have to say something."

"All right, I get it. Is the first week after winter break soon enough?" Thomas regretted the offer as soon as he said it. That would only give him a couple weeks to prepare.

"Perfect and thanks. Looking at the calendar, it looks like the first colloquium opening in January is Friday the eighth. Because that is so close to the holidays, no one wants to travel so we haven't been able to fill that date, and it's free. We will advertise it and answer media inquiries with that schedule. Please write me a few sentence statement about your work that I can distribute. I will make an announcement later this morning. I hope that satisfies the hoards at least until the colloquium. Also, we will anticipate a very large crowd, given the recent gatherings outside and the press interest, so we will use the large auditorium."

Thomas left her office feeling even more uncomfortable. If he had to spend the next two weeks preparing a major presentation, it meant less time working on the data. It would be a busy break. Once he made it back to his office, he called the lab to let them know about the requested talk and to expect requests for data plots as he prepared his presentation. He called his sister to let her know he was OK and that he and Sam were looking forward to Christmas Eve. Finally he called Sam. She hadn't heard the news reports but was very concerned about the day's events. She asked a lot of questions about exactly what Harold said, how scared Thomas was during the chase, and whether the Chair sounded worried about him. The long conversation was very cathartic and it was good to discuss the morning's adventures with someone who was not only supportive, but was actually interested. It helped Thomas relax.

Change is the Only Constant

Christmas fell on a Friday this year and the campus was closing for the winter break on Wednesday evening. The ET team was anxious to complete their work by then. They were all going their separate ways before nightfall. Today, they were readying the fifth week of results since the onset of the change.

Tomorrow, Christmas Eve, Thomas and Sam planned to drive to Tanya's house for the night. The weather was unseasonably warm today for his walk to work, but if the forecasters were right, this wouldn't last. The area was preparing for a very white Christmas. He wasn't thinking about the coming snow and enjoyed the days of mild temperatures. In celebration of the holiday, the Brewers Cup featured a cinnamon spice coffee and cranberry scones. Averse to variety, Thomas stuck with his regular brew however, his favorite muffin (blueberry), and carried them to the lab to enjoy. Despite the mild temperature, he did not want to linger in the quad, sunshine or not.

The walk to campus was uneventful, but today would present another block of data to assess and Thomas was anxious about what it would show. He avoided walking directly by the large quad crowd. After yesterday's run-in, Thomas didn't stop to listen. He was no longer entertained by their antics. He proceeded briskly to Grunderson Hall.

Entering the building and turning toward the hallway

door to the stairs, Thomas came face-to-face with Harold Simpson and four of his followers. Thomas startled to a halt just before colliding with the CUS leader. "Professor Conrad," Harold began, "Just the person I was hoping to run into here. Although perhaps not literally." His smile coincided with widening eyes in a rather unnerving expression.

"I have nothing to say to you, Simpson," Thomas barked. His anger finally letting loose, he pointed his finger in Harold's direction. "You broke into my house, You hacked my lab computers, Your goons chased me yesterday. You may have the upper hand at the moment, but now that I realize what a danger you are, I'm ready for you."

The four supporters stepped between Harold and Thomas. "Settle down, boys," Harold instructed in a calm and fatherly voice. "He's understandably upset." Turning his attention back to Thomas, Harold's voice became very soothing and he patted the air with his right hand in a gesture to lower the tension. "Now Professor Conrad, I don't know what happened to your house or your computers, but I assure you, I am on your side. Your work is very important to us. We would not do anything to disrupt it or slow it down. But we do need the results you are finding. It is critical that we know the time frame for the coming of the MUTs."

"You people are deluded idiots," Thomas yelled as he pushed through CUS members and stepped into the access to the basement stairs. He nearly ran down the hall, fumbling with his keys the entire way to the lab. He felt a sigh of relief when he realized they hadn't followed him. Making sure he had the correct key selected and ready for use, he took several deep breaths to collect himself before engaging the team.

As he entered the lab, Kathy and Adrian were looking at the previous week's results and Carl was preparing a presentable plot of all the data for review. Adrian looked up to say hello to Thomas as he came in, but was a bit surprised by what she saw. "Are you OK?" she asked him. "You look like you just saw a ghost."

"Not a ghost, just Harold Simpson," he answered. "He and some of his enforcers are on the first floor. They confronted me when I came in the door. They seem to be getting bolder and more intrusive. Everyone needs to be extra careful."

"You think they might actually be violent?" asked Carl.

"I have no idea, but they have already done things that make me worry," Thomas explained. "Kathy what is the status of the cluster? Can we get it back on line so we can reduce our trips to the lab? I think it would be smart to break our routines and be less predictable."

"I talked to the Department IT guy," said Kathy, swiveling in her chair to face Thomas. "He had some suggestions to improve our security. I should be done implementing them by tomorrow. None of it is very hard to install, but it means a lot more passwords and two-factor authentication. It might be annoying, but I suggest we password protect all the devices on the local area network and the key applications we use. I will certainly do that for the data files and log books."

"Good. A bit of log-on annoyance will be less grief than these other things," said Thomas. "I sure do miss the days when we rarely talked of anything but physics." He took a deep breath and tried to relax. "What does the data say *this* week?"

"The new data set is ready although it'll be a few minutes before we have decent plots. I fear it indicates further acceleration. The rate of change is increasing," explained Kathy. "The doubling time is short, or at least short compared to any time frame I would have predicted beforehand. We now have five weeks of data since the charge started changing. As a result, we have limited sensitivity and, therefore, a lot of uncertainty."

"Please," interrupted Thomas. "We have all day to discuss the details, nuances and science philosophy. What is the doubling time?"

"Sorry. It's about four weeks. But with the uncertainty, the results are consistent with any value between two and five weeks."

"Shit," hissed Thomas.

Thomas almost never used any crass language, even something this mundane. Adrian certainly took notice and exchanged a meaningful glance with Kathy.

"If this acceleration is real," added Kathy, "the world could be in for it. Two to the power of fifty-two is a very large number." She pulled out her calculator and started typing. "Wow," she whistled. "In a few years, the charge will have changed a huge amount. In fact, to change by a percent, we only need forty-four doubling times. If the four week number is correct, we talking just over three years."

"Sorry, but I can't accept this as real," said Thomas with exasperation. "It goes against all we understand about the laws of physics. It isn't possible that this just turned on. We should focus on making sure things are working properly and not on wild interpretations."

"But Thomas," protested Adrian, "don't we have to go where the data takes us? We have been over this thing many times and still the data look solid. We all agreed to publish, no matter the answer, after twelve weeks of data.

We now have twelve weeks. We should publish this, no matter what."

"We can't publish something we don't think is right," responded Thomas.

"Just because you don't like the answer, is not a reason to claim it's wrong," countered Adrian. Kathy was nodding her head emphatically.

"I updated all the environmental and monitoring plots last night," explained Carl. "Those plots are as flat as ever. But the charge value plot has a definite uptick."

"Can this really be true?" asked Kathy. "We can't seem to find anything experimental that explains this and it doesn't seem likely that we will before your colloquium."

"That colloquium will be a challenge," admitted Thomas. "We will have to acknowledge that we have some concerns, but we can't hide that we see a trend in our data."

"I almost hate to bring this up but Winter Break starts tonight" began Adrian. "This a bad time to remind everyone that I have been planning my vacation for a while now and I leave tomorrow? I'll be gone until just before your talk. I hope that's OK." She finished with a defeated whispering sigh. "Not knowing the answer to this will drive me crazy and probably ruin my vacation."

"I understand Adrian," answered Thomas. "You've done great work getting this experiment up and running and Kathy deserves great credit for her tireless analysis. You both deserve a break. I hope everyone just has a nice Christmas and tries to avoid thinking about this."

Carl noticed he was left off that list.

Resisting Change

The Christmas Eve drive to Tanya and Mark's was tense, not just because of the snow-packed slick roads, but also Thomas' foul mood about his upcoming talk. They had gotten a late start as well and got caught up in holiday traffic as students were rushing to leave for the winter break and the townies were zipping to parties and pageants. Thomas planned to take the state highway to Tanya's as the interstate did not go to her part of the state. A few miles out of town, the highway narrowed to two lanes. He was very familiar with the route, having used it several times a year but the snow, quickly icing over once the sun set, and the likelihood of drunk drivers, made the journey dangerous. Several state and county highways intersected frequently, and he had to be alert the entire way.

"I don't understand why you are so worried about this talk," Sam said with exasperation. "You've given a thousand talks. This is just one more." She was wearing a fashionable parka with a velvety green fabric and tawny faux fur trim; she had already unzipped it to enjoy the heat of the car.

"It's not the act of speaking that has me worried," he explained. "It's that we don't understand the experiment well enough yet to be sure of our result. I want to focus on that, not a presentation."

"It sounds to me like you claim you don't understand

the experiment when, actually, you just don't like the answer," she tried to suggest without confrontation. "If you didn't see a trending change in the charge, would you be worried about this talk? I think it's good that you are getting the result out there."

Despite her effort to sugar-coat it, Thomas was clearly irritated by that question but he had to admit there was some truth to it. "When an experiment finds the answer that was expected, no one really scrutinizes it. But if you find an extraordinary result, you have to provide extraordinary evidence," he explained.

"You have made a big deal about the use of blindness in your work," Sam countered. "To truly follow that philosophy, don't you have to accept what the apparatus tells you?"

"The community doesn't examine a null result where one was expected," he said in an attempt to rephrase his point. "It will go over *this* work with a fine tooth comb."

"But if you don't follow your blindness protocol, doesn't that introduce a very strong bias? One that blindness is supposed to avoid?"

"Damn Sam, you really sound like Adrian today. The answer is yes, of course. And in fact, I think a lot of experiments that find null results make claims that are probably right, but aren't supported by their data. Such results just don't get the same level of scrutiny as evidence for something new. If we are shown to be wrong after making a spectacular claim, it will greatly damage our careers."

"So, the bottom line is that you're worried about tenure and your career crashing," Sam concluded.

"Of course I'm worried about tenure," he responded bitterly. "A garden variety result with a best-to-date limit would effectively ensure I'd be promoted. But now, I have no idea how this will play out."

As Thomas' frustration boiled over while snapping at Sam, he missed the stop sign at an intersecting highway.

"Thomas!" Sam screamed as the other car bore down on them from the left. He caught a glimpse of the impending collision out of the corner of his eye in time to slam on the breaks and jerk the wheel hard to the right. Luckily, the other driver jerked to his left and the cars avoided each other. The whole incident took place in slow motion. Not only was time slowed down due to flowing adrenaline, but both cars were driving at a modest speed due to the snow. The speed was so slow, that Thomas kept expecting the car to come to a stop, but instead, the car continued to slide on the slick road. Seconds ticked by as the car spun around in a large arc, gradually edging off the pavement and down a shallow embankment. The car eased to a stop.

"Are you OK?" he asked Sam.

She nodded. "You?" He returned her nod.

They took a few moments to let their heartbeats settle. As they sat looking into each other's eyes with a feeling of salvation that was hardly deserved by the slow-motion near miss, a knock came on the driver's side window. Thomas, was quickly brought back to the situation. He turned to look out at the other driver looking in. Thomas rolled down the window and the cold air rushed in.

"Are you two OK?" asked the elderly man.

"Yes, but a bit shook. Are you all OK?"

"It's just me and I'm fine. My car spun but stayed on the road. Do you need any help?"

Thomas said, "We're fine! I'm just going to reverse out of this."

The old man stepped back a few paces while Thomas shifted gears. They heard the wheels spinning but the car didn't move. Wordlessly, Sam stepped out and assessed the situation. Leaning against the open passenger door, she bent her head to tell Thomas, "It looks like we're high centered. You're not getting any traction."

Thomas thumped the steering wheel and swore. He jangled the door handle and stepped out. The snow in the ditch was deeper than on the road and covered the tops of his laced boots. He marched to the back of the car to confirm what Sam reported. The car exhaust puffed into the chill air.

The man repeated, "Do you need any help? I have a tow line, but I don't have a hitch."

Thomas glanced over at the man's vehicle, safely pulled to the side of the road, with the emergency lights flashing. It was a sedan, a grampa car, not up to the task off hauling.

"I will have to call roadside service to get towed out. But otherwise, we will be OK. I know this is my fault for missing that stop sign and I apologize for frightening you" responded Thomas.

"I understand and I'm just glad everyone's OK. But you should be more careful with the weather as it is."

"You're right and I do apologize for my driving," answered Thomas. He really just wanted this to end.

"Why don't you call the service? I'll hang out for a while to make sure you can get the help you need. I was on my way to St. Albertus. I'm supposed to usher for Midnight Mass."

"I appreciate that," answer Thomas

A call to AAA confirmed Thomas' fears. It would be an hour or so before the tow truck would get to him. The other driver went on his way. Sam waved at his departing car.

"Damn it, my sister already worries too much about me," Thomas complained to Sam. "Now I have to call her and and explain this to her."

153

"So just call her and say we'll be late. What's the big deal?" During the time they were dealing with the car, the steady snow had dwindled to big flakes falling lazily. Sam scanned the horizon to see her surroundings - mostly farmers' fields in every direction.

"You don't understand! She will make a big about it!"

Sam looked at him oddly. She smiled and took his phone, thumbing the contacts and pressing call. "Hi, Tanya! This is Sam, Thomas' girlfriend. Yes, Merry Christmas to you too."

Thomas frowned and tried to snatch the phone back, but Sam spun away and continued talking. "I just wanted to let you know that we're going to be a bit late, a little road trouble."

"Give it back, Sam!" Sam continued, but Thomas could only hear her end of the conversation.

"We slid into a ditch and need to get towed. No, we're fine! It was all slo-mo. We've called Triple A but they're going to take a while to get here, being Christmas Eve and all."

Then Sam gave a series of "Uh-huhs" and "Yes, I knows" in response to Tanya's chatter. He tried to grab the phone, but Sam was too quick. Then Sam let off a peal of lush laughter and that infuriated him most of all. He made a lunge and started to slide and threw out his arms for balance.

"No, we fueled up before we left town - you know Thomas! Yes, I'll be sure to tell him. He's making snow angels now. See you soon! Bye-bye! Merry Christmas!" She clicked the phone off and cocked an eyebrow at Thomas. "And that's how it's done."

"That was mean, Sam!"

"Oh hush," Sam replied. She walked to him and slid the phone into his jacket's breast pocket. Then she slid her cold fingers inside his shirt along his warm ribs. "Where would you be without me?"

"You shouldn't have..."

"Shhh!" said Sam. "Listen!"

Thomas cocked his head. "It's just coyotes. They won't..."

"No, not that! Listen!" She smiled. "It's church bells, Thomas! Do you hear?"

He listened and he could hear the faint peal. "I think there's a monastery in those hills."

"It's a magical night, Thomas!" She tilted her head back and opened her mouth wide to try and catch the big fluffy snowflakes. She laughed again, and this time he could hear the joy in her voice.

"At least we have plenty of gas," he said. "We can keep warm by running the engine."

"Oh, I can think of other ways to stay warm," Sam said mischievously, snuggling her cold nose into the warmth of Thomas's neck.

"Sam, I love your love of life." He tangled his fingers into her silken hair to turn her face toward him and kissed her deeply and passionately. With an impish giggle, Sam hopped back in the car and Thomas crawled in on the driver's side.

The snow covered the car gently and persistently, as did their hands on each other. The kissing became more desperate until the inhibitions of being in a publicly parked car were overcome by passion. Thomas slid his hand up under Sam's sweater and released her front clasping bra. As he firmly squeezed her breast, Sam's hand made its way down Thomas' chest and undid his pants and reached in. Soon they were both partially nude. The fogged windows hiding the building layer of snow.

The tow truck driver came upon the snow covered

car just where he was told it would be. He parked and walked over while assessing the situation. "Not all that bad," he thought. "Just a short winch job." He went up to the car and wiped the snow off the driver's side window. He smiled when he realized the couple was too busy to notice him. He gently tapped on the window and the lovers jumped like they had heard a gun shot. He started laughing and walked back to this truck so they could gather themselves in private. "This will make a good story to tell the wife tonight," he thought.

"You're lucky. No damage to the car that I can see. The underbelly looks fine." The truck driver was quick and efficient, which Thomas and Sam appreciated. They were still embarrassed after getting caught.

"Thank you for your help," Thomas answered while handing over his credit card.

"You're welcome. Be careful," he advised, "and not just while driving." The driver laughed as he handed back the card and boarded his truck. Thomas lowered his head upon hearing the wisecrack. He guessed he'd hear similar advice all weekend.

"Wait," Thomas called. He pulled a twenty from his wallet and handed it to the driver. "Thank you again."

The driver winked and said, "Much obliged, sir!" He chuckled and with a grinding of gears disappeared down the snowy road.

As Sam and Thomas reentered the car, Thomas tried to be consoling. "Some day we will look back at this and laugh."

"Perhaps," she answered. "But why wait? I'm already laughing." She patted his lap and Thomas edged back in the road and they continued their journey to Tanya's.

Thomas and Sam pulled into Tanya's driveway a bit after eleven. Even before Thomas was fully out of the car, his sister was running toward them. He knew his sister was going to lecture him. "She didn't even take the time to grab a coat," he muttered to Sam.

A slight giggle escaped Sam. "I don't know. This could be fun. She looks like a woman in charge to me." Thomas groaned in response.

Thomas instinctively stiffened as he climbed out the car, ready to withstand the onslaught of his sister's greeting. She gave him a violent hug that almost made him lose his balance. "Thank goodness," she cried. "I was so worried. The weather is horrible. I don't understand why you can't drive more carefully. You're lucky you weren't injured. Don't you look for stop signs?"

"Yes the weather *is* horrible," he answered glancing around. "Let's grab the bags and get inside. It's cold."

Inside the warm house, Thomas handled the introductions. "Mark, Tanya, this Samantha. She goes by Sam." Jazzy holiday music played in the background.

"I am so excited to meet you, Sam," exclaimed Tanya as she leaned in and gave her a hug. "Welcome to our home. I know its late, so Mark will show you to your room. In the meantime, are you hungry or would you like a drink? I have hot cocoa and Christmas cookies. Or maybe a nightcap? Some brandy?"

"To be honest, I'm just tired," answered Sam. "I might have a glass of water but I think I'm ready for bed."

"Let me take your case and follow me," offered Mark. Your room is right down here."

When Thomas woke and rolled over in bed, he realized Sam was already up. Fearing that she was alone with Tanya, he quickly showered and dressed, releasing a brand new shirt from its wrapper. He made a detour to bring the gifts to the living room and added them to the pile under the tree, before heading to the kitchen. Sure enough, the two women were drinking coffee and laughing it up. When they saw Thomas, the laughter just got louder. "Enjoying yourselves at my expense, I assume?" he asked.

"Of course," teased Tanya. "Sam is just delightful, Thomas. We have been having a great time getting to know each other."

Thomas leaned over to give each woman a kiss on the cheek. "Merry Christmas."

"Yes, and Merry Christmas to you too," answer Tanya.

"Well don't let me stop you two from your gossip," he said. "I'll just fix myself something simple to eat. Since I probably don't want to suffer through your depiction of my life's story, do you need anything done that will get me out of the kitchen?"

"No," answered Tanya, "I'm actually way ahead of the game for once."

Thomas toasted a bagel, coated it with butter and orange marmalade, poured a cup of coffee, and headed out to the living room. He sat in a big chair near the Christmas tree. He tried not to think of work. It was painful to be idle with that presentation haunting him. Fortunately, Mark came by and sat in the other chair. They spent the next couple hours drinking coffee while debating and predicting football championship outcomes.

The diversion worked and before he knew it, Cole and Kelly arrived. With a new round of introductions and the serving of drinks, the day's festivities began. After a toast to acknowledge the season and spending time with friends, the three couples exchanged and opened gifts. The others were so animated that Thomas could just relax and listen, which he was very happy to do.

"OK everyone," announced Tanya, "dinner is ready, so please refill your glasses and have a seat. Mark if you will bring the ham in from the kitchen and place it by me, people can pass their plates and I'll serve."

Once everyone had full plates of ham, scalloped potatoes, asparagus and rolls, it didn't take long for the conversation to turn to ET.

"So let me see if I understand correctly," summarized Mark, "you have twelve weeks of data, but the last five indicate the charge on the electron is increasing. This change started just before Thanksgiving and if it continues to increase, life as we know it will cease to be possible in a few years. Good thing Cole and Kelly came for dinner. I can't wait to hear Cole's take on this!"

"Really?" asked an exasperated Thomas. "I already feel like I've transitioned from the proverbial 'turkey before Thanksgiving' phase to the 'cooked Christmas goose' endgame of this situation. Not sure I need to hear further philosophical dissection of the topic."

"Look," began Cole, "this is most likely an experimental artifact."

"Thank you," interrupted Thomas loudly.

"And even if its real," continued Cole, "it is most likely that the change in the charge will not be catastrophic. What you've described is a long way off from mass death. It assumes the extrapolation of an abnormal doubling effect for an extended period. The phenomenon isn't even understood well. We have no idea yet how this will transpire. For all we know, the charge could stop changing next week. Claiming doomsday at this point is fear mongering."

"Simpson, the nutter who founded the CUS lunacy, keeps pushing this extinction event conspiracy," moaned Thomas. "It won't be easy to drag people back to reality once they hear the basis for his claims."

"Most conspiracies are built of melting snow on a slope of grounded truth," added Kelly. "They have to be plausible enough to get the snowball rolling. Once it starts downhill, though, no telling what it'll pick up."

"If it isn't real and you are convinced that you have checked all the apparatus, could it be sabotage?" asked Mark. "I mean could someone have intentionally done something?"

"Our lab is always locked and there are a lot of interlocks that would provide a sign of tampering," claimed Thomas. "If you damaged some piece of apparatus or adjusted something, it might cause a shift in what we see, but not a sudden or ongoing increase. We wrote all our own code and it would be almost impossible to corrupt thousands of lines of software in such a specific way. You would have to be very intimate with it. In any case, why would someone sabotage a scientific experiment? What would anyone have to gain? Science will eventually find the true answer. If you faked a result, the gains would be short lived and perhaps ruinous once the claim was refuted. Such a move will destroy a scientist's career."

"Harold Simpson has credibility to gain with his followers for one thing," answered Kelly. "Since the Changing Universe Society derives its income from new recruits, there is a financial motive. I doubt that CUS cares about your career."

"Although it's true that CUS raises some funds from newcomer donations," responded Sam, "most of their money comes from Harold Simpson's wealth. He seems to have become completely focused on these MUTs and has little interest in anything else. In fact, their plan to join the MUTs involves leaving their bodies behind, whatever that means. If so, I'm not sure what more money does for them."

"It's a suicide cult?" asked Mark in disgust.

"I don't know for sure," answered Sam. "but I've gotten a vibe and the end of days focus comes across loud and clear in meetings."

"Meetings?" asked Cole. "You meet with them?"

"Yes," answered Sam, "I'm their bookkeeper. I work mostly with Harold's son, Jonathan. I meet with him a couple times a month at his office and we discuss financial details by phone fairly often. We don't discuss the CUS tenets very often, but it has come up on occasion."

"Thomas, my brother," interjected Tanya, "will you help me in the kitchen with the dessert, please."

"Certainly," he replied and got up to follow.

Tanya was cutting the pecan pie and putting slices on plates, while Thomas added whipped cream and a fork. After the first couple slices were ready, Tanya asked, "is Sam a member of this CUS?"

"No," answered Thomas, "she just works for them. Sam has a lot of clients. CUS is just one of them."

"I didn't realize how scary that group is," said Tanya. "They are harassing you, they may have sabotaged your experiment, and they are planning to kill scores of people. You need to convince Sam to step away from them before she gets hurt."

"Sam has a less harsh view of them," explained Thomas. "Although the possibility that it's a suicide cult concerns her, she thinks of them more as an emerging religion. She is adamant that the members are happy and get a reasonable exchange for the money they contribute. And in my own defense, I must insist that it's not possible for someone to sabotage our experiment. I am sure whatever is going on in my laboratory is not underhanded."

Tanya turned to face Thomas head on. "Look, the suicide thing trumps everything else. If that is the group's plan, Sam needs to steer clear. And *you* need to be careful yourself. If they're willing to kill themselves, who knows what else they might do. I know he was joking when he said it, but there is wisdom in Dad's words, 'Never trust anyone who wants to get to heaven too fast."

Thomas just nodded but felt his tension return.

The two siblings were able to carry all six servings to the table in one trip. Tanya went to grab the coffee pot, and they all began to eat. Thomas was thankful the conversation turned to more mundane topics. Not too long after dessert, Cole and Kelly caught their Uber for home. They were worried about the roads and didn't want to stay too late. Mark and Thomas cleaned up while Sam and Tanya relaxed by the tree.

After finishing the dishes, the men came to join the women. Mark brought a Chateau de Monbel Armagnac and provided everyone with a small stemmed glass of a couple ounces each.

"How are the nightmares, Thomas?" asked Tanya.

"Nightmares, what nightmares?" asked a surprised Sam.

"Thomas is under a lot of stress about this tenure decision. He has had a recurring nightmare," explained Tanya.

Thomas rolled his eyes. "You just won't give me a break will you. Yes, I have nightmares and the tenure decision is a critical milestone in my career. The experiment that will impact that decision is having issues. Why would you be surprised that I am stressed."

"I understand all that, Love," consoled Sam. "But I'm hearing this nightmare thing for the first time and I am a bit surprised. And worried, I might add. I wish you had confided in me."

By Saturday morning, the road crews had finally won their battle with the snow. As a result, driving home was easy and uneventful. The previous day's conversations, however, had hit all the touchy points. The two lovers traveled in silence.

Upon arrival at Thomas' house, Sam got ready to leave. "Love, I have to take a swing by a number of clients before the New Year. Tax deadlines and all," she explained. Thomas frowned his disappointment. "I also plan to see some family tomorrow and for New Year's. I'll be back in time for your colloquium." She gave him a lover's kiss goodbye, tossed her bag in the car, and off she went.

Thomas understood she had work, but he was still disappointed. He thought it was strange that she always found a way to avoid telling him where she was going. She hadn't talked of her family, but seemed to see them on occasion. "I wonder if I'll ever meet them," he thought. He unpacked the car and checked on the house. He found some relief that everything was as he left it.

The rest of Christmas break wasn't much of a break, at least not for Thomas. "Why did this have to go public?" He asked himself over and over. "It would have been so much easier if we could have worked this out on our own time." He felt they should publish, or at least submit a paper, before discussing the results publicly. But he didn't know how to write the paper.

"What does the conclusion say in a paper with an extraordinary result that implies worldwide destruction?" Thomas had always made publishing before presentation his policy, but this situation put him in a difficult spot. Some scientists preferred to present results at a conference and get feedback from other experts before they wrote their final paper. But that was a bit old school. In today's scientific culture, any public announcement was taken as a final result. If a scientist then made changes, it was now considered justification for skepticism, or at least, an indication of sloppy work. This ethos intimidated Thomas.

He dedicated the entire week between the holidays developing the presentation. He had to get this right. His scientific reputation hinged on how he handled this situation, to say nothing of his tenure case. He had to walk a thin line between being open about what they saw and not emphasizing what was likely to be a spurious result. He didn't want to discredit his own work by advertising an outlandish claim.

He decided to describe the data, but not discuss any potential implications. He would focus on the systematic tests they were conducting. That approach worried him a bit because they were mostly done with these tests and out of ideas of additional things to check. Even he had to admit that the result was surviving scrutiny. He didn't want to be dishonest about their work to understand the apparatus, but he didn't want to create a stir either. He decided he would dedicate much of his talk to the upgrade. He wanted to discuss this approach with Adrian, but she was on vacation. He thought about asking Kathy, but he didn't want to start a debate about publishing. "I wish Sam was here," he thought. "I could use a bit of distraction."

New Year's Eve was a stupid excuse for parties in Thomas' opinion, and he worked the entire day, but he relaxed on New Year's Day to watch the games and drink a few beers and eat a pizza. Late on the Saturday night after New Year's Day, Thomas was focused on fixing one particular slide in his presentation regarding the scientific method and its application to ET. Some experiments were designed to falsify a hypothesis, while others were designed to measure some physical value. He wanted it to make it clear that his experiment had been designed to falsify a hypothesis. The design of ET was based on the premise that any change would be exceedingly small. With that assumption, the experiment was unlikely to see a change, but instead would falsify the hypothesis that the charge *was* changing. The result would be a limit, determined by the sensitivity of the effort, on the size of any change. The interpretation of any experiment intended to falsify a hypothesis can become complicated if, instead, one used the data to claim an observation of an effect.

Thomas knew it was difficult to prove the observed result is due to, and only due to, the physical process investigated. Often in such cases, the measured effect was near the experiment's ultimate sensitivity and therefore the evidence was marginal with a premium on how well systematic errors were understood. For ET, however, the result was much larger than its sensitivity. In fact, it was large enough to have been seen by previous searches. However, ET also implied the change commenced only recently. Since the previous experiments were no longer operating, those searches wouldn't have seen it because they weren't looking at the right time.

Thomas struggled to capture these concepts clearly. He wanted to be open about their work, but worried his explanation would come across as claiming the charge was changing, something he was loathe to do. He had less than a week to get this talk ready and his nerves were fraying.

Thomas' concentration was broken by the tell-tale creak of his front porch step. He was well accustomed to the time span between the creak and the doorbell ring. He saved his work, took a drink from his neglected and now warm beer, and stood to answer the door. But the delay had expired. That no ring came was more startling than a sudden noise. He went to the front window, and glancing out, saw no one. "I know that sound too well," he thought. "Someone was on my porch. I'm sure of it." He opened the door and inspected the porch. Nothing was out of the ordinary. He slammed the door shut. "Leave me alone," he screamed at the ceiling.

Lecture with Changes

The week flew by and Thomas was nervous when Friday the eighth arrived. He was as ready as he was ever going to be. Arriving at the colloquium site, he made sure the audio visual equipment was in good shape. He was thankful he could do it without an AV tech assistant. He then stepped into the auditorium's support room for some water to calm himself. That didn't work so well, because he could hear the increasing murmur of the audience as it began to fill the auditorium. He knew it was going to be a big crowd, but nothing prepared him for the standing-room-only vision as he re-entered the room.

Every seat was taken in the six-hundred capacity room; one of the largest lecture halls on campus. Two film crews had set up cameras on tripods in the back of the auditorium and Thomas saw news reporters doing sound checks. A couple rows on the left side of the hall were full of tan collared pull-over shirts with light blue arm bands. The front row on the right was filled with media people. Thomas wasn't sure who to be more afraid of, CUS or the press. He took a seat while DeeDee introduced him to those assembled.

Once Thomas started talking, his nerves relaxed a bit. Public speaking about his science was something he truly loved and the more he explained his work the calmer he became. He projected a slide with a cartoon of the experiment's layout. "ET is an experiment that monitors the wavelength of two atomic transitions that depend differently on the electric charge," he explained. "Our team uses lasers to excite the transitions of interest and we detect the emitted light." He moved to the next slide which described how the data was processed. "It's important to know that the data is blind to the experimental team until the analysis is finished. We also fixed the length of time we would collect data, twelve weeks, which ended just before Christmas."

Thomas knew his next slide was likely to cause a stir and he hesitated a bit before clicking his remote controlled mouse and advancing. "Beginning the week of Thanksgiving, the data indicate that the charge is changing. The rate of change is about a part per quadrillion per week. This is a very, very small number. It is about ninety-three million miles from the Earth to the Sun. If that distance increased at the same rate, it would increase by about half the diameter of human hair in a week. ET is a very sensitive apparatus. But let me emphasize, we are still working to verify that the experiment is working properly." The audience began to murmur, and not in a good way. Thomas worried.

As he prepared to evolve his talk toward ET-2, he realized that Harold's group had attended in especially large numbers. Not only was there a collection of them in one section, but many others were scattered throughout the audience. A shiver ran up his spine.

He advanced to the next slide, with its description of ET-2. "The present experiment compares transition wavelengths in two different elements," he lectured, "mercury and cesium. But we have developed a technique using two nearby transitions in ytterbium and hence we won't require a relative standard to compare the wavelengths. This will be a significant improvement even though the new version won't be an extensive modification beyond the present configuration. It will only take a few months to get it running. If the presently indicated rate of change of the electric charge is true, it will only take a few days to confirm or refute the present result."

A hand shot up from a tanned shirt sitting near the center. Harold didn't even wait for Thomas to acknowledge his request to speak. "Nice presentation, Professor Conrad," complimented Harold, but the niceties ended there. Thomas raised his hand to ask that questions be held till the end, but Harold barreled on. He stood in front of his seat and projected his voice to be heard through the entire hall. "But you spent so much time backing off the obvious conclusion, that I'm sure many in the audience have missed the significance. The Universe, as we know it, is changing and will soon have no place for us in it. You had a chance to tell people the truth but you dodged it. I am very disappointed in you. As an intellectual leader, you should be more intellectually honest."

Harold's voice and posture were that of a disappointed parent. The audience responded in many ways. A few laughed taking Harold to be a crackpot. Others gasped, struck by the lack of manners. Still others nodded and verbally agreed.

"I don't know what you are referring to," stuttered Thomas. "I described our result and our concerns." He was a bit shook by the atmosphere the room had acquired.

"You did not address the impact of a changing charge," Harold accused.

"No, I didn't Mr. Simpson," defended Thomas. "This is only a lone experimental result and it requires review and confirmation." Once again, numerous disappointed groans sounded throughout the hall.

"You are very misguided, Professor Conrad. Be sure, your future will certainly not be what you think." Those accusing words were haunting and reminded Thomas of the past Thanksgiving dinner conversation at his sister's house.

"We have not looked at possible consequences," said Thomas.

"You have too," yelled a CUS member from the other side of the auditorium. Thomas' head shot to his right as he tried to see who made the comment. Several other audience members started their own catcalls. "There will be cancer clusters," called one. "The climate may change," called another.

Thomas tried to calm the disturbing trend in the room. "Now, please, this is not the time to be alarmist."

"Oh, but it is exactly the time to be alarmist, Professor Conrad," interrupted Harold. "The populace must make preparations. By ignoring the inevitable, you are putting them in unnecessary danger." Every line Harold proclaimed was punctuated by clapping and cheers from his followers, like a congregation approving a preacher.

The University did not provide security at its colloquia. As people began to leave their seats and crowd the stage to confront Thomas, he feared things were getting out of hand. He tried to address questions as he quickly packed his things, but the questions seemed to be mostly rhetorical and accusing. The newly formed mob didn't really want answers. Harold, remarkably spry for his age, stood on his seat and Thomas could hear him address the CUS members. Other people were hurrying out the back doors of the auditorium. The media teams were trying to capture as much of the activity on tape as possible. DeeDee tried to recapture control but she couldn't be heard over the increasing noise. Thomas was trapped behind the podium, but DeeDee and two other faculty helped to make a path to the back door for him to escape. Once through the door, DeeDee made sure it was locked and she asked one of the other professors to call campus police.

DeeDee was not happy. "Why didn't you answer the question, Thomas? You just threw gasoline on this fire. Some of those people are genuinely concerned and you should have anticipated someone would ask about what this all means."

"DeeDee, I'm sorry," apologized Thomas. "I sincerely thought I could avoid that topic by convincing them that we still need to better understand how ET works."

"Just great, Thomas. Just great," snapped DeeDee. She shook her head and glanced around, clearly in thought. She then added, "We will wait here until the campus police arrive. We should get an escort out of here. Who knows what some of those people might do."

Thomas' phone rang. It was Sam. "Thomas," she panted. "Are you alright?"

"Yes, but I'm stuck here in the building until the campus cops come and rescue us," he answered. "What about you?"

"I'm fine. I snuck out the back as soon as people started rushing the stage. Send me a text when you're clear so I know you're OK. I have to prepare for an unusual Saturday meeting in the morning, but I will see you tomorrow night."

"OK, see you then," said Thomas as he hung up.

Almost before the call disconnected, he got a text from Kathy. "With Adrian. Couldn't get thru crowd. See U @ Lab tomorrow."

"Am I just a doomed turkey?" Thomas asked himself. "What are my chances for tenure?" He hung his head and waited for the rescue.

171

Thomas walked home after the colloquium. The campus police had Thomas wait for over an hour while they dispersed the unruly crowd. It was very cold, early evening. He didn't feel like cooking for just one, so he stopped and picked up a chicken Caesar salad to go. As he made the final turn down the street to his place, he passed a house with a small pond in the garden. The pond was near the sidewalk and as Thomas glanced at the ice on the pond surface, he did a double take. He came to a complete stop and stared at the water feature. He completely forgot the horrible afternoon as the frozen layer of ice struck him. "Ice floats," he said out loud to no one.

Thomas picked up his pace and hurried home. Entering, he set his salad down on the counter and immediately forgot about it. He took a beer from the fridge, opened it, set it on his desk and then forgot about it too. He pulled his private notebook out of the covered bookshelf, opened up to the first blank page and wrote the date. He made a list of all he knew about the water molecule. When he finished that, he did some web surfing to complete his thoughts. At that point, he began to write a summary of what he knew and learned about the topic.

The water molecule contains two hydrogens and one oxygen atom. One might imagine that the atoms in the molecule lie on a line, but that is not the case. The hydrogens provide one electron each and the oxygen provides six. Each hydrogen-oxygen bond takes two electrons, which completes an atomic shell. The remaining four electrons form two lone pairs. Without the constraint of being bound to two atoms, the lone pairs are mobile. The electrostatic repulsion of these lone pairs, and the electrons forming the bonds, push the hydrogens off to one side of the line with the two lone pairs inhabiting the opposite side. As a result the hydrogen-oxygen-hydrogen arrangement forms an angle of about one hundred four degrees. This molecular shape is responsible for many of the unique properties of water required for life. As a result of this shape, when it freezes the molecules arrange themselves so that water expands instead of contracting like most materials. Since ice is less dense than water, the bottom of deep ponds will not freeze permitting fish to survive through the cold winter months.

If the electron charge increases, the repulsion will too. This pushes the hydrogens further away from the lone pairs and decreases the angle. If the angle decreases too much, ice would be more dense than water.

Water is a polar molecule. That is, the charge is not evenly distributed. This uneven distribution results in stronger electric forces between water and other molecules. This feature leads to water's ability to dissolve a large number of common substances. Many of these dissolved compounds are necessary as nutrients for life. This polar feature also means that water adheres to itself strongly. That feature allows trees to lift water high above the ground. If the electric charge increases, this polar feature would decrease with disastrous consequences for life as we understand it.

As he finished rereading his entry, he realized two things. First, the size of the change implied by his data seemed too small to distort the shape of water enough to cause any science-fiction-like consequences. His initial excited panic about water diminished. Two, he was hungry. He took a sip of his beer and grimaced at the warm drink. He got himself a fresh cold beer and started in on the salad. Looking at his watch, he figured it was too late to call Sam. He finished his meal, put the notebook back in its place, and headed to bed. The evening's research and journal writing mitigated the feeling of dread from the debacle at the colloquium; he felt refreshed confidence – he could deal with DeeDee and all the expected fallout.

Yearning for Change

Kathy and her younger sister talked by phone a few times each week. Their joint love of science was instilled by their parents. Both engineers, they were always working with the girls on a technical project, or building something, or visiting a museum. The family's enjoyment of all things technical influenced the impressionable young women. A year apart, both graduated first in their high-school class, completed the undergraduate studies in three years and then went to graduate school.

"Kathy, put a big red circle on your calendar for the last weekend in May – that's the graduation weekend and Mom and Dad are coming. They promise a celebration."

"I am so proud of you, Judy. My sister, the Ph.D. chemist. I finished reading your dissertation last night. It was fascinating. You did a great job."

"Thank you, Kathy. Mom has picked this really upscale restaurant on the beach for a family dinner the night before the ceremony. They rented an Airbnb – a large house on the water that can sleep the whole family and is big enough for a party. They are really going all out."

"It will be a lot of fun. I wouldn't miss it for the world, even if there was no dinner or party."

"I can't believe I'm done. It seems like it took so long."

"Five years isn't that long, little sister," Kathy responded with thinly veiled frustration. "I have done all they have asked and more. Still they won't let me go. I'm beginning to feel used. Student labor is cheap and how else do you get such expertise at the cost of my salary. I am about ready to scream." She loved her sister, but her comment drove home a painful point.

"I'm sorry Kathy. I didn't mean to be insensitive. I know you're having issues with Thomas. I'm just excited for myself and got self-absorbed. I hope you aren't mad."

"Judy, I am very happy for you. You have worked hard and deserve this. I do not blame you. But I do think that I deserve it also. So I am upset, but don't let that keep you from enjoying your time. I'll get mine someday."

"Maybe you should talk to Thomas and tell him what you're thinking. He might be distracted and just hasn't thought about how long you've been there. You said he just hired another student and you have gotten the planned twelve weeks of data. Throw that at him. It's time for him to let you go."

"I think you're right. I will talk to him."

As Kathy hung up the phone, her anger was starting to build. "I have to talk to Thomas," she told herself. "If I don't I'm going to explode."

The following morning Kathy woke up and ate breakfast across the table from her roommate in silence except for the methodical crunching of granola mixed with yogurt. She lived in university housing for graduate students and married students, where she shared a two bedroom apartment with a medical student. The two of them were very diffcrent and really didn't talk much. She rinsed her bowl, and rehearsed the speech she had constructed before going to bed last night after talking to Judy. The roommate pointedly cleared her throat, and Kathy sighed and sheepishly washed the dish and spoon thoroughly; that was one issue they had discussed. Kathy muttered the lines of her argument as she wrung out the dish cloth. When she was finally happy with her argument, she walked over to Grunderson Hall.

She stopped at Thomas' open office door, knocked and asked, "Thomas, can we talk?"

"Sure Kathy. Come on in. I need a break from this anyway."

"Thomas, I think I need to start writing. We have our twelve weeks of data now and I helped build and operate the experiment. I have finished the analysis. It's time."

"Kathy, you *have* done a great job, but you have to resolve the complication that arose in your data. Good scientists work through these things."

"Thomas, I have been a grad student for six years now. Four of those I have worked for you on this project. We now have a result and I want to write it up and graduate. I know our result is anomalous. So I propose I write a thesis with a weak limit and say that although our result is consistent with a dramatic change in the charge, we don't want to make such a dramatic claim without further confirmation."

"Wanting to graduate is a good thing, but there is one more hurdle to jump. You have done everything that you need to do to learn the tools of science. I agree with that. But the next step is to become a full colleague and not just a student. We have a surprising result that we don't fully understand. We need to better assess what could have gone wrong. A colleague does that."

"Easy to say on a professor's salary, Thomas." Kathy's eyes were blazing as her frustration was evolving toward anger. "I have worked hard to look for experimental problems. You know that and you know that we have found nothing. It's time to write up what we've done and then prepare for the new effort. ET-2 is Carl's experiment, not mine. I'm working for next to nothing here. It's time for me to graduate. I would be willing to accept a short-term postdoc or research position to help solve this mystery, but I need to graduate."

"I'm sorry Kathy. We just don't see eye-to-eye on this. I think seeing this through is part of the educational process."

"Oh screw this," Kathy snorted as she stormed out of Thomas' office.

Thomas sighed. "This just keeps getting better," he thought.

Kathy was too angry to work, so she headed out to the student union building. The SUB was a favorite hangout of the students and Kathy loved the place, especially its coffee. She bought a cup and a scone, picked up a student newspaper, and went to sit at a table by the window. She took a sip of the coffee, a bite of the scone and then laid the paper out on the table.

After staring at, but not really reading the paper for twenty minutes, she started in on the crossword puzzle. It was a moderately difficult puzzle. Hard enough to take time, but easy enough to keep her working on it. Soon an hour had passed.

A man approached her table. "May I join you, please? I would like to discuss your research with you."

Kathy looked up and was confused. "Do I know you?" Kathy was struck by his resemblance to Thomas. For a second she thought perhaps Thomas had followed her.

"Probably not. I am Jonathan Simpson. My father, Harold Simpson, leads the Changing Universe Society. I have seen you at some of his rallies near the physics building and it didn't take long to figure out you work with Thomas Conrad."

"I'm not sure I really want to talk to you. Hacking our systems and breaking into Thomas' house were really low."

Jonathan looked at her quizzically, but then went on. "As you know CUS is really interested in your research. We just want you to drop by our compound and give us a summary followed by a Q&A. We'll compensate you. Two hours of your time and we'll give you a thousand dollar honorarium. What d'ya say?"

Kathy hid her reaction with a quick swallow of coffee. A thousand dollars? With that amount, she would be able to buy a ticket to Judy's graduation without having to beg Mom and Dad for it. Maybe she could get a gift too, or a fabulous outfit for the event. "Wow, that's a lot, but I don't know. I could use the money, but I have some concerns about your group. I'm not sure I should support it."

"Kathy, we are a serious group. We are not a dangerous cult, but we do have a set of beliefs that are founded on a specific sub-field of science. That sub-field just happens to be your area of expertise. Therefore, we'd like to hear your take on it."

"Why me? Thomas gives all our talks, and I mean all of them. Why don't you want him to speak?"

"Honestly, we'd love that," explained Jonathan, "but that relationship is too far gone. That colloquium event got out of hand. Thomas won't discuss such things with us."

"Can I think about it, Jonathan?"

"Certainly, here's my card. Think about it and if you decide to do it, give me a call."

"Good bye." Kathy knew she should just say no, but she was mad at Thomas and wanted the money. She was tempted and stared at the crossword without reading it.

A shadow fell on the puzzle page and Kathy looked up. Adrian stood there, a fresh cup of coffee in her hand. She hooked her thumb in the direction of Johnathon's departure and asked, "Who was that?"

Kathy shrugged, reluctant to tell her thoughts.

"I was watching from the coffee bar. He doesn't look like the usual campus kid."

Kathy shrugged again and shook her head. "Some guy from that CUS group. He wants me to visit and talk about our work."

"Whoa." Adrian sat opposite Kathy and sipped her hot brew. "And you said?"

"I said I'd think about it." Kathy rolled her eyes for comic effect. She wanted to hide how sorely the offer tempted her. She went on, "Look, all I want to do is graduate. I don't want to deal with all this other nonsense. But Thomas is insisting that I stay until we are one hundred per cent confident in our result. I get the impression he doesn't believe our own data. But what else can we do. We have checked everything more than once."

Adrian nodded knowingly. "Kathy, you know that Thomas needs this experiment for tenure. He has a lot to lose as we delay. I am also worried that we aren't getting a paper out, but you can't claim he has no skin in this game. We all have career issues with this thing."

"OK Adrian, I hear you, but I am very frustrated and it's hard to cope. And what about you? You were angry that Thomas didn't let you give that talk."

"Yes and I'm still angry about that. But the colloquium got the result out, so I am optimistic Thomas will agree to submit a paper soon. What choice does he have? He'll need to get an official statement about ET before the rumor mill destroys our credibility. A publication will help all of us."

Kathy sighed, "Anyway, I better get back to work. I've been sitting here quite a while now. Want the paper?" She reached out, offering it to Adrian.

"Yeah. Thanks." Adrian watched Kathy walk back toward Grunderson Hall. She couldn't help but think that something wasn't right. Kathy seemed more agitated than normal.

Another Change

Mid April, Thomas walked to campus with a sense of urgency while mentally revisiting the last few months and the upcoming summer. The NSF money had arrived a bit earlier than expected. He had begun ordering the new parts in February as soon as the money was in his university account. Some items were delivered rather quickly, within a couple weeks. Once they arrived, Thomas had turned off ET and the process of upgrading the experiment commenced. There were some parts, however, that had an anticipated twelve-week lead time. These were the more complicated and custom designed parts, so by the time they were ordered, delivery was expected to be late May. If all went well, the apparatus could be ready to run in fall. After a vibrant debate, the team finally agreed to a one month data run for ET-2, all blind. They would take the data and then analyze. There would be no intermediate result stages as with ET. With the rate of change being so large, ET-2 would easily confirm or refute what ET saw with that month.

Thomas had a lingering concern about the NSF view of things. Fareed expressed strong disappointment with the CUS situation when he called last January to let Thomas know the money was being transferred. "Your colloquium energized that group," he complained. "They are very active with their social media and have made quite a stir. The online news media now have routine updates on the group and even the network news groups mention them every now and then. Be careful how you interact with them in the future. The NSF does not want our science investment to become a circus act. The film clips of you being chased and of the talk are all over the internet. That is not the type of publicity we are looking for." Thomas heard him loud and clear.

When they turned off ET the first week of February, the change rate in the charge was three parts per quadrillion per week. Kathy's initial guess of a four week doubling time was just about right. Although they had operated ET for over a month longer than planned, the team had an acrimonious debate about the wisdom of turning ET off.

"It is the only experiment making these types of measurements," argued Carl. "If the charge is really changing, we are required to monitor it. The world will need to know what ET has to say."

Thomas, sure the result was spurious, countered, "We need to focus on ET-2. It's the only way we can prove whether this is real or not." Thomas insisted they stop the data collection and they had begun the disassembly.

To further add to his stress, the delay in publishing the results from ET was taking its toll on his tenure case. DeeDee was struggling to keep the department on his side and used much of her political capital convincing her colleagues to give him an extra year. It was tricky argument to make, but in the end, the speed with which the new experiment was progressing tempered even the most impatient.

Life with Sam, however, was certainly going well. They had fallen into a routine usually seeing each other four days a week, Wednesday through Saturday. Sam would leave on Sunday morning to prepare for her work week. She would visit clients on Monday through Wednesday, returning that evening. His life was complicated, but it certainly had its pleasures. He looked forward to seeing her tonight. When he saw her walk up his driveway, his heart skipped a beat.

Sam entered the front door but their embrace immediately signaled something was wrong. "What's bothering you, Love?"

"I'm not sure," he replied. "I am so grateful for the NSF support and the progress on ET-2. But the vibe in the lab is all wrong."

"How so?"

"Both Kathy and Adrian are upset and getting more disagreeable by the day. I understand Kathy's anger well enough, but I don't see why Adrian is so put off. She has plenty time left on her postdoc clock."

"What about that conference she wants to go to?" asked Sam.

Thomas hesitated a bit, wondering when Adrian told her about that. "I know she's upset about this summer's talk, but once we understand the ET result, she will be sitting pretty."

"How's Carl doing? He always seems cheerful," said Sam, trying to find a bright spot.

"Carl is very quiet, and building ET-2 seemed to keep him satisfied for a while. But, even so, he is drifting away for reasons I can't put my finger on."

"Love, let's eat and forget about work for a while. You need to take a break."

Thomas smiled, and kissed her.

It was an unseasonable hot April Wednesday morning as Adrian walked into Grunderson Hall, descended the stairs and turned down the hall toward the lab. It was the warmest spring on record and she was feeling pretty good. Things were going well with ET-2 and she was confident they were going to get better. She was smiling and walking with a kick in her step. Adrian always seemed to be a bit late on Mondays and in a good mood. Whatever she did on weekends was working for her.

As she entered the lab, Thomas, Kathy and Carl were fixated on a paper. She joined their huddle and peered over their shoulders at their object of interest.

"A group in Japan claims to have observed a change in the charge," answered Kathy. "This paper just appeared on the archive. It reads like we could have written it. It's a similar setup and process. They are even getting an answer comparable to ours."

"That's not possible," replied Adrian in shock. She was almost desperate. "There's no way."

Thomas acted like he didn't hear her. "I don't like this. They don't have any sort of blindness scheme. They have much less data than we do. How can they be so sure they don't have an experimental problem."

"Because they know we see it too," enunciated Kathy slowly and precisely. "Since they aren't first, they aren't so squeamish about describing what they've found. I can't believe they scooped us. Now I won't even get a first result pub. We should have submitted a paper a long time ago. You really blew this." Kathy was angry and it showed. She glared at Thomas.

"Kathy," Thomas looked her in the eye, "we have been doing all our cross checks and this Japanese group certainly hasn't. They jumped the gun. Everyone knows we have this result and are checking it. We will get credit. But worse, if it is right, it won't matter. Things will not be good. Don't you realize yet what a charge changing at this rate means? If it's changing as fast as these data imply, we are looking at a world-ending event. How can you worry about graduating? Graduating to what?"

"That paper can't be right," Adrian barked in interruption.

Both Thomas and Kathy looked at her, surprised at her emphatic attitude. "How are you so sure of that?" asked Thomas. "Have you read it?"

"Uh, no, just the abstract," She stammered. "As you said, they don't have enough data to do the required cross checks," she answered a bit hesitantly.

Thomas gave her a baffled glance. Kathy continued her tirade. "Clearly they consider us their cross check. We need to get our result posted ASAP. Shit! They even took the opportunity to define the unit of change. They denote parts per quadrillion per week by the short-hand PQW and even indicate how it should be pronounced, peek-week. This is exasperating."

Thomas' frustration with Kathy was building but Carl spoke before he could respond. "From data taken in March, they quote a result of four PQW," he noted. "That would agree with our estimate of the change if you account for the four week doubling time, but we never told anyone about the acceleration, did we? Shouldn't they be thinking our result is 1 PQW? That is quite the coincidence if the paper is wrong."

Thomas and Kathy looked at Carl with shock as the reality of his observation sank in. If there were two experiments seeing evidence for the same rate of change, it implied the change was real. Although they had open mouths, neither said anything. Adrian just kept reading the paper.

"Why did we turn ET off?" complained Carl. "If this is real..."

"If the press follows up on this, things are going to get interesting," said Thomas, changing the subject a bit. "Considering how they responded to our colloquium, imagine what they'll do now. And that doomsday group is going to have a field day. They will consider this to be confirmation of their beliefs."

"Why do you care what that cult thinks?" lectured Kathy. "I want a career in science and this will not help. Poor Adrian here has worked on this project even longer than I have. What does she now have to show for it? Sure we can still publish, but now we are also-rans when we had this result for weeks. Actually it has been four months. When will we publish?"

"I'm sorry, Kathy," responded Thomas. "I can't help but think something must be wrong. I am focused on understanding our apparatus better."

"What does blindness mean then?" asked Kathy. "Didn't we all agree that we would publish regardless the answer? You sound like you're afraid of your own result."

"Kathy, don't go too far," implored Adrian. Thomas was just staring at Kathy in silence. Adrian hoped to tamp down the tension. She knew Kathy had a point, but Thomas wasn't going to see it her way if she backed him into a corner. "Thomas, we need to understand what you have to see before you will agree to publish."

"I," he stuttered. "I don't know. This result is so strange, I just can't get my head around it."

"Uggh," groaned Kathy. She stood abruptly, grabbed her pack, and stormed out of the lab.

"Thomas, you need to be careful with her," advised Adrian. "We need her. She wrote all the analysis code. If we had to figure out how to revise it without her, we would really be delayed."

"I know. I know." Thomas prepared to leave himself, and just as he got to the door, there was a knock. Thomas opened the door revealing Harold Simpson standing in the hallway.

"Did you see the paper out of Japan?" Harold asked.

Thomas just stared, too shocked to respond. Adrian flanked Thomas in the doorway and she spoke first. "We saw the paper but we are still digesting it."

"Interesting how their result matches yours if you account for the increasing rate of change," Harold prodded. "You must have noticed that. You don't have any thoughts on what this all means?"

"How the hell could you possibly know those details of our analysis," Thomas barked. "We haven't told anyone about the accelerating change."

"Ah, so it is true," smiled Harold. "Thank you for confirming the rumors."

Thomas realized he had lost his composure and said too much.

"Why are you here?" asked Adrian. "Can't you just leave us alone until we finish our work?"

"Several PQW and increasing," Harold answered. "The world is headed for a difficult future. The climate is already affected and we will soon start to hear of cancer clusters. The Changing Universe Society will depart before these catastrophes take their toll, but I needed confirmation before I could make final arrangements to meet the MUTs. Thankfully, I now have that."

"When do you plan to meet them?" Carl asked. He was still at his desk, but his voice carried and they all wheeled to face him.

"We have many preparations to make, but I think we would be ready this fall. We still need to hear from the MUTs, but it's exciting to know that the time is finally here."

"Mr. Simpson," finally spoke Thomas, "I ask that you stop your harassment. Please leave us."

"Certainly, Professor Conrad," he politely responded. "I now know what I need to know. I will no longer be concerned with your efforts. Instead, I will work on my own obligations." He gave a brief wave, "You all have a good day." After his words of good bye, Harold turned and walked down the hallway, whistling the old Styx song, *Come Sail Away*.

Thomas didn't notice Adrian's eyes widen in disapproving amazement. He swung the door, but overcame his desire to slam in time to firmly close it. He turned back to the face the lab, and put his hand up to his forehead in frustration. "How did he know about the acceleration of the change?" Lowering his hand, he looked at his colleagues but saw no indication of guilt. "The rumors must have originated with one of us." he concluded. "We must be more careful of what we say and to whom." He grabbed his things and left. It was still early in the day, but he went home.

Sam's arrival couldn't come soon enough for Thomas. She had called to say she was done at the gym and was going to pick up supplies for dinner. In the meantime, Thomas cleaned up the house a bit and set the table. Anything to keep busy. The exchange with Harold had him spooked and he couldn't sit still without thinking about it.

It seemed like forever, but finally he heard Sam's car pull into the driveway. He almost ran to the front door. He had an overwhelming desire to hug her, but when he opened the door, she was carrying a number of packages. "Hello Love," she said cheerfully. "I got dinner."

"Here let me help," offered Thomas as he grabbed the tote bags she was carrying, leaving her with the box. "What's to eat?" he asked while not even trying to hide his stare. Coming directly from the gym, she was wearing a pair of grey yoga pants and a bright blue, cropped wide-strap exercise tank top. She kicked off her slip-on tennies as she set down the bags.

Sam gave Thomas a knowing smile. "I got a couple Cobb salads at that new restaurant, Edible Plants. Turns out it is not a vegetarian place like I thought. It focuses on eating healthy, but this salad still has bacon and chicken."

"So the owners aren't fanatics, I take it," Thomas replied while taking the salads out of the box and setting them on the dinning table.

"No, they aren't. I also got some brie at that cheese shop next door to Wine Importers. That cheese shop has opened an adjoining boulangerie, so I got a baguette also."

"This all sounds great. I hope you got something at the Wine Importers?" Thomas asked hopefully.

"Yes I did," she answered playfully. "They had a great looking Clos Guirouilh Jurancon that should pair with the salad well. At least I hope so. It sounded so good when the guy described it."

"Let me open the wine while you get a cutting board and knife for the bread and cheese," offered Thomas. "I am so glad you are here. This was not a great day."

Sam set the cheese board down on the table. "I'm sorry to hear that, Love. What happened?"

"You remember I told you the NSF told me to be careful with CUS," he began. "Well today I had a confrontation with Harold Simpson and I let on that the rate of change we saw was increasing. He made a big deal out it. I'm sure it will be all over the online systems. I didn't mean to tell him. He hinted that he knew and I lost my temper. "

"Oh Thomas," Sam sympathized. "I'm sorry. Maybe it won't be so bad."

"There was also a new paper out today from a Japanese group. They claim to see the same thing we do. Kathy and Adrian are furious that we haven't published yet."

Sam gave Thomas a hug. "Don't worry, they'll come around. But you should get that paper out."

Thomas frowned, but didn't argue. He continued describing the day. "Simpson said now that the Japanese have a result like ours, he's now confident the charge is changing and he is going to start preparing to meet the MUTs."

Sam stopped her arrangements of the food and drink. "What!?" she asked in shock.

"He plans to organize whatever it is they need to organize to become MUTs," Thomas answered. "Why does that surprise you so much?"

Sam looked wide eyed and didn't immediately respond. When she finally gathered herself, she asked a bit desperately, "Did he say *when* they planned to join the MUTs?"

"He thought they could be ready this fall. But it's not like there is any such thing as the MUTs. Why are you so interested?"

She had a distant look, like she was thinking about something while trying to carry on a conversation. "I think they may shut down their operations as they get ready. I am worried about losing a major client."

"Of course. I'm sorry Sam," Thomas said consolingly. "I was so concerned with my own problems, I forgot you have yours. Do you know what they have to plan? What do they need to do that takes months?"

"No idea," she answered. "I may figure it out, if it involves expenditures, but otherwise I may never know."

"We should eat," Thomas tried to change the subject. "This looks great. Thank you very much for picking it up."

After dinner, Sam made a quick stop in the bath. Thomas refilled their wine glasses and sat on the couch. When Sam returned, he invited "Come have a seat," as he patted the spot next to him. "Let's see if we can't figure out what Simpson has in mind."

"Hmmm," Sam hummed seductively, picking up her glass from the coffee table. "Do we really want to talk about Harold?" She took a sip of wine leaving perfectly imaged lip prints on the glass from recently applied lip gloss. The effect on Thomas was as intoxicating as the Jurancon.

Sam stood in from of Thomas. With her bare right foot she pushed his left leg to the side. She smiled at him while pulling off her top. Her torso was bare and she showed no concern that the window blinds were open. Thomas was mesmerized as she knelt between his legs. She placed her hands on his thighs and looked into his eyes. "We could talk about the Changing Universe Society," she said as her hands slid up to undo his belt, "or we could spin one." Thomas took a deep breath as she reached inside his pants. He forgot all about Harold Simpson.

As the World Changes

It was a late May Thursday evening and Sam arrived for her extended weekend stay with Thomas. Today, she didn't even wait for dinner, but amorously attacked him immediately upon entering. The suddenness of the encounter sent Thomas reeling. "How is she able to always find a new way to fire things up?" he thought to himself as he was carried away with excitement. After the heated encounter, the couple laid in bed and caught up on the week's events with pillow talk.

"This was a good week for ET-2," Thomas explained. "All the parts have now arrived. Well, most of the parts, there are still a few things on back order. But we have all we need to finish assembly. Putting things together, making sure it all works, and then turning on - we should have a running experiment this fall."

"Great news, Love. Have you heard anything from Simpson lately? He is certainly ramping up his activities at CUS. I'm not sure what they're all up to, but they are buying lots of stuff. Some of it above board, so to speak. They bought a lot of nice audio-visual equipment and computer networking equipment, for example. But they also are buying a lot of stuff under the table. Not sure what it all is, but its expensive and is requiring a lot of paperwork."

"I heard him speak on campus this morning," Thomas replied. "He's claiming the change in the charge is real and they are preparing for 'departure', whatever that means. He is warning that everyone needs to join him as soon as possible."

"Well, lots of people are joining," she said. "The intake of money is remarkable."

"It's getting a bit late, I'm gonna start dinner," announced Thomas as he stood. He began to pull on his pants as Sam rose.

"I'm going to take a shower. Between my workouts at the gym and with you, I need one."

Thomas pulled out the recipe for their planned dinner, a spicy shredded chicken dish he had made many times before. He had cut it out of a cooking magazine a long time ago and taped it into a book Tanya had bought him for just that purpose. He collected each ingredient for the dinner on the counter, and selected a vegetable to round out the meal. "I could use some music to temper this chore," he decided. He turned on his stereo, which was still tuned to a news station he had listened to that morning. As he reached for the knob to change the station, the headline struck him like a thunderclap.

"The changing electrical charge is causing global warming. We will have the details just after the break."

Thomas almost went into shock and started talking to himself. "Even if the charge was changing, can that be true?" He tried to think through the physics of the question, but didn't make much progress before the commercials were over.

The news program was talking with a geophysicist who was channeling his inner teacher. "There was a drill project just off the coast of Hawaii a number of years ago.

The goal was to drill through the Earth's crust and into the mantel. That project followed a number of previous attempts, and thus its success was exciting to the community of geophysicists. The project collected all the core it needed for its primary goals, and then they abandoned the hole."

"And you were able to gain control of the site for your own studies," interjected the host.

"Yes. Our team saw an opportunity and placed a series of instruments at different depths within that hole. One set of those instruments included precision thermometers. We placed fifty of these at various depths. By monitoring the temperature, we can study the Earth's energy balance. These instruments took data for about three weeks last December before our transmitter failed. We are waiting for a replacement to arrive and then we'll start collecting data again. Even with that mishap, however, our data has some overlap in time with the one of the experiments that seems to see a changing electrical charge."

"That is really interesting," commented the interviewer. "For our listeners who just joined us, I am talking with geophysicist, Professor Robert Goldman, who leads a team of researchers studying the deep Earth. Professor, why would a change in the charge be seen by thermometers underground?"

"Thanks for that question, Charles. There are a lot of atoms within the Earth. Each atom has electrons bound to it. The energy of that binding depends on the electron's charge. If the charge increases, as indicated by the laboratory experiments, the electrons will become more tightly bound. That is the binding energy increases. As the electron becomes more tightly bound, that excess energy is released as heat into the rock containing all those atoms."

"But that must be a small amount of energy, isn't it?" the interviewer asked.

"Of course, the predicted release of energy from each atom *is* very small, but like I said there are a lot of atoms in the Earth. If you wrote out the number, you would have fifty zeros after a one. It's huge. All that extra energy is flowing out of the Earth. The Earth releases energy produced by primordial radioactivity within the planet and what remains from the gravitational formation of the Earth. This is a new source of energy from the Earth and it is about a factor of five higher than those other contributions."

"Fascinating, Professor. Should we be worried? How does this compare with other energy sources that affect global warming?"

"What we are seeing is an energy source that is about a tenth of a percent of the energy radiated onto the Earth from the Sun. A one percent change in the energy from the sun would increase the global temperature by about one degree celsius. So the present value is not anything to panic about, but if the charge change accelerates, it might become a serious concern. There are online reports that the change is accelerating, although the researchers doing the measurements haven't made any claim. If those reports are true, I, for one, will be worried."

"Professor, quickly before we have to wrap up. Is the size of the change implied by your measurements consistent with the laboratory measurements?"

Thomas didn't like these references to laboratory experiments. The Japanese had published, but he hadn't. People were drawing conclusions from the story that Harold was spreading and not the scientists.

The professor continued on. "Yes, those measurements found a charge change of about one PQW. That is a very small number and it's remarkable that they are able to do that. But as I mentioned earlier, there are many atoms in the Earth. The total power that comes from this is about one tenth of a per cent of what the Sun provides."

Thomas' couldn't believe what he was hearing and didn't wait for the sign off. He just turned the radio off. The argument seemed plausible, but sounded too fantastic to be right. He walked toward his desk to work out his own estimate of the magnitude of this effect. The news story confirmed his earlier thought about a collective effect he hadn't considered. Now there were three claims of evidence and Thomas knew he couldn't dismiss their result for much longer.

Sam took a long shower and did some unpacking. She fully expected dinner to be nearly ready when she returned to the kitchen. Instead she found a gathering of ingredients on the counter and Thomas working at his desk.

"What's up?" she asked. "I thought you were cooking." She glared at him while standing with her hands on her hips.

"Sorry," he answered, "I got distracted by a news report. A geophysics group is claiming they see a change in the energy balance from the Earth and they attribute it to the charge changing. I just had to see if I agreed with their numbers."

"Well, do they?" asked Sam. She approached the desk and glanced over his shoulder at his work.

"Amazingly, yes," he said. He was shaking his head and staring at his private notebook.

"How does this relate to what you and the Japanese are seeing?" Sam asked.

"The numbers all agree, at least roughly," he answered. "These experiments are all new, so it wouldn't be surprising that there is some variation at this stage. But I just don't see how this result can be right. I keep going over this, hoping to figure out what's wrong, but everything keeps coming up OK."

"I wonder how Harold will react to this," said Sam. "He got so excited with the Japanese claim, I can't imagine how this will affect him."

"I can't really think about him," Thomas responded. "The NSF is already angry about our interactions with CUS. I need to stay clear of them."

"OK, but I can see the web-o-sphere getting spun up about this."

"I agree," Thomas replied while lifting his notebook and showing it to Sam. "This is my private notebook that I used to keep on that shelf. It's the one that the burglar must have been reading and misplaced when he saw me coming. Now I keep it hidden in the pan drawer in the kitchen."

"Interesting place to hide it. Why don't you just keep it in your office for the time being?" she asked.

"This notebook is more like a diary. It's where I consider very speculative thoughts before I'm ready to consider them serious science. Just didn't seem like a good idea to keep it in my office where one of my colleagues might find it. That would be uncomfortable."

"I'm going to get dinner going, while you figure this out," she said. "I am starving."

As Sam started reading the recipe, Thomas' phone rang. "Hello Kathy, how are you?" Thomas asked, knowing full well how she was.

"Did you hear that news report about the deep hole

temperature measurements?" she asked.

"Yes, I did. It was an interesting if a rather disturbing summary," he replied.

"They quoted us as a lab measurement, but we haven't published," she said. "Shouldn't we say something?"

"I don't see what we could say," said Thomas. "The public is going to react whether our results are in a paper or not."

Sam smiled as she listened to Thomas' side of the debate. As it became increasingly contentious, she shrugged her shoulders and focused on cooking dinner. When the two physicists finally stopped arguing, Thomas sat down to dinner and they ate in relative silence. After dinner Thomas sat back down at his desk. He was obsessed with the comparison between his results and that of the geophysicists. Sam looked at him a bit disparagingly. "If you are going to work, I may as well just go home and get some of my own work done. I'll talk to you tomorrow." Thomas acknowledged her departure briefly.

Fareed Raja took the subway from his Arlington office to the Smithsonian stop at the National Mall. He exited, glanced at the Washington Monument, turned and walked along the row of museums and stopped near the Grant Memorial. A modest gathering of a few thousand people were listening to a lecture. One of Fareed's colleagues had told him about these gatherings and he decided to check it out for himself. They had taken place every day for a few weeks now. However, since the media covered the deep Earth measurements – another damned NSF project – the numbers had grown.

The speaker was calling on Congress to take action. "There is a great deal of evidence that the charge of the electron is changing. Soon it will pose a threat to life on this planet. What will our government do?"

The speaker went on and on, frequently quoting the experimental results and even mentioning the NSF support. "Just great," sighed Fareed under his breath. But the worst part came when the speaker implied that somehow the research was to blame. Fareed almost exploded from the frustration. "Measuring something changing doesn't mean you caused the change," he said out loud, but only the few people next to him heard him.

Fareed had had enough and turned to retrace his steps to the subway. "If this effect is real, what do these people suggest the government do?" he thought. As he chose a seat, he checked the news for any stories about the Mall. His worries soared when he not only saw coverage of DC, but also that similar demonstrations were happening in Europe, Japan and South America. He put his phone away and leaned his head back to stare at the subway ceiling. After a bit of thinking, Fareed finally decided that the best course of action was for the NSF to focus on the science. He quietly practiced the speech he would give if asked. "Our official line is that all measurements need confirmation. Our Foundation will continue supporting efforts to better understand these results and we will let policy makers concern themselves with policy."

A Message of Change

Kathy arrived at the compound at the agreed-upon time, seven p.m., one hour prior to her talk. The July evening was still well sunlit and she found her destination without any difficulty. When she entered the main hall, Jonathan was there to greet her. "Thank you so much for coming. We are really looking forward to your talk. We don't get many external speakers here, so this is a treat for us. Come with me," he said while directing with his open palm. "We have a variety of finger foods, wine and beer available. Let me show you around."

Kathy nodded and followed Jonathan over to the refreshments. She had eaten dinner so wasn't very hungry, but to be polite, she took a finger sandwich as Jonathan poured her a glass of white wine. Jonathan introduced her to so many people so fast, that she couldn't keep track of who was who. She found it uncomfortable that everyone was calling her by name, but she couldn't reciprocate.

As the talk time neared, the common room seating filled up. Kathy was both scared and excited by the number of attendees. She was surprised they weren't wearing their uniform. Only a couple wore the tan shirts and most were variously dressed. Kathy had dressed professionally for the occasion in a navy blue skirt suit. She considered this a dry run for any job talks that were in her future, and acted as if the event was an interview. The memory of Thomas' experience with this group last January weighed heavy on her.

A young man came over to help Kathy set up her talk. She had brought her own laptop so it was a matter of connecting cables to the correct ports. The aide was quick and effective. Kathy thought the University should hire this guy.

Kathy had prepared a talk that was mostly based on the public lecture and colloquium that Thomas gave. However, she did add in a few details covering the data, which weren't available for Thomas at the time of those talks. Since she knew this group wanted to hear that the charge is changing, she decided she would include a slide on other results and some possible consequences. She also knew Thomas wouldn't like that, but she was past worrying about pleasing Thomas. Thomas wanted her to become an independent colleague. Well that autonomy meant that she not only made her own contributions to their research, it also meant she had her own views and opinions. Thomas would just have to accept that they might not always agree.

In her final slide, Kathy did emphasize that extraordinary claims require extraordinary evidence. Therefore the ET team was being very careful in what it claimed. It was at this point that Harold Simpson stood and introduced himself. Kathy found his command of the room to be very intimidating. He was tall up close and the assembled people showed him obvious deference.

"You only require extraordinary evidence because you refuse to acknowledge that this claim is not extraordinary," he lectured confidently. "Those of us in the Changing Universe Society know many things about our Universe that you refuse to accept as true. Once you accept the truth, this claim fits in nicely with a coherent world view. Therefore, there is no need to be skeptical. There is nothing extraordinary about any of this."

Kathy didn't want to offend her hosts, but she had to counter. "With all due respect, Mr. Simpson, your world view is based on claimed communications that you, and only you, have had with these MUTs. That is hardly a well-reviewed source."

"But Ms. Dotson," Harold responded, "there are three results now that have been reviewed by methods that you do approve. It's time for you to accept the inevitable."

"Kathy, look around." Jonathan waved over the common area as he spoke, "there are a large number of believers, not only in this room but worldwide. We now have associates around the globe. Furthermore, not only do laser experiments see the effect, but also geology provides evidence."

"The MUTs will be arriving this fall," said Harold to the room as a whole and not directly to Kathy. The date isn't specific yet, but I am informed that it will be in November. We must continue our preparations."

"Yes," Jonathan added, "mid November. That will allow time to finish arrangements."

"Jonathan, really," said Harold, "you and your arrangements. We will meet the MUTs when they are ready whether we are or not."

A woman in the audience center spoke up. "I can't wait for departure day. Giving up my body is a small price to pay to cross into a new and better Universe."

Kathy was shocked. What did she mean, "give up her body?" Did that woman just say she was going to kill herself in November? Surely, she didn't mean suicide. She was becoming scared and she began to subtly pack up her things. As she disconnected her laptop from the AV system, a group of women surrounded her at the podium and peppered her with questions. One woman in particular put her arm around Kathy, whose unease rose with the touch. She pushed the arm away and stepped back.

Undeterred the woman spoke directly to her, "I think you would make an excellent addition to the Changing Universe Society. Your work with lasers and your discovery that the charge is changing makes you one of the prophets. We would greatly benefit from your insight."

"Prophet," Kathy mouthed. "Who are these people?" she thought loudly.

"Yes," added another. "Harold is always saying that we would benefit from a science advisor."

With each inch the crowd pressed closer, Kathy's panic built. Although no one was constraining her, she felt claustrophobic with a need to escape. One arm around her was already too many, but when a second woman tried to clasp her hand, Kathy grabbed her bag, said good-bye and thank you to Jonathan for his hospitality, and walked quickly out the door. When she reached her car, she felt a wave of relief when she realized she wasn't followed.

Later that night, Kathy saw that CUS posted a recording of the talk, along with the question session afterwards, online. She noted the exchange about giving up one's body for the MUTs was edited out. CUS then advertised the presentation heavily through its social media emphasizing scientific support for their beliefs.

Fareed sent the link to Thomas with a short all-caps message, "ARE YOU NOT LISTENING TO ME?"

Thomas' walks to work were less eventful these days. Harold had been true to his word and mostly ignored

Thomas. CUS had what it needed from him. As he passed the gathering in the quad, he heard Harold's speech, but Harold didn't acknowledge him. He was very happy to be able to pass through the quad without hassle.

Thomas needed to finish his progress report for the NSF so he went to his office before going to the lab. He opened his laptop and began reading email. He stopped reading as soon as he read the note from Fareed. Thomas wondered how Fareed always seems to know what CUS was doing. Thomas opened the link to Kathy's talk and his fury surged. He punched Kathy's contact on his phone. "When will you be in?" he asked abruptly. "We need to talk about your presentation at CUS."

When Kathy arrived, the argument started immediately. "How could you discuss our data with those people?" Thomas asked her. "Haven't you been following what the NSF has been telling us?"

"I saw an opportunity to give a practice talk and took it. You do realize that you give *all* the talks on our work, don't you? In four years, I haven't seen Adrian give more than a short contributed talk at a local American Physical Society meeting. You reserve all the glory for yourself. I needed to give a real talk."

Carl opened the door and entered the lab. He could sense the tension right away and tried to be unobtrusive. Thomas was too angry to concern himself with any audience. "But why would you speak to them? Are you part of that group now?"

"No, of course not," Kathy said defensively. "They offered me five hundred dollars and I wanted it. But I don't believe their nonsense."

"That's not what the internet says this morning. Tell me Kathy, were you the one who hacked us? Did you tell them how to gain access to our analysis?"

205

"Absolutely not," she yelled. "I can't believe you think I would compromise my own work."

Carl was shocked at the exchange. This was nuts and not the type of graduate school experience he had been looking for.

After a brief pause, Kathy calmly and firmly spoke. "I have begun writing my dissertation." She then turned and left the lab. Carl put his lunch in the fridge and then went to check on the bake-out of the vacuum chamber containing the optical resonator. Thomas didn't even seem to notice Carl was there. He just grunted and then left. Carl assumed he went to his office and continued working.

Kathy almost ran out of the building. She stopped and sat on one of the concrete planters nearby. She was so angry she was almost in tears. Although she would never admit it, she did agree with Thomas that the talk at CUS was a mistake. But that was all they agreed on. "How could he accuse me of that hack," she said aloud.

"Who accused you?" asked Adrian. She had been on her way to the lab when she noticed Kathy sitting on a planter outside Grunderson Hall.

Kathy was startled and sat up straight. "Oh, it's you Adrian. I had an argument with Thomas. He thinks I'm in with CUS and am responsible for that hack we had last year."

"That's crazy." Adrian was incredulous. "Doesn't he remember that you were the one who recognized the break in?"

"Probably he does. I think he is mostly angry about the talk I gave. CUS posted it on line and promoted it. A number of people, including Raja from the NSF, commented. I guess Raja was pretty upset about the publicity."

"I'm sorry Kathy. How was the talk itself? Must have been strange being inside the compound."

"Scary is a better description," Kathy answered. "I think they are a suicide cult. A woman was looking forward to departure day and 'leaving her body behind'. They made a big deal about the day being set."

"The date is set?" asked Adrian. "Did they say when?"

"It's not specific yet. But Harold said November. They are doing a lot of preparation to get ready."

"No specific date, just a month?"

"Yep, just the month. Harold said the MUTs haven't been precise yet."

"November is four months away. Wonder what they have to do that takes so long."

"Adrian, why do you care about the date so much?" Kathy's frustration was turning to anger. "I just had this big blow out with Thomas. Our careers are falling apart here because he's afraid of his own data and you are obsessing about that cult."

"I'm sorry," conceded Adrian. "You're right. What that cult is doing may be interesting, but it isn't what we need to focus on. I should get to work. I'll work on Thomas for you. You just finish your dissertation. There is one good side to this. Thomas hasn't mentioned a Cow-Tippers outing this year."

Kathy smiled at the mention of their mutual lack of interest in all things baseball, but didn't feel that cheered.

Even More Change

The second Monday morning of July, Thomas was making himself breakfast and taking things a bit slower preparing eggs, over easy. The bacon was crisp and the toast would be popping any second. Thomas took a sip of coffee when his phone rang.

"Did you see the archive this morning?" asked a clearly agitated Kathy.

"Not yet. I was just making breakfast. Is there something interesting?"

"Interesting!" exclaimed Kathy. "No, it's infuriating. The Mortis group in Europe posted a paper claiming they see a change in the charge. And, spoiler alert, they get the same value the Japanese get."

"You've got to be kidding," said a surprised Thomas as he poked at the nearly perfect eggs with his silicon spatula. "Last I heard, they were still nearly a year away from data taking."

"Well," Kathy replied sarcastically, "they knew this topic was of interest. They also knew that the effect was relatively large so they could cut a lot of corners and still have sensitivity to what we're seeing. They scooped us too, Thomas."

"Kathy," Thomas pleaded, trying to be patient, "they didn't scoop us. We were first and everyone knows it." He turned off the heat under the eggs.

"But they have submitted a paper and we haven't,"

cried Kathy.

"Ok, look. I'll be in the lab within the hour. I just have to eat and then walk over. When I get there we can go through the paper."

"Assessing their paper isn't my concern, Thomas," Kathy said almost yelling at this point. "When will we publish our result?"

"I'll talk with you when I get to the lab," answered Thomas curtly and he hung up. He shoved his phone into his pocket. He took a bite of bacon, but decided he was no longer hungry. "Damn it!" He put his food-filled plate in the sink, grabbed his pack and left for campus.

When Thomas arrived at the lab, Adrian and Kathy were there, but not Carl. "Where's Carl?" he asked, clearly frustrated, as he put his lunch in the fridge.

"He's been coming in a bit later these days," explained Adrian. Thomas made a face but dropped it.

Both Kathy and Adrian were looking at copies of the new paper and Adrian handed Thomas another. She had also printed out four copies of the Japanese and geophysics papers. Thomas realized he was in for a day of it. Kathy did not even acknowledge his arrival.

"All four results find roughly the same size of change," observed Adrian. "Can they really all be wrong?"

"I agree that multiple results using different techniques lend credence to such a claim," Thomas said philosophically. "But that doesn't necessarily prove it's right. I have seen cases in the past of a kind of wrong-result feedback. When I was an undergraduate I did a paper on neutrino mass. A series of experiments were trying to see if this sub-atomic particle had any weight or was

209

pure energy like light. These experiments used different techniques and not only found evidence for a large value, but they agreed as to what that value is. Once, however, a new experiment showed convincing evidence that the neutrino mass had to be much smaller than these claims, each group *discovered* a systematic error that had been overlooked. That study of history really struck me and I admit it's on my mind now."

"So your saying that you think all four groups have missed some aspect of their efforts and are all wrong?" said Kathy with skepticism. "That sounds like a conspiracy theory to me."

"I'm not saying it happened in this case," replied Thomas, "I'm saying it's a possibility. These efforts are not done in a vacuum. They all know about each other and each positive claim gives confidence to the others. This is an extraordinary claim and we have to consider alternatives."

"Well both the Japanese and European groups will be at the Rome conference next month. Since you're going, you can ask them what they screwed up," snarked Kathy.

Adrian looked up from her phone. "While you two are bickering, the news feed is churning with stories on this topic." She handed her phone to Thomas. "Look at this, there are already six stories on the topic from various news operations. We are front and center in most of them. A couple of the articles criticize us for not submitting a paper, especially since the others have."

"See! What did I tell you?" Kathy said with exasperation as Thomas quietly studied Adrian's phone.

Kathy stared at Thomas waiting for a response when Adrian jumped in to try to keep the conversation civil. "Isn't it a bit strange that so many teams see this all of a sudden?"

"Not really," responded Thomas. "As technology improves, its not unusual for a number of research groups to develop similar capabilities at similar times."

"Oh come on, Thomas," countered Kathy. "This isn't about technology advancement. Lots of groups have had the technology required to see this for a long time. The issue is that the charge started changing."

"And how does that fit with our understanding of physics?" asked Thomas. "The laws of science don't just switch on or off one day."

"That is your understanding, but you can't ignore the evidence in front of you," Kathy argued.

"It is true," added Adrian reluctantly, "that there is an astounding agreement. This European paper reports a result from data taken in May. That would be six doubling times from when we first noted a change and they see thirty PQW, which agrees with that prediction."

Before Thomas could respond, Carl entered the lab. "Good morning, everyone," he said cheerfully.

"Where have you been?" Thomas asked angrily. "Your thesis topic is based on data that will come from ET-2. You should be here putting the upgrade together."

Carl was taken aback and couldn't respond any better than saying, "I'm sorry. I'll come in earlier from now on."

"Good, make sure you do," scolded Thomas, who left the room and walked up to his office.

Thomas entered his office, closed the door, pulled his laptop out of his pack and sat at his desk. He opened his mail application and scanned his inbox. He had a larger volume of email this morning than usual. The time stamps indicated that his colleagues in Europe and been writing him since the Mortis result news broke during afternoon across the pond. Asian night owls chimed in as well. Deeper into the queue, he could see when the East Coast woke up following with a wave of inquiries that washed across the continent. Some of the messages were asking about certain details of ET, but many others wanted to know when he thought he might publish. The most worrisome email was from Fareed. He wanted a schedule for publishing ET, and a progress report on ET-2. His email did not mince words and Thomas knew he had to be careful and prompt in his answer. He was almost thankful for the knock at the door. "Come in. It's open," he instructed.

When Kathy walked in, he knew this was not going to be a reprieve but just a different twist on the same pain. "We need to talk," she said.

"About?" he asked, although he had his suspicion.

"I have done the work required for a Ph.D.," she said. "I helped build ET, I wrote the analysis software and produced our results. I have a physics interpretation. I insist I be allowed to write up and graduate."

"Kathy," he said with a sigh, "we have been all through this. Don't you want to see the result from ET-2? It will be ready by November."

"No, I don't," she answered. "ET-2 is Carl's project."

"It's all our project," Thomas said defensively.

"OK, it's all our project, but it's Carl's thesis, not mine. I have mine and it's done. I am here to tell you that I don't plan to come into the lab anymore unless it relates to my dissertation. I will be at home or in my cubicle writing. If you need something, you can always call me, but I will not be routinely in the lab anymore."

"Kathy," Thomas started, but she cut him off.

"Thomas, this is not negotiable," she stated firmly. She turned and left the office, shutting the door behind her firmly but quietly, an act that symbolized the finality of her message. Thomas took off his glasses, squeezed his eyes shut hard, and rubbed them. After a few seconds of introspection, he decided to stop fighting that battle. He needed to focus on the wars he needed to win and not lost causes. He returned to reading and responding to email while considering his response to Fareed.

He only had a few additional minutes of quiet when another knock came. This time it was Adrian. "Thomas, as you know I have been applying for jobs. I have gotten some interest from a couple companies. One in Germany and one in Italy. Without a publication or a highly visible talk, I don't see any hope of an academic position, so I will likely take one of these opportunities."

"Adrian, don't you want to see the results of ET-2?" he asked. His desperation was obvious, but he seemed to completely overlook the reference to the conference.

"I will continue to work on the upgrade and its start up until I leave. With immigration issues and other relocation logistics, I expect to move sometime in fall. But I don't have a date yet."

Again Thomas felt rather defeated. "I guess we'll plan for that then."

DeeDee was in her office reading the abstract of the new report from Europe. "This will make things worse," she said aloud as her words were transcribed to a note-taking application on her laptop. She had been following the public's response over the past few weeks and it was unnerving. The size of the demonstrations worldwide were increasing. The media coverage, both commercial and social, was intensifying. Although the implications of impending doom hadn't caused a panic yet, one could sense the public's growing unease. "People will soon begin to make irrational decisions," she said. "Panic buying, job quitting, reduced inhibitions and law breaking. It is going to get ugly if these results all hold up." She sighed as she closed the laptop.

Talking about Change

Thomas Conrad was sitting at his office desk, wearing a feathered turkey costume, trying to estimate the laser power required for his proposed next experiment. The door to his office burst open, shattering his concentration. His department chair, DeeDee Champton, stormed in wearing denim overalls and a wide brimmed hat. She was carrying a pitch-fork, tines up. She was attended by Fareed, Harold, and Kathy, each wearing jeans and flannel, leaving two security guards, wearing tan shirts and arm bands, standing just outside in the hall.

"Thomas, your work has been awful. Not just sub-par but awful." She pounded the floor with the pitch-fork handle and his desk, along with everything on it, disappeared. "We have decided to take early action to rid our department of your unsuccessful program."

She pounded the floor again and all the other furnishings, books, and Thomas' backpack disappeared. Even the chair was gone. Thomas was now standing in front of her, stiff with fright. "We have talked to the bank and your house and its furnishings have been repossessed. Your car has been towed."

She pounded the floor one last time and the turkey outfit lost all its feathers. He desperately tried to cover himself with his unwilling hands. "This academic life you have taken for granted is over. Good luck in your future endeavors, as if you have any future. Security, escort Dr.

Conrad off campus. You are no longer welcome here."

As DeeDee turned, she disappeared along with the nodding approval of Fareed, Harold and Kathy. Handcuffs appeared on Thomas' wrists and the security guards were instantly next to him. Each took an elbow and they began pushing him out the door. "We're going to meet the MUTs," one said.

Thomas woke suddenly with a jolt that woke Sam. "What was that?" she asked, leaning over to see if he was all right.

He was breathing quickly and sweating profusely. He took a moment to look around the room and then at Sam. He put his arm around her as he relaxed. "That damn nightmare, again."

"Are you OK, Love? That was really dramatic."

"I don't know. That is the first time I've had the nightmare when you are around. And this time the dream had Harold in it. I guess the stress is getting worse. Either that or I'm having a harder time coping."

"Is it always the same dream?" she asked.

"For the most part, it focuses on our department chair firing me. But it does evolve over time. Tonight, Fareed, our NSF manager, Harold Simpson, and Kathy were there showing their approval of my firing."

"Well," she consoled, "it is just a dream, even if it is disquieting. In any case, it's about time to get going. Let me make breakfast while you take a shower."

Thomas leaned over and kissed her shoulder. "I have a better idea. Let's take a shower together and then walk over to Brewers Cup for coffee and a scone."

She gave him a sly smile, patted his leg, and then walked toward the bathroom.

At Brewers Cup, Thomas ordered his usual, Sam ordered a hazelnut latte and they kissed outside the cafe door before parting. He felt buoyant as he strode to the office. At Grunderson Hall, Thomas picked up the mail that had been collecting in his department mailbox. Among the various University memos and junk mail was his July issue of *Physics Today*, which he placed on his desk. Normally, he would check email before continuing onto the lab. But today he had to prepare his talk for Rome and only planned to check in on the lab. Even so, he lingered beside the desk procrastinating and flipped opened the magazine. The first thing he noticed was a letter to the editor regarding the changing charge. The long letter received an extensive response from the editor that Thomas knew would be widely read. Thomas sighed, profoundly knowing that this would be a lousy email day.

He sat down to read the letter and response. The writer, a scientist Thomas knew on the faculty at Boston University was Professor Sidney Perkins. Perkins argued that a sizable fraction of the population now believes, or at least worries, that the charge is truly changing and that their lives are at risk. The letter continued,

> *Even if this scenario is nonsense, the physics community needs to respond more effectively. Researchers cannot assume they are detached from the impact of their work. They had to get out of their ivory tower and engage the public on this topic. It is especially egregious to not publish results in a timely manner so that the whole community can assess the situation and contribute to educating the public as to what the risk really is.*

The editor's response defended the researcher's right to publish only when they are confident in their result, but otherwise agreed with the letter writer's views.

"That's just great," Thomas began talking to himself. "The whole world demands that we publish this." He mulled the consequences of giving in, and having Adrian take a stab at producing the draft, a plum assignment. That might convince her to stay longer.

Thomas put down the magazine and called Adrian to ask if she wanted to take that on. To his surprise she was a definite no. "Why not?" he asked. "I thought you and Kathy were upset that we haven't published yet."

Adrian didn't answer right away. After a bit of stammering she finally offered, "I think Kathy should do it. It's her thesis topic and she is close to finishing her dissertation, if she isn't done already. She should have first crack at the initial draft."

Thomas was confused by her reluctance, but agreed to ask Kathy. With that settled, he gathered his strength and began work on his talk for the conference in Rome. Since they were going to publish and since their results were made public by CUS, the talk was less difficult to prepare. He did not need a nuanced report or to straddle a fence to retain plausible deniability. He would just summarize what they have found, make a statement about what they have checked, and then describe ET-2. Giving an honest and open talk on data was easy to prepare although responding to questions afterwards may be more difficult.

He made his slides rather quickly since he had been pouring over the data and the cross checks nearly continuously during the past weeks. Since he didn't want to sit on anything, the content came easily. However, his was the first talk at the conference on this subject matter, which meant he had to also spend time providing an introduction. All in all, he carefully considered what to reveal and what to hold back because of the talk's time limit. In the end, he just put the extra content into backup slides in case there were questions. He assumed his talk might be controversial, so his final effort was to make a list of tough questions and his planned answers. The first one on the list was, "Why haven't you published yet?"

The list of potential questions was long and Thomas prepared an email to Adrian, Kathy and Carl for feedback on his proposed answers. He wanted them to not only wordsmith his responses but also point out issues he missed. He hadn't quite finished rereading the message one last time before hitting send, when he was startled by a knock at the door. A flashback to his nightmare gave him a start, but he called out to come in.

Kathy came in and handed Thomas a tall stack of paper. "I have finished a first draft of my dissertation. Can we distribute to the reading committee and schedule my defense?"

"Wow, this is a lot of paper, Kathy," Thomas said. "You could have just emailed a pdf."

"I know, but I wanted to make a statement," she said with an ironic smile. "It's time I graduated, Thomas."

"I leave for Rome in a few days. I'll be gone about a week and then we need to focus on getting ET-2 running. Once it's running, I'll turn my attention to this."

She frowned and shook her head emphatically. "I don't understand," Kathy complained. "It doesn't take that much time to schedule a meeting, but it is likely to be several weeks in the future before we can get everyone in the same room. Why is setting a date so difficult?"

"Like you said, getting everyone on the same page takes time. Let's get ET-2 online and then this can be priority one."

Kathy gave a deep exhale and then calmly stated, "I am going to talk to Professor Champton." She left before Thomas could debate further.

"Damn," he said, "I forgot to ask her about writing the paper."

Kathy went straight to DeeDee's office. Assuming she would have trouble with Thomas, she had printed out two copies of her dissertation. Handing one to DeeDee, she said, "I have finished a draft of my dissertation and I want to schedule a defense. But Thomas is putting me off. He wants us to get the upgrade running before we pick a date."

"That does sound a bit unreasonable," sympathized DeeDee. "Let me talk to him and see if we can find some common ground. I will give you a call after I have a chance to see him."

"Thank you Professor Champton," said Kathy as she departed.

DeeDee scanned through the dissertation. At three hundred and seventeen pages, it was an impressive piece of work. Although longer than most dissertations, the few pages DeeDee read carefully were well written. It covered each point, but was still concise. The detail on the experiment and the analysis was very comprehensive. Even with a scan, she learned a lot about Thomas' experiment. DeeDee took time to read the conclusion chapter, which was a real gem. It was clever how Kathy had addressed the significance of the result, if taken at face value, without making any sensational claims. She had presented two results - the measured rate of the change and an upper limit if one concluded that the charge can't be changing. She addressed the philosophical issue of the apparent sudden turn-on of the effect in a way that appeared to deflate the issue in DeeDee's mind. The summary of potential consequences was treated as a summary bibliography without trying to estimate magnitudes. "Maybe she should go into politics," thought DeeDee. "She sure knows how to ride a fence and serve a constituency."

DeeDee didn't look forward to talking to Thomas. This whole thing had gotten out of hand but she couldn't let a student become collateral damage of a difficult situation. She picked up her phone and dialed his number.

"Thank you for coming to see me, Thomas," DeeDee said as she shut the door behind him. "Please take a seat."

"I assume you have talked to Kathy?" asked Thomas.

"Yes, I have and I must say I am a bit disappointed in the way you have handled this, Thomas."

"DeeDee, we need to get ET-2 going. That is my priority now. It'll only be another four, maybe five weeks. Then I promise to focus on Kathy."

"If getting ET-2 is your priority, why are you going to Rome?" asked DeeDee. "You have to balance these priorities. All three, Kathy's defense, ET-2, and the conference are all important for your tenure case. Kathy has been an outstanding student. I scanned her dissertation and it looks very impressive. I agree with her on this. You need to arrange a time for her defense and make sure it happens. Graduating students is what Universities do. Your conduct has the appearance of exploitation."

"OK, OK," Thomas conceded the argument. "I will work with the committee to schedule her exam."

"Thank you," DeeDee said. "And by the way did you see the *Physics Today* letters to the editor section this month?"

"Yes, I did," Thomas answered.

"Sounded like good advice to me. You should take it." As Thomas got up to leave, DeeDee instructed, "Thomas, I expect a date within a month. Set it up before you leave for Rome." Thomas nodded and left.

Back in his office, he made the arrangements for Kathy's defense. The earliest everyone was available was the last week of August, more than thirty days away but Kathy seemed OK with that. She just wanted to see serious progress. She was also happy about the suggestion of writing a draft of the paper.

***

As typical for many flights from the US to Italy, Thomas arrived at the Rome-Flumicino International airport in the morning. After an extended wait for his luggage to come out on the carousel, he took a thirty minute taxi ride to his hotel. The hotel Sam suggested was a nice boutique hotel, Hotel Pace Helvezia. It was well situated and a reasonable price. Here he had a bit good fortune as they let him check in at eleven a.m., even though the official time was three p.m.. Thomas had a routine for dealing with jet lag and early access always helped. He unpacked in his room and then took a quick shower. He then got dressed and prepared to head out on the town. If he could stay awake until at least eight or nine that evening, he would recover a bit faster. Thomas planned to attend the reception at six to help him reach his bedtime goal.

The sessions of the International Conference on Fundamental Symmetries were held at the Pontifical University of Saint Thomas Aquinas. The Dominican university, nicknamed 'Angelicum', was an imposing compound near the Colosseum and only a five minute walk away from his hotel. The Baroque façade with its white stone flourishes welcomed students and visitors into a grand complex that included classrooms and massive tiered lecture hall, where Thomas would be presenting tomorrow. The eight hundred year history of the Angelicum impressed him. The detailed written history of Europe extended much further into the past than those of his home country so it was always exciting to attend meetings at these revered locales. His first act of business was to locate the meeting hall and confirm his route.

The conference location was also within walking distance of a number of the venerable sites of Rome. Thomas spent the afternoon being a tourist. After he made sure he knew how to find the meeting rooms, he began the fifteen minute walk along Via degli Annibaldi to the Colosseum.

As Thomas crossed Via Cavour, Jonathan exited the Crèdit Agricole Italia. Jonathan saw Thomas across the street, but Thomas didn't notice him. Jonathan decided to change his plans and go the opposite direction to avoid being seen. He wasn't worried about being identified, since he was a registered attendee at the conference, but he didn't really want to engage him. He knew Thomas would probably recognize him at the conference before too long, but he didn't want to be seen going in and out of financial institutions. Even though he was traveling under his own name, he was using his alias for the transactions, and if Thomas caught wind, it would be hard to explain. He next stopped at the Bank of Italy instead of his planned stop near the Parco del Colle Oppio. "Only two more banks today anyway," he thought. "Doesn't really matter what order I do them."

Thomas felt the scooters, the horns, the smell of diesel, and the sense that he took his life in his hands with each street crossing. As he arrived at the Piazza del Colosseo, he gazed ahead at the ancient structure to assess the long line of tourists getting tickets. He was startled to pick out three people wearing the tell-tale tan shirts with blue arm bands. "They came to Italy for this conference?" he asked himself in disbelief. "Who are these people?" At least they didn't notice him, so he didn't have to deal with them. He finished the walk and joined the line to buy a tour ticket.

Thomas took his tour, although his mind was elsewhere and he didn't get much out of it. As jet lag was beginning to set in, he went to a small bakery to get provisions for a light dinner, and ate it while walking along the River Tiber. The inexpensive, but delicious, ham and cheese sandwich definitely hit the spot. The peaceful walk along the river contrasted with his earlier battle with Rome traffic. He began to relax.

When it started to get close to reception time, he found his way back to the conference site. The organizers served a very nice array of Italian wines and the finger foods were tasty. Thomas enjoyed the capicola, mixed cheeses, grapes, and the array of olives. The wine was served in carafes, so he didn't know the label, but he found it excellent. He found several old friends at the dinning credenzas and the conversations quickly passed from family updates to topics of physics. This was the third time Thomas had attended this conference series as it was held every other year. The meeting typically attracted about two hundred scientists, although attendance was closer to two hundred fifty this year due to the appeal of the venue's location. Thomas considered this to be a perfect size for a meeting, large enough to attract the key people, but small enough that you could interact effectively with anyone. A number of the participants brought their spouses to the conference, making Thomas wish that Sam had come. As Thomas sipped his wine, he pulled out his phone to check the time at home. He figured at this time, Sam was up. He sent her a text, "Made it to Rome, wish you were here." After a few moments he got a reply. "Enjoy, Love."

The conference covered a wide range of sub-topics. The presentations included both theoretical and experimental studies. Thomas reviewed the conference agenda, and was pleased to see studies of the Pauli exclusion principle and a variety of conservation laws. There were searches for violations of various symmetries and searches for new forces or particles. There were studies of the limitations of special relativity and the theory of gravity. Scientists were doing measurements with anti-matter and some were looking at possible anomalous decays of fundamental particles. Like Thomas, some were looking at the steadfastness of the fundamental constants. The common theme was a collection of tests of the accepted models of physics to better understand the world. From discussions at the reception, one thing became clear, the second day of the conference with the session including Thomas' talk, would be very popular.

Thomas had twenty-five minutes for his presentation, with an additional five minutes for questions. He spent the first five minutes giving an overview of the motivation and another five describing ET. He spent ten minutes describing the results, including their evidence for an initial turn on and that the rate of change was increasing. During that section of the talk, the audience was as silent as a stone. No murmurs from whispered conversations, no clicking sounds from those working on their laptops instead of paying attention, and no rustling of people coming and going from their seats. The audience was so silent it almost distracted Thomas. He had never given a talk at a conference when not even a small fraction of the audience was uninterested and hence doing something other than listening. His final five minutes was dedicated to ET-2. He included a final slide that thanked the NSF for support, mentioned a paper was in preparation, and had summaries of what Adrian and Kathy did for the project and mentioned they were job hunting. The latter was an honest effort to help them find a position, but it was also true that if he could point to a successful career step for his mentees, it would help his tenure case.

To Thomas' surprise, and a fair amount of relief, the session chair decided to defer questions. "Let's hold questions until after the final talk of the session," he instructed. "We will combine all the question periods along with some extra time due to the cancellation of a talk scheduled for later in the day. That way we can have time for an extended discussion of the situation."

Next up was the Japanese group, who was represented by one of their postdocs. The young man was a bit stiff and wore a suit but was also very professional. The official language of almost all physics conferences was English, and this young man certainly mastered that skill. He accent was slight and easy to understand. He didn't once say "uh," which was rare for even most native speakers. Thomas was impressed with the presentation. The group presented twelve weeks of data. The data was taken during March and May, which didn't overlap with Thomas' group's data. They saw a comparable result and also saw the increasing rate of change. Their doubling time was also about four weeks. The rate of change at the end of the presented time period was thirty-two PQW.

The European group presented their results, which were also in agreement with the Japanese. The audience was stunned by the presentation of Elgin Mortis. He was an entertaining speaker with an opening joke that received a roar of laughter. The plaid sport coat with black slacks and neon orange tennis shoes really captured his personality. At nearly seventy-five years old, he was a respected elder statesman of the field. Anything he said carried a lot of weight. Although their result was based on only a few weeks from May, the consistency of the three experiments was striking. Once the result was projected, the audience went from silence to near chaos. The audience chatter crescendoed.

The chair struggled for several minutes to recapture the room's quiet. Once he did, a theorist presented a coherent interpretation on the situation. Dickson Trundle was a particle physics theorist from the European Organization for Nuclear Research, more commonly known as CERN. Dickson was only in her late thirties, but she already had quite a reputation for insight into leading scientific questions. Her review talk covered scientific theories that could include a change in the value of the charge, but also spent a great deal of time on the implications. She covered the doubling time issue in detail. "One has to accept a doubling time hypothesis for the three laser experiments and the geophysics result to present a consistent picture," she explained. "If one does accept that premise, it implies we should start seeing a variety of effects, some of which will have serious consequences within a few years." The session chair actually winced. He really didn't want the meeting to degrade into a disaster movie plot device.

When the chair asked for questions, hands shot up across the entire hall. The organizers had assigned four local students to carry wireless microphones about the room. The chair selected a person seated on the aisle near one of the volunteers to get things rolling quickly. While that question was being asked, the chair was arranging for the following questions. The young assistants got their exercise running up and down the stairs of the auditorium helping to make the questioners heard.

The first question was more of a comment. "There is no way this can be correct. It's too dramatic and implies we live in a special age. This is a case of one wrong result followed by other sloppy work by scientists who want to believe the answer." The chair swiftly thanked him for his contribution and went to the next in line.

"I have a technical question about temperature control in the three experiments. Did you maintain a controlled environment?" The answer was yes, of course, and all three experimentalists confirmed that. The chair acknowledged the exchange and moved on.

"It's too bad the geophysics group is not represented here. I think they ignored the chimney effect in their work. They weren't measuring the true temperature of the rock because they ignored the impact of rising hot atmosphere from the depths. Since they had technical problems with their deep sea communication, it will be quite a while before they can do any more measurements. I wrote to them but they have not replied to my concern. Does Dickson have any comment on this?" She said she wasn't expert enough to comment on experimental techniques. No one in the audience volunteered any insight into the question, so the chair moved on.

The next question, regarding the frequency standard, was from someone who was not expert in the field. Elgin answered it succinctly. "Next?" asked the chair.

"What evidence is there for the existence of the MUTs and their role in all this?" The chair cut the discussion off. Not only was it not scientific, but he had a hunch it was not a serious inquiry but just an attempt to stir things up. If that was the intention, it worked. The auditorium got loud from a resurgence in isolated conversations. Once again, the chair struggled to get things under control and several more minutes passed before order was restored. Looking up at the audience, Thomas realized several media reporters were present in the room, furiously typing on their tablets, which he took as a bad omen.

"One last question," the chair announced.

"It seems strange that this just turned on," began an ancient man in the front row. Victor Heinlein was a Nobel Prize winner from two decades past. He was well into retirement but enjoyed the conference circuit and organizers were only too happy to accommodate him so they could advertise his participation. He was a bit feeble and had an attendant who helped him negotiate the landscape. "Is it possible that this doubling process was always taking place but only recently got large enough to be observed? As the effect increased, there would always come a time when our technology would just reach the required sensitivity. That would eliminate the turn-on concern. Furthermore, it would eliminate the implication that we live in a special age."

This comment struck Thomas hard and he didn't hear the discussion that followed. His experiment was the only one that might address this question since they had a fair amount of data before the turn-on date. He knew that before the turn-on, any effect was too small for ET to observe and thus Heinlein's hypothesis made perfect sense and was insightful. The idea seemed obvious now that he heard it and he was upset that he hadn't realized it before now.

The debate became heated and unruly. The implications of a changing charge and what it meant for humanity became the primary topic. Some of the discussion bordered on panic, and the chair became concerned. He closed the session, although it wasn't clear anyone heard him. The acrimony extended into the coffee break. Most of the disagreements centered around the validity of the evidence but the implications had disturbed the attendees. The debates were passionate and initially nonviolent. One of the scientists, however, saw the tan-shirted CUS members and confronted them. Jonathan tried to intervene to protect his younger colleagues but the man was very angry. The facility security personnel stepped in to stop the altercation. Thomas recognized Jonathan from the University quad events and decided he would make an effort to avoid him over the remaining couple days of the meeting.

The next session was poorly attended. The arguments in the coffee break room were not yet settled and many conference goers wanted to watch the show. Thomas was exhausted from the pandemonium and decided to skip the conference dinner. He went to bed early that night.

Change for the Worse

Kathy's thesis defense was scheduled for the end of August on a Thursday afternoon. Given the interest in the topic, the seminar room was full. Normally, the department advertised these events publicly and Thomas was grateful they made an exception in this case. No one wanted CUS in attendance. The members of the audience included many people from the department and some close, non-scientist friends of Kathy's. Her parents were unable to travel to make this date, but they were flying in on Friday evening for a weekend of celebration. Her sister, however, wasn't going to miss this for the world. Judy flew in on Wednesday.

Thomas introduced the five members of the committee. Three were designated to read the dissertation and an additional two were participants in the oral defense. In addition to Thomas, the readers included Robert Thibodaux, a particle theorist, and Cheryl Hodgens, a nuclear physicsist studying beta decay. The final physicist on the committee was Eric Leverson who studied plasma physics. Chandler Parsons was from the Economics Department and was the graduate school representative. Once he was introduced, he clarified his role to the audience. "I am not an expert in this field and will not be providing any technical assessment of the work presented. I am here as a representative of the University to make sure its processes are properly followed."

231

Thomas explained that the afternoon would follow a process that was traditional within the Physics Department. Kathy would give a public lecture followed by questions. Once the public had exhausted its questions, everyone except the committee will step outside and the committee will ask their own questions. That would be followed by an *in camera* meeting of the committee and finally an announcement regarding the outcome of the exam. There was a plan for to celebrate with pizza afterwards. It wasn't announced, but Kathy and Judy planned a party at Kathy's apartment that evening.

Kathy spoke confidently and answered questions well, both to the public and the committee. As the committee discussed among themselves, however, an issue arose. Eric asked, "Why is there no chapter in the dissertation outlining a plan for a future research program? Since this result is controversial and clearly needs further experimental work, such a chapter seems critical." Since Eric was not a member of the reading committee, he felt a bit odd criticizing the written document, but he considered this important.

"Good point," said Cheryl. "I agree such a chapter is necessary. Since you already have ET-2 well on its way, most of the chapter should be easy to write. She just needs to put that in the context of the existing results and implications, ET, the Japanese, the Europeans, that geology measurement."

"I also agree," said Robert. "I can't imagine it would take more than a day or two for her to add that."

"OK," said Thomas indicating the discussion was concluded, "Let me just write up a summary of what we want, then everyone can sign. I'll bring Kathy back in and we can tell her the news."

Once the committee members had signed the graduation sheet, Thomas opened the door, found Kathy and congratulated her with an out stretched hand. Adrian remembered the hug the two shared when the experiment started operation and thought how strained their relationship had become.

With Thomas' congratulations, pizza boxes were opened with commotion and the remaining crowd voiced their good wishes to Kathy. After a few moments things quieted down enough for Thomas to take her aside and explain the one requirement the committee had. Kathy was visibly upset, but didn't complain.

The party at Kathy's apartment later that night was a was quiet affair despite the heavy drinking. A friend brought a bottle of tequila and soon everyone was doing shots with salt and lime. Kathy couldn't decide whether she was relieved to have finished or angry that she had to write another chapter. Judy was finally able to get through to her. "Look," she said, "this will only take you a little while. Just get it done. I suggest you ignore it for a few days or a week and then just sit down and knock it off. We're talking five pages of content that you already know."

"You're right," conceded Kathy, her drunkenness making her melancholy rather than confrontational.

"That's the spirit," encouraged Judy. Then, in an effort to change the subject to something lighter, she added, "That Carl guy is kinda cute. Maybe you should start thinking of something besides science."

"He's just a friend. There is five years between us and I will be leaving soon. Seems like a bad idea to start something."

"I'm not suggesting you marry him, just get to know him better." Judy smiled at her sister, "much better." Kathy smirked back. "Now let's turn this sob fest into a party," Judy said loud enough for everyone to hear. Since the immediate neighbors were also attending, the decision to turn up the music was unanimous.

Thomas hosted the family Labor Day cookout at his house. Even though he didn't want the extra stress of hosting a party, he knew it was about time he took a turn. It gave him the opportunity to have the team over and he couldn't let Tanya do another dinner without returning the favor. However, Tanya and Mark seemed to be doing everything anyway, so maybe it wasn't much of a payback. As he watched them work, he commented to Adrian, "I should have catered this thing. Then they would be able to relax and enjoy themselves." Adrian smiled.

Kathy and Carl arrived together. This was not the first time Thomas got the impression their relationship was something more than they were letting on. "Good for them, if they are together," he thought.

"Hi Thomas," Kathy started, "thank you for the invite. I hate to bring up work at a party but I wanted to check whether we can submit the paper." Kathy had quickly written a draft of the ET result and the team had been debating prose for the past week. Her efforts writing her dissertation minimized the time it took to get the paper complete. She cleverly wrote an overview chapter that was effectively the draft. That impressed Thomas, even given his reservations about the result.

"Yes, I read the paper again yesterday and some this morning," he answered. "It's really good. You write well. If Adrian is good with it, then submit."

"Great. We talked to Adrian last night and she's on board. I will submit in the morning. And with that done, I promise no more shop talk."

Thomas noticed the use of we. "The drinks are in the coolers on the porch. Please help yourselves. I need to check with Tanya and see what I can do to help." Kathy and Carl picked out the local brews and settled into a couple lawn chairs.

Thomas found Tanya in the kitchen chopping chives for the potato salad. Thomas would have bought it at Whole Foods, but Tanya insisted hers was better. Adrian was sipping from a glass of wine across the kitchen island. "Thomas," began Tanya, "I can't believe Adrian has worked with you for so many years and we haven't met. You really need to host these parties more often. She is just a delight. You do have a talent for surrounding yourself with beautiful and intelligent women."

"Speaking of beautiful and intelligent, where is Sam?" he asked, but didn't notice the smirk Adrian gave.

"She's in the back changing. She came from a workout I hear."

"Unless you need help, I'll go see how Mark is doing with the grill. When Sam comes out, tell her I'm out back." Thomas headed out back to make sure things were going as planned.

Mark was making sure the condiment table was set to his liking as Thomas approached. "Even when I host the party, you two host the party."

"We love this stuff, Thomas," replied Mark. "But we'll let you clean up. How's that?"

"Perfect, and I can't wait for that special Mark-burger with that unique secret ingredient." Thomas winked at his brother-in-law and Mark laughed back.

"It's not much of a secret, but don't tell your friends. I need all the mystery I can get."

"Hi everyone," called Kelly as she and Cole came round the side of the house carrying supplies. "Sorry we're late. The hot water hose to our washer split this morning. Quite the mess."

"Damn," said Mark. "Did it do much damage?"

"Not much. The water ran over tile and out the garage," explained Cole. "The drywall behind the washer might need some work, but other than that it was just a lot of cleanup and mopping."

"Well that's good," said Thomas. "That could have been a lot worse if the water had flowed toward the carpet."

"Anyway, our washer isn't the big news of the day," said Kelly. "We saw a report on our iPhone news app that cancer rates are up and one quote attributed the increase to the changing electric charge."

"What?!" asked Adrian as she and Tanya came to the backyard to meet the new arrivals. "What news feed reported that?"

"It is a new outlet, NewsWire," answered Cole. "In fact, it's the first time I've seen them quoted. But I'll tell you, that CUS group has a huge following worldwide. This report is just going to encourage that movement."

"Let me see that report," said Thomas.

"I'll play the video so everyone can hear," said Kelly. "The screen is too small to gather around, but it's just a talking head anyway."

Kelly played the video and the party was silent as the reporter spoke. "The Centers for Disease Control announced today that the number of cancer diagnoses significantly increased over the past half year. Over the recent few years, the number of new cancer cases has been about five hundred per one hundred thousand residents per year. This five hundred number varies somewhat year to year. The general trends decrease due to improved treatments or preventative measures but increase due to earlier diagnosis techniques or a new carcinogen exposure. That variation is about ten or so in those units. This past half year saw an increase of about fifteen, which is large enough to be of a concern to the CDC. The report also noted that increases were reported around the world this past quarter. It is very anomalous and not associated with clusters. It is a general, overall trend.

"Some statisticians have speculated that this increase could be related to the observed change in the electric charge. The hypothesis is that distortion of the carbon bond undermines the stability of DNA base pairs. Furthermore, the DNA repair process would be hindered by this bond distortion altering the relative rates of damage and repair. This might lead to a higher rate of consequences from damaged DNA. With nearly four hundred million people living in the United States, even a small increase in the probability will result in an significant increase in the number of cancer diagnoses."

"Thomas," Adrian asked, "I thought you said that you estimated this effect and it wasn't significant?"

"I estimated how large the charge change would have to be for the bond to break. That would require the change be a sizable percentage of the charge itself. That is much too large compared to what ET sees. But I did not consider what it means if the bond is simply distorted."

"So this is possible then?" asked Mark.

"I didn't mean to imply that," answered Thomas. "I didn't consider it so I didn't try to do that estimate. But my intuition tells me that what we are seeing is still much too small."

"It doesn't matter if it's true or not," said Carl.

"Many people will believe it and that alone will cause problems. Look at this article." He presented his phone for others to see. "There is a rally in Los Angeles tomorrow for believers in CUS. This movement is really spreading."

The burgers, potato salad, baked beans and corn delicious, with Mark and Tanya's special flair. Even so, dinner was a fairly quiet affair. When talk was had, it tended toward CUS. After dinner, Carl left with Kathy and Sam left soon after Adrian. Thomas was grateful that no one brought up his tenure situation. He didn't want to explain the year delay.

The following Wednesday, Sam entered the compound door behind the kitchen and walked over to Jonathan's office door and knocked.

"Come in," she heard called from within.

As she opened the door, she glanced at the combination lock. The dial was set to sixteen. As she entered the room, she gave the inside handle a gentle twist, and sure enough, it worked just fine. "Sixteen," she thought as she spun the exterior dial.

"Sam," welcomed Jonathan, "thank you for coming by the compound today. We have lots to discuss."

"Hello Jonathan," she replied. "I hear you have big news for me?"

Sam could hear Harold speaking in the common room. He certainly had an orator's voice. Although she couldn't quite hear his message, she knew he was excited.

"Yes, I do have news," said Jonathan. "The date for the departure has been set. The event will take place on Saturday, November twenty. We have a number of things to prepare and we need your help." Jonathan laid a variety of advertisements, order forms, and hand-written notes on the table in front of Sam. "We need to place these orders immediately and make sure we get delivery no later than November thirteen."

"What is this order for compressed air bottles from Tyson Welding for?" she asked. Many of the other items were listed with just a generic product number with no description.

"Don't worry about that. I need the gas bottles and the air is just a convenient way to get them. They are critical for the departure and so the order has been placed. You just have to make sure about delivery and paying the invoice."

There was also a large compressor and a natural-gas combustion engine on the list. Sam found that suspicious and made a mental note to follow up and figure out what they were for. There was also a list of items under a heading of exhaust. She was struck by the cost for these items, which alone was enough to draw attention. "This is also a lot of plumbing supplies. Are you installing something? If so, there might be some tax implications." She knew this was a stretch, but was hoping it would get Jonathan talking about the purpose of this collection.

"No, it's all parts of a system for the departure program. And I don't plan to worry much about taxes this coming year."

The rest of the items seemed clear although their purpose seemed a bit strange, new CUS shirts, a very impressive new video and sound system for the common room, the cost to install the AV, lots of duct tape and caulk, and a rather expensive pre-prepared catered gourmet meal with drinks. "This looks like it will be quite the evening."

"Yes, and unfortunately, I have to be there, at least at the start. But it will make an impression, that's for sure."

"How about the money transfers? Is that going as you hoped?" Sam asked.

"Yes. I branched out as you suggested and visited Europe for some of that. Thanks for the hotel suggestion in Rome, by the way. It was a great location. South America was a mixed bag, however. Some of the banks were so easy to deal with, but others were very strict. I fear I may have stranded some money."

"Give me a list of the problem accounts. I will see what I can do. You did put my name on all those new accounts, didn't you?"

"Yes I did. Thanks for looking at it. It is a fair amount of money."

"My understanding was that this 'departure date' would coincide with CUS no longer requiring my services. Should we discuss any close-out actions?"

"I don't think that will be necessary. I anticipate still requiring some of your expertise over the coming months."

"OK, then I guess I'll be off to work on this. May I exit through this back door so I don't interrupt the meeting in the common area?"

"Certainly, you know the way."

Sam stood and turned the door handle, but the back door wouldn't open. "Darn it," said Jonathan. "I really should have gotten that fixed by now. Sorry but I guess you will have to sneak through the common room."

Sam smiled and exited as quietly as she could.

Adrian was at the quad picking up a banana nut muffin to go with her coffee to eat when she got to the lab. As she grabbed her thermal cup and turned from the pick-up window, she saw Carl hand Harold something. "That's interesting," she thought. "What could those two be up to?"

Adrian called to Carl and joined him on his walk toward Grunderson Hall. Carl mentioned that he was surprised to see a quote from the President's science advisor in a news article. Dr. Florence Ignacio, M.D. Ph.D., was trying to tamp down the building worry over the value of the electric charge. "People should not panic. Cancer rates fluctuate year to year for a variety of reasons and there is no convincing evidence that this increase is related to the electric charge changing. The epidemiologists are studying the situation and we should wait for their analysis. In the meantime, we will convene a panel to look at the situation regarding the charge."

Carl was not impressed. "That statement is not going to calm anyone," he said. "If the highest levels of government are concerned enough to convene panels, the public *is* going to panic."

Adrian nodded understanding, but otherwise didn't comment.

Change of a Change

At the beginning of October, ET-2 was almost ready to start. Carl arrived early at the lab. He ate breakfast at home being worried that he was developing scone overload. He avoided the quad while coming in and made a pot of coffee as soon as he entered the lab. With his lunch in the fridge and workspace arranged, he sat down to work on his blindness code.

The algorithm for blindness was his final task before the experiment was ready to begin. The old code, with its weekly data update wasn't intended for this upcoming data-taking period. Instead, they planned to collect one month of data in a lone batch. Over the past month Carl had written computer code to perform that task. The new blindness scheme was different than the ET version because the offset wasn't tied to the calibration. The new method generated a random number to shift the answer and simply hid that shift within an electronic envelope. Once the data analysis was complete, the envelope would be opened and the answer adjusted for the shift. He was confident his code was correct, but some of the numbers were coming out a bit different than what the old code calculated. The algorithms were similar enough to concern him. It was a small effect but the discrepancy was clear.

Carl opened up the source of the previous code in an editor and began to study it. "Adrian writes good code," he thought with admiration. The code almost described itself, even if she had omitted the numerous embedded comments. She had at least one line of descriptive comment for every line of code. But her blindness component was intermingled with the calibration and getting the big picture of what she did was slow going. "It's almost like she tried to make it complicated," he thought.

The lab door opened, startling Carl.

"Good morning, Carl," Adrian said cheerfully as she put her lunch in the fridge and set a bag with her scrambled-egg filled croissant by the coffee pot.

"Hi Adrian," he acknowledged her with a brief nod.

"What are you working on today?" she asked as she poured a cup.

"I'm implementing the blindness code and I'm glad you're here. I don't quite understand how you did this. Something looks funny."

Adrian looked over his shoulder and recognized her own code. "You shouldn't worry about my code," she said a bit harshly. "The new planned algorithm is different, so don't waste your time on old news."

"The two codes are differing on calculations where I think they should agree," he responded defensively. "Why are you upset? I just want to get it right."

"I am not upset. I saw your algorithm and it's right. You shouldn't waste time when we need to get this experiment running." Despite her protest, she sounded upset to Carl.

"OK, OK," he acquiesced. "You're the boss." Carl closed the file and returned to interfacing his new code in the data acquisition framework. He avoided further conversation after the strange exchange. He did not take long to get the code working. Once he did, he left for a break.

As Adrian was finishing up the calibration of the various sensors, Thomas came into the lab. "Hello Adrian, how are things?"

"Good," she answered. "Carl has the blindness code finished and he took a break after installing it. After lunch we'll do the final testing to verify everything is working together without any conflicts. All the sensors are working well and I'll be done with the calibrations today or tomorrow. We are ahead of schedule to start next week."

"Great news," he answered. "You two have done a good job. I guess I'll head to my office since you have it under control here."

"Thomas, before you go there is something I want to talk to you about."

"What is it?"

"A few days ago I ran into Carl on the quad. As I was walking toward him, I saw him hand some sort of document to Harold Simpson. I don't know what it was, and I was too shocked to ask him. But it seemed strange and I thought you should know."

"God damn it! First Kathy and now Carl," yelled Thomas. "Why can't they see how dangerous it is to get involved with that crackpot. Fareed has warned us more than once about our interactions with them. And I still wonder who is responsible for that hack. I'll talk to him." Without even waiting for a response from Adrian, Thomas stormed out of the lab.

Adrian gave a knowing nod and returned to her work.

Data taking for ET-2 began on October thirteenth, keeping with their Wednesday to Wednesday schedule. Although this would be a monolithic data set with no need for a weekly schedule, the team had become accustomed to a pattern and they kept to it. Thomas was grateful that he had Adrian and Carl's help getting ET-2 running. They had gotten much done in a short period, a tough slog. The upgrade sounded straight-forward, but broken parts, shipping delays and other mishaps had kept them very busy.

Kathy was a disappointment, however. Thomas knew she was very unhappy, and even worse, so did many in the department – another blow to his tenure case. Once the ET paper was finished, she had a couple interviews for postdoctoral positions. She had success with a school on the West Coast that had a strong atomic physics program. She planned to start in February and effectively stopped coming into the lab. She did help with some of the text for the developing paper on ET-2, but otherwise she was not very involved anymore.

Thomas was struggling with his frustration about Kathy and his nagging feeling that maybe she was responsible for the hack, when Carl entered the lab. Thomas frowned and narrowed his eyes. "What was it you gave to Simpson?"

"What?" Confusion played on Carl's face.

"On the quad, you gave a document to Harold Simpson. What was it?" Thomas' voice was controlled, but the anger came clearly through.

"Adrian." Carl whispered.

"What?" Thomas couldn't quite hear him.

"Harold requested a copy of our paper on ET. Once we submitted to the archive, I printed a version and put it in my pack. The next time I saw him on the quad, I gave it to him."

"Why are you cooperating with, or even talking to, that man?" Thomas demanded.

"I'm not cooperating with him, I just gave him the

paper."

"Don't you and Kathy realize how dangerous that man is to our program? We could lose our funding."

Carl picked his pack up and left without saying anything more.

"Where are you going?" Thomas barked, but got no response.

Thomas' alarm went off and he rolled over and turned it off. He really didn't want to get out of bed this morning. He certainly didn't want to go to work. With ET-2 running, he had nothing to do until November tenth when the four-week data set would complete. The wait was killing him and the tensions in the lab were just getting worse. Since he didn't teach on Tuesdays, he rolled over and went back to sleep.

He usually arrived at Grunderson Hall by eight each morning and checked in at the lab either first thing or after checking email. Rarely later than nine. His phone rang at half past nine, startling him awake. He reached over and glanced at the caller ID. "Adrian?" he thought. "She never calls me at home." He picked up the phone and touched the answer icon. "Hi Adrian. What's up?"

"Did you see the archive today?" she said excitedly.

"No, I'm afraid I don't feel all that great. I haven't even gotten out of bed yet."

"Oh." He heard her sigh before she continued.

"I'm sorry," She sighed again. "But I am sure you will want to hear this." She paused again. "The Europeans have recanted."

"What?" Thomas sat upright on the side of the bed.

"They recanted. They withdrew their paper from the archive and posted a brief one-page note explaining that they had a failing power supply that resulted in an offset variation."

"Amazing. Any details as to what they plan next?" He tried to wrap his sleep-addled brain around this news.

"They say it wasn't until the drift started shifting the other direction that they figured out what was going on. That's when they tested how its output corresponded to the readout."

"Unbelievable. Sounds like a good case for blindness to me. They got an answer that agreed with previous results and they just ran with it." Thomas felt a bit vindicated for being such a hard nose on publication, but he knew it was unlikely to be acknowledged.

"Probably right. Anyway they now say their experiment does not support or refute the charge changing hypothesis. They have ordered a new power supply and will start data taking again once it arrives. They claim it will only take a couple weeks to see the effect."

"Thanks for calling Adrian," Thomas said. "This is very interesting, although I'm not sure whether it's good or bad news. Anyway, it got my blood flowing so I'll be in the lab before long."

It was the last week of October when Adrian came to Thomas' office. He gestured to a chair, but she remained standing. She seemed agitated. "Thomas, all this drama with our efforts and CUS has just stressed me out. I have accepted an industry job in Europe. They want me to start on December sixth, so I am giving my notice.

The fifth of November will be my last day. I have a lot to do getting ready to move so I really need to move on."

"But Adrian," Thomas pleaded, "don't you want to be around for the end of the run on the tenth?"

"Not really Thomas. It took us so long to publish the first result, I really don't want to be involved in that process again."

"We published though, Adrian. We published." He sighed as he saw she was unmoved. "And we already have a draft of our next paper. Once the data is in, it should only take a few days."

"I feel like my value as a scientist has been decreasing because of all the delays and competitors beating us to the punch. In fact, I am just disenchanted with the idea of a career in physics. I think I want to try something new. I'll spend my last few days making sure the documentation on my subsystems is complete so others can maintain the hardware."

When Adrian stared at him steadfastly, he dropped his gaze to his desk and exhaled slowly. He paused for a long moment before replying. "Is there nothing I can say to change your mind, Adrian? This is really a shock. I thought you loved this work."

"I did love it and I am proud of what we did, but it's time for new adventures."

Thomas was left speechless. After a moment, Adrian said good-bye and left.

Thomas sat in a state of shock and confusion. "Christ, she never even asked me for a reference letter. That company didn't want one?"

The morning of November ten was an early one for Thomas. The excitement of the data run completion made him eager to get to work. Technically, the four-week run didn't end until mid-afternoon, but the anticipation was driving him crazy. He was out of bed, showered and dressed well before his alarm was scheduled to ring. He mixed a yogurt, fruit and muesli breakfast and then headed to the Brewers Cup for a scone and cup. His walk to the cafe was a messy slog, with typical November sleet and wind. Thankfully, his umbrella was up to the task and the cold and wet kept CUS off campus. He stamped his feet to shake off the rain and left his umbrella outside his office door to drip dry, although he was able to keep his scone dry. He ate the scone and drank the coffee in his office while he read his email.

Around ten a.m., Thomas worked his way down to the lab. When he arrived at the basement and turned the corner, he saw one of the CUS shirts at the far end of the hall moving quickly away. Thomas stopped for a second and closed his eyes tightly. He instructed himself to relax, took a deep breath and then opened his eyes. The figure was gone, thank goodness, and Thomas continued onto the lab.

Entering, the smell of brewing coffee was strong and Carl was sitting in front of the monitoring computer. "Hi Carl. How's everything look?"

"Looks good. The month's data collection went without a hitch. I think you'll have a great data set."

"You mean we'll have a great data set. You were a big part of this."

The student shifted in his chair and paused a moment before responding, not meeting the professor's gaze. Thomas could tell that Carl was having difficulties speaking up. He perched on the edge of Kathy's desk, just opposite Carl and waited till the young man spoke.

"I need to talk to you about that. I have decided to work for Cheryl Hodgens on her new experiment on angular correlations in nuclear beta decay. She is willing to take me on mid semester, so I am going to switch starting Monday."

Thomas was stunned. He knew he should pause before speaking to collect his thoughts but plunged ahead anyway "Carl, that is quite the surprise. We had agreed that you would take three one-month data sets over the next six months and then your dissertation would be on the rate the charge change is changing. You did a good job building the upgrade and you could be one of the fastest PhD's in the department."

Carl was a bit annoyed that Thomas complimented him only now, when he was worried about his departure. "I understand and I'm grateful for the opportunity, but I really think working for Cheryl is a much better fit. I find the work environment here a bit too tense. I am sorry if this leaves you in a tough position, but I have to do what's best for me."

Carl got up to leave. "All right Carl," sighed Thomas as the student walked out the lab door. "Best of luck to you and your work with Cheryl."

After Carl left, Thomas stared inattentively at the data monitoring screen. An overwhelming dread began to cover him. "I was counting on Carl for analysis. Without him, or Kathy, it will be quite an effort to analyze the data." Thomas swore and violently kicked a metal file cabinet.

Day of Change

In was Saturday, November 20, and the Changing Universe Society was meeting in the large common room on the first floor of their condominium facility. Nearly all the members attended this meeting. Some of the men were finishing affixing a number of gas bottles to a rail along one wall and making plumbing attachments to distribute the gas throughout the room. Once the bottles were set, they moved a heavy bench up against them to make more room near their makeshift stage. The stage was basically a very large table with a step-stool adjacent and a music stand strapped to one of the legs extending to a speaker's height.

Sam parked her car and entered the building through the door that led to the hallway behind Jonathan's office. Once inside, she verified no one was in the hall and then ducked into the stairwell, descending into the basement. This old factory was constructed largely of wood. Numerous work benches previously used to support heavy machinery, some wood and some heavy metal, were distributed throughout the basement and the common room. An extensive plumbing and pneumatic communication system ran throughout this structure and to the numerous rooms throughout the building. Neither Harold, nor Jonathan, however, spent much time in the lower floor of the facility. They did not appreciate the the danger of the legacy waste there. Leftover and neglected bags of fertilizer were piled in the old packing plant basement. Even with the ongoing installation of the laundry room, the basement was mostly ignored.

Sam negotiated a path around bags of fertilizer, and found the gas hookups intended for a line of dryers. Only a few were used for dryers. There were three that were plugged last time Sam was here. But now one was connected to a large Natural gas boiler. "That's new," she said. The exhaust of the boiler was connected to a compressor that in turn was connected to a compressed gas bottle. Over the boiler was an exhaust system with duct work connecting to one of the dryer exhaust lines. Sam looked closely at the boiler and realized that a water line snaking back and forth was welded to a large metal block situated just above where flames would burn when the system was on. She shook her head thinking it was a very clever way to create incomplete burning to produce and collect carbon monoxide.

Sam refocused on the job at hand and walked over to the last of the unused gas lines. Either no one noticed, or they didn't care, that this connection was near the old abandon chemicals. She used a wrench to remove the pipe plug and then took a modified regulator out of her purse and screwed it in. Taking out a wrench, she tightened the fixture and opened the gas line valve. She operated a valve on the regulator momentarily to confirm that her addition worked as planned. Tossing the wrench to the side, she rotated a curved nozzle on the regulator to point toward the wooden wall structure. She returned upstairs.

As Sam walked past Jonathan's back door, she glanced at the combination lock and gave the dial a spin. She continued along the hallway and then turned right into the common area. She crossed the room in front of the arranged chairs and walked along the gas bottles. She smiled while reading the misleading bottle labels indicating they contained compressed air. After standing there for a minute, she made the rounds saying hello to a number of members. She shook hands with Harold and Jonathon. When Harold began to climb the stairs up to the stage, she moved to the back of the room. Standing near one of the metal work benches, she opened a drawer and put her purse inside. "It'll be safe there," she said to a woman walking by who took notice.

Harold said something to Jonathan. He stood, seemed to look right at Sam and smile, then walked into his office. Through the door she saw him push a few buttons on a panel. She assumed that was the video and sound recording of the event. He closed the door, obviously working on something he didn't want others to see. She looked up and noted that she was presently standing behind the ceiling mounted camera. She walked forward a number of rows and knelt next to a woman sitting in an end chair. "Hello Tammy, I haven't seen you in a long time and just wanted to touch base."

"Hi Sam. It has been a long time. I hope you're well."

"Yes, and tonight's the big night. It looks like Harold is getting ready to start so I'll let you go." Sam, turned and walked erect so she was clearly viewed, although she was careful to not look directly at the camera.

"My fellow future MUTs," Harold thundered in an attempt to get everyone's attention. "Tonight is the night we have all been waiting for." The applause and celebration was deafening. Harold smiled and allowed the members to express their excitement. "In a few moments, we will begin our planned journey. It is clear from recent new reports and scientific results that the charge is changing and our Universe will not support life within a few years. The Multi-Universe Travelers have informed me that now is the time for our departure. If anyone is not sure about our journey, feel free to leave us. Soon we will be sealing this room for our planned departure. I will wait five minutes to allow any doubters to give up on the chance of departure. Sam was surprised that only a few CUS members chose to leave, when Harold made the offer. She took notice that Jonathan had not returned from his office.

After the allotted delay, Harold nodded to two young men in the front of the gathering. They picked up a box of duct tape and started sealing the windows and interior doors. The exterior doors, one by the kitchen and the one on the far backside of the room, had good weather stripping and didn't need an extra seal. The back door also had a wind wall so the room stayed warm even if it was open. The wind wall blocked the view of the door from the majority of the room. The two men made quick work of the major cracks around the room and returned to their seats.

After another short wait, Harold nodded again and the two assistants went to work opening the valves of the large pressurized gas bottles. Even from the back of the room, Sam could hear the hiss of their contents flow from the bottles. She walked backwards slowly the few steps required to reach the enclosed hallway at the back of the room, making sure no one paid attention to her. Once concealed by the wall that protected the room from the weather of the open door, she hurried out of the building and crouched behind a CUS operations truck where she would not be seen by those who chose to leave instead of joining the departure. Those members quickly walked to the parking lot and entered their cars. It was clear they wanted to get away promptly. That provided Sam the opportunity to relocate unnoticed to a spot where she could watch the common area through a window. It wasn't long before she noticed people slumping in their chairs as they became unconscious. She could see Tammy as one of the slumped victims. Children were leaning into their moms as if they were sleeping.

Jonathan stood from his chair and went to leave by his office's back door. As he grabbed the knob, it wouldn't turn. Panic struck him as he struggled with it. Finally, he went to the front door, took a deep breath and held it. He opened the door and exited. As he turned right to hurry to the exit door, he bumped into his father. "Isn't this a glorious day," Harold said as he grabbed onto Jonathan and gave him a stifling hug. "I'm so happy we could share this event together." Jonathan struggled but couldn't break his father's grip.

Sam pulled a phone from her pocket and dialed a number. She heard the tone she was waiting for and then hung up. She opened the back door of her car and took out an overnight bag. Closing the car door, she began to walk the mile to the blue metro line bus and shook her head as she boarded and sat down. "Why do people believe the things they do?" she spoke to the empty metro car.

Fire erupted violently in the basement. Through the bus' rear window, Sam could see the smoke begin to rise. The wooden structure imbedded with legacy chemicals burned quickly and very hot, if unevenly. Many of the bodies in the common area were entirely consumed.

The following day, as Thomas read the newspaper reports of the mass suicide, he was horrified. Between one hundred fifty and one hundred eighty people took their own lives. Worse than that, a number of satellite groups around the world also participated. Individual suicide deaths worldwide were exceptionally high. The total number of deaths due to the CUS departure wouldn't be known for days or maybe weeks. The police and fire department couldn't tell for sure how many people died in the local compound fire because of the devastation. The film and narration by Harold Simpson posted to the internet as the event took place made it clear it was a cooperative event. No one was forced to participate. Thomas didn't watch TV often, but he turned it on this morning. He watched in shock as reporters conducted their interviews. "How do you convince so many people to kill themselves?" he thought. "And if you have that ability, how could you bring yourself to do it?"

Seven people had decided to not partake in the event. The young newsman from the local ABC affiliate interviewed an older man. "I am here talking to Jack Stanis, a member of the Changing Universe Society cult, but one who lived through last night's horrible events. This loss of life reminds us of the Jim Jones incident in Guyana. People committing suicide because of belief in the message of one man. But this time, there were survivors. How did you manage to escape?"

"I didn't have to escape," answered Jack. "No one was forced to participate. I, and six others, simply left when Harold announced the last chance to leave."

"So, does that mean you had doubts about the CUS message? Did you believe that MUTs were going to rescue you from the approaching calamity?"

"Yes, I do believe that the MUTs are coming to take us. But I wasn't ready to take that next step. Maybe we'll start again. I don't know at this point."

"One of the other survivors told me that all members gave over all their assets to the CUS. Is that your understanding?" asked the reporter.

"Yes. I gave over all my money to them. Those monies helped operate the compound and get our message out. I was happy to do it."

"But what happens with all that money now?"

"I don't really know. Jonathan Simpson was the treasurer for CUS. I have not seen him since last night, so I assume he joined his father on the journey with the MUTs."

"That is quite the story," exclaimed the reporter. "All that money and the compound. I suppose it will take the courts years to figure out who it belongs to. I hope you and the other six survivors will be OK."

Thomas picked up his phone and dialed Sam's number – no answer and he hung up. "She still isn't picking up. Where is she?" he said out loud. "Why did she stand me up last night?" His stomach had an ache that he refused to acknowledge. "She wouldn't have gone to that meeting," he assured himself.

Thomas switched the channel to the NBC affiliate and their reporter was talking to the city's police chief. The two were standing in a parking lot with a smoldering shell of a building behind them. "Chief Dominguez, how long will it take you to understand how many people died here?" ask the young woman.

"That is a good question. We may never know," answered the chief. "The fire burned very hot in spots. That building used to be a fertilizer factory and it wasn't entirely cleaned out. Much of the wood, especially in the basement, was impregnated with chemicals that made it very flammable. Those spots of left-over chemical really burned hot. Certainly, the large quantity of wood in the building provided a lot of fuel. Some of the bodies were burned beyond recognition. In fact, we aren't even sure how many bodies are there. The film that the Changing Universe Society posted to the web is helpful in that regard and we have received some useful information from the seven people who chose not to die. But we may have to identify the dead by the process of elimination. We are trying to figure out who was there from the film."

"Chief Dominguez, what about the money? Any idea how much there is and what will happen to it?" she asked.

"We will have to look into that and the lawyers and accountants are getting organized. But I have no information for you at this time."

"Thank you Chief." Turning to the camera, the reporter signed off. "This is a real tragedy at the Changing Universe Society compound in downtown. Details are emerging and we will bring them to you as they become available. Back to you George."

Thomas turned off the TV. "Wow, all those people just killed themselves," he said to no one. "All those times I dismissed them, I never thought they would take it this far." He tried to call Sam again. She didn't answer.

Everything Changes

The Wednesday after the mass suicide, Thomas was working in his office. He had been there almost continuously since Sunday. His calls to Sam went unanswered and he was worried about her. But obsessing about the changing charge dominated his thoughts. Sometimes his thoughts wandered over his missing colleagues as well. He was very disappointed, and a little peeved, that Kathy, Adrian and Carl weren't here today. If they had been around to help him, this analysis would have gone much faster. He'd lost all three of them in a few short months. He wouldn't win any mentoring awards this year. Certainly the departure of three good scientists from under-represented groups will be noticed. That will be hard to explain as he prepared his statements for his tenure package.

Thomas rubbed his eyes, sighed and lamented aloud, "all this nonsense started exactly one year ago when we noticed the charge changing."

He felt alone. Sam was nowhere to be found and tomorrow was Thanksgiving. He had been invited to Tanya's for the weekend, but he had avoiding accepting until he heard from Sam.

He felt the impact of his colleagues abandoning him. He sighed again, but this time with determination, knowing he *would* get the paper out, albeit without their help. Even that, however, was a conundrum. He knew it was not ethical to submit a paper with collaborator's names on it without them reading and approving. But then on the other hand, it wouldn't be right to not include them as co-authors either. They worked hard on ET and ET-2. They had seen the draft before numbers were available. They were all so adamant that the paper get written first and, when available, just insert the numbers and publish, regardless the answer. They had been tired of delay and they insisted on a strict policy on how to implement the unblinding. Write the paper with a blank for the answer, unblind, see the result, put that number in regardless of what it is, and submit. Their strict view is how he rationalized including their names on the paper. They had seen the text and expressed a strong opinion about how to handle publication. He was just following their wishes, even if they didn't see the result before submission.

Today he would do the final unblinding. The paper was written, just the final number was missing. Thomas was a fastidious writer and the team had been frustrated with how slow things went. His first draft got only a few significant comments, but still it took him a couple weeks to incorporate them. Kathy had been convinced he was scared to own up to the ET data. She accused him of being afraid of the result, which led to the delay of that publication. He had to admit there was some truth to that. Too bad she wasn't here to witness today's events.

Adrian left only a couple weeks ago but she had effectively checked out of his program some time ago. She never got over the argument about the conference talk. She didn't bother to leave a forwarding email address, so Thomas couldn't send her the paper in any case. Thomas was disappointed she didn't go for an academic science job. She was so talented and he was optimistic she would have been successful.

Well, here he was, all alone and ready to put the final number in. He only had to open that electronic envelope and see what the winning number was. He smiled at his own poor attempt at humor. He knew he was procrastinating because in many ways, Kathy was right. He was scared. What if ET was right? What if it says the charge is changing? Will that claim be so sensational and controversial that it will jeopardize his tenure. What if the answer is no? Would there be a backlash because the past erroneous hints were so impactful? The answer from ET-2 will be dramatic no matter what it is. He expected fallout regardless the answer. "So yes," he said out loud. "I am scared."

Carl was an especially sad case. Thomas lost him rather early in their time together. "I chased him off somehow." The sad part was that Thomas wasn't even sure what he did to upset Carl. He assumed his own hidden biases must have come through. Probably biases he didn't even know he had. "Carl is a promising student and will likely make some other professor successful. Young physicists work hard to make older physicists famous," his monolog continued. "I used to lament that as a student and postdoc. Now it seems that coin flipped and I didn't even see it coming."

"Time to do this." Taking a very deep breath, Thomas typed the password into the program that would reveal the artificial shift. But he hesitated and didn't hit return. After a moment and several more deep breaths, he pressed the key. He stared at the result for over a minute.

"I did not expect that," he said with resignation to no one in particular. "That will certainly interest the surviving CUS members. I guess it's also clear what measurement I should do next." Without any further delay or emotion, he typed the result into the paper. He uploaded the paper to preprint server. From there, it was a direct submission to the journal. He filled in all the electronic forms and hit submit. Next, he made sure all the data and computer codes were backed up to his cloud account.

"OK, it's done." He pulled a bottle of Maker's Mark from the cabinet in his office. He poured some into his coffee mug and then stood in front of the window. "Where is Sam?" he said with fearful frustration. He looked aimlessly at the grey day framed by his office window.

"I need her to help me through this moment." He sat back down at the computer and wrote an email to the team with a copy of the paper and congratulating them on a job well done. He didn't know if they would ever see it, but he felt it was necessary. He figured it must be time for another drink, but he'd rather have it at the The Gulpers' Guild. He packed his pack, turned off his computer monitor, put away things on his desk, and stood to leave.

A knock at the door made him look up. The door was rarely shut when he was in his office and the opening framed the view of DeeDee stepping into the room with a man in a worn suit and a police officer standing behind them.

"Thomas," DeeDee started with a wave of her hand. "These officers are here to talk to you."

"Professor Conrad?" asked the man in the suit.

"Yes, I'm Thomas Conrad," trying not to let the distinction between assistant and full professor bother him.

"I am Detective Lanstrom and this is Officer Baca. We'd like to talk to you about the Changing Universe Society incident."

"OK, but I only know what I've read in the papers."

"Professor Conrad, we believe you orchestrated a financial embezzlement by exploiting this mass suicide. You faked a scientific result to get more people to join Changing Universe Society. You established inside access by getting romantically involved with one of their members. When they all died you absconded with the money they donated to CUS. There is an account at the University credit union in your name that received a hundred grand on the Saturday of the catastrophe. It matches well with a similar account that the leader's son had that also had a hundred G deposit."

"Romantically involved with a member?" Thomas asked rather distantly. "I am confused, I have no involvement with CUS."

"Your girlfriend, Samantha Hendrix, was one of the victims of your scheme. We found what was left of her purse, including her cell phone, wallet and passport. Her car was found in the parking lot of the compound."

"Sam was at that meeting!?" Thomas was stunned. "Is that why I've been unable to reach her?"

"We haven't found her body yet. Many of victims were incinerated, so we may never find her. But we found her purse. She is seen on the streaming download that Harold Simpson made, so she was certainly there."

"Oh my God, Sam," he cried softly. "Can it be true that you were there?" He turned and stared out the window.

"Professor Conrad," insisted Detective Lanstrom.

"She never indicated she was a member. Just that she did their books and gave them financial advice." Thomas was in shock. He was talking to no one in particular.

"Thomas," DeeDee said, "We should wait to submit your tenure package until after this is cleared up. Don't concern yourself with getting that paperwork ready. You can do that when things are back to normal." She did not sound comforting. "I will leave you all to your purposes." And with a wave of her hand, she left.

The detective took a couple steps toward Thomas. "We would like you to come down to the station, make a statement and answer some questions. I want you to know that we have warrants to search your home and office. In fact we have already been to your house. Curiously we found a passport in a nightstand drawer under the name of Dobbins with your picture and a number of recent entry-exit stamps to Canada, along with a variety of other countries. We also have a positive ID from a teller at a Regina bank that has a dormant CUS account. There were bank transactions by Dobbins in Rome during the time you were attending a conference there." After a slight pause, "I am really looking forward to your explanation for that."

As Thomas was escorted out of Grunderson Hall to the government sedan, his thoughts were panicked. "That fucking dream came true."

The Change Revealed

Sam walked along the beach carrying Mai Tais. "Ah, there," she thought and made a slight turn away from the water. "Hi Love," she whispered to the napper on the beach lounge. Leaning over they shared a deep kiss.

"Here's your drink." Sam removed her beach wrap to reveal her new bright solid yellow bikini and matching belt purse. She reclined on the neighboring lounge. "The weather sure is nice here near the equator, even the day before Thanksgiving. Just love it. The beach is also so empty. Hardly anyone here. If it was dark we could spin one right here. I bet we could walk around that jetty and be completely alone, huh Love." She heard a low chuckle and smiled as she was pulled in to share a longer kiss. Sam reached over and slid her hand up a leg. "Yep, you could make my gucci quiver right here, Love."

"Delicious! What a long wait for this moment. Not that we didn't have our delights. But your relationship with Thomas, if I can call it that, was hard for me. I could hardly take it. We got to spend only half of each week together for over a year. At night I would just scream thinking of you two together."

"Yes, it was a long year," answered Sam. "Thomas is good guy, but he isn't you. I had to fantasize about you to get through some of those nights. You and I did have some good times though. He went on travel a few times or to his sister's giving us more time together. And he was too trusting to ask many questions about what I did without him."

"True, but it still hurt. Lounging here today, though, it all seems worth it. Tell me again how you arranged the accounts."

"Oh I do love you Love. She entwined her fingers with her lover's.

The only hard part was the fake passports. Luckily one of the cult members had a sketchy past and he connected me with 'a guy'. Moving the money to an offshore account was easy because it was legal. Jonathan completely trusted me and followed my instructions perfectly. And, since I never joined the cult, there is little paper trail of my presence. Since he moved money promptly as it came in, the size of the accounts never got large enough to attract undue attention. Moving the money to a second foreign account, and then buying a bunch of cryptocurrencies, means that the final conversion back to currency will be very hard to trace. We arranged so many small transfers and conversions that the accounting is all over the place. It will take a long while for the police to figure out where the money went, if they even look. The amount of money was not documented anywhere and a lot was left behind, especially in the operations account. Since Jonathan died in the mass suicide, no one remains who knows how the accounting was done. Jonathan wanted it all hidden, and I took advantage of that. He wanted direct help and thus allowed me to access all the accounts and I took advantage of that.

"Jonathan clearly planned to run off with the money so he was not going to let anyone in on to the money laundering advice I gave him. Plus like many men, he was very easy to manipulate. Thus it was easy to make sure eyes would be on him if he survived the *departure*.

I even made a couple small local accounts in Jonathan and Thomas' names with last minute transfers to bring attention to them. Because Jonathan gave me all the account information, I was able to make additional accounts that he didn't know about. All in all, there was so much money moving around that one could use some of it to divert attention away from the primary pot that we are going to live on. To be successful, one can't get too greedy in the money laundering game.

"Near the end, I placed a passport with the same false ID that Jonathan used for some of his trips in Thomas' house where police are likely to find it, but Thomas wouldn't. I feel a bit bad about setting him up, but not all that bad. He was just too exploitable to respect.

"The most tricky part was timing our departure to the *departure*. That hacker ploy of yours was brilliant by providing an explanation for how the results got out. Letting Jonathan know about the existence of Thomas' private notebook also helped. Not only did their burglary really direct attention far away from us, that notebook provided a lot of material to get people worked up and worried about their future. The release of the results greatly increased pressure on Harold to set a date. Once everyone knew ET's results, it really sped things up. And then, other science teams wanting to get in on the action created a feeding frenzy. Who could'a predicted that? We lucked out that Harold chose to join the MUTs before ET-2 started and that he defined a specific date well ahead of time. That made it easy for us to make our final plans. It was hectic those last few days making sure all the accounts were right and installing the ignitor was away from my comfort zone, but it all worked better than we had hoped.

"And then the guy decided to record the whole departure thing! That clip certainly clarifies where to place blame for the deaths. I was able to get myself on video and leave some of my things behind. The police will think I died also. That small ignitor you made worked like a charm and that old building and its chemicals burned fast and hot." Sam raised her arms above her head and pointed her toes for a satisfying stretch. "Your turn. Tell me again how you did it."

With a long sip of the Mai Tai, Sam leaned back to hear the other half of the story. "Thomas, like most scientists, was so trusting, he was almost naive. He never thought anyone, especially someone on his team, would tamper with the data. It was impossible for him to consider intentional sabotage. And even if he had, his training and disposition just wouldn't have provided him the skills needed to discover any malfeasance. He never changed passwords and the blindness technique assumed that we would all cooperate. It was an honor system. The computer code used to calibrate the atomic transition energies was written so long ago that the team had pretty much forgotten about it. In addition, we had simulation software that would mimic a small change in the electric charge so we could do sensitivity studies back when we were designing the experiment. These two codes were intertwined, although the simulation code had long been modified to do nothing once ET was running.

"But, we had everything set up for blindness. The calibrator added a small offset to the measured value of the charge that could only be subtracted back off once all the verification checks were complete. This procedure had become very routine because we always saw what we expected; no change in the electric charge. So routine, in fact, that no one noticed when a new modification was made to the simulation code. This tweak reconstituted an additional offset determined by the simulation code in addition to the offset calculated by the calibration code. Hence, when the calibration offset was subtracted, it no longer cancelled the full value's offset, giving the impression of a changing charge. Just like our test studies before the experiment, except I put in the acceleration to increase the tension. All to get Harold motivated to declare the departure.

"Because the simulation code was considered dormant, no one checked it when we began to see an effect. It was a good thing that I had plenty of lab access by myself because I didn't have a lot of time to make that alteration once we decided to do it. I had to do it fast. But it was such a subtle change in such a large, complicated program that it would have been very difficult to find, even if you were suspicious. And Thomas isn't capable of suspicion. No one will ever connect me to that feature of the code, especially now with the emphasis on ET-2.

"I did have a scare when Carl started looking at the code, but I think he was already planning to quit and didn't really care that much. When I told him to stop, I think he was relieved to have less work. We did get lucky with the timing though. It would have been very hard for me to do something similar with ET-2. It was such a change in how we took data that I would have had to completely recode the deviation. Since everyone was hyper aware of all the experimental details at that point, it probably would have been noticed. Thankfully, the timing of the decision of Changing Universe Society to depart and join the MUTs came when it did." After a pause she added, "and you, your handling of this was perfect.

"I must say though I was shocked by the other results. I knew they couldn't be true, but I couldn't tell the team why. The scientist in me had a hard time with that. But that did speed things up."

Sam squeezed her companion's thigh and leaned in for another kiss. "This afternoon is getting hotter by the minute," she smiled.

"You know one thing nice about this island? Being topless." Adrian sat forward, reached behind her back and untied her bikini top. Seeing the lust in Sam's eyes, she smiled. "Yep, that is a very nice thing about this island."

"Boy it definitely is hot though," said Sam. The two shared another long kiss.

Adrian saw a beach waitress working her way toward the two women. She finished her drink in one large gulp. "I'm going to order another drink and a snack. Do you want anything, Sam? Or should I call you Denise?" Adrian smiled.

"Cute Love, or should I call you Becky."

"I will say that friend of Jonathan's can sure make a fake passport," commented Adrian.

"I'm just glad Thomas arranged that baseball outing. Otherwise we wouldn't have met."

"So true. That was a seminal day."

"But boy, do I feel sorry for those idiots that followed Harold Simpson," said Sam. "They are all dead now and for what?" After a pensive moment, she continued. "Well, I guess I don't feel so guilty that I won't enjoy spending their life savings."

"No I won't either," agreed Adrian. "Sometimes, I wonder about the result of ET-2. I guess Thomas must've submitted the paper by now. When that number comes out as no charge change, Thomas will be driven nuts wondering what went wrong with ET."

"Adrian, one thing I still don't understand is the Japanese result," said Sam. "How could they get the same result that was faked by ET?"

"Hmm. No. I don't get that either. They must have done something wrong."

"I certainly hope so," emphasized Sam. "The MUTs have already left without us."

Laughing, the two clicked glasses, and the lovers smiled at each other. "Let's have a toast," said Adrian. "To all the lives that changed suddenly last Thanksgiving."

For Further Reading

A number of reference works were used to develop the technical ideas in this story. Below is a list of references for various topics if the reader wants to explore some in more detail. This is not an exhaustive list but would certainly get an interested person started.

- Physicists characterize the strength of the electrical force by a dimensionless constant called the fine structure constant. The fine structure constant, written as α is proportional to the value of the electric charge squared. The are a number of efforts looking for a change in α as a function of time using laboratory experiments, and astrophysical observations. Some references looking at the possibility of the fundamental constants changing include, F. C. Adams, Phys. Rep. **807** 1 (2019); J. D. Barrow, J. Phys.: Conf. Ser. **24** 253 (2005). There is an interesting discussion of the consequences in an online forum, Physics Forum under quantum physics dated Aug. 17, 2012 (https://www.physicsforums.com/threads/change-in-fine-structure-constant.629286/)

- There are a number of experimental groups looking for a change in the fine structure constant by measuring atomic wavelengths precisely. Their research is an offshoot of work to improve atomic clocks.

Recent examples are described in N. Leefer *et al.* Phys. Rev. Lett. **111** 060801 (2013); T.M. Fortier *et al.*, Phys. Rev. Lett. **98** 070801 (2007); M. S. Safronova *et al.* Phys. Rev. Lett. **120** 173001 (2018).

- A naturally occurring nuclear reactor was discovered in Oklo, Gobon. The argument that natural self-sustaining nuclear reactions took place about two billion years ago in a uranium ore body is based on an anomalous isotopic ratio of ^{235}U and ^{238}U. The rate of neutron induced fission would depend on the fine structure constant. The result has also been used to place constraints on the rate of change of the electric charge. Wikipedia has a good summary of this phenomenon and a recent technical reference can be found in E. D. Davis and L. Hamdan, Phys. Rev. C **92** 014319 (2015).

- The Anthropic Principle is discussed in numerous places. Some references to the anthropic principle or the required fine tuning of the constants for life are, B. J. Carr and M. J. Rees, Nature **278** 605 (1979); L. A. Barnes, Pub. Astron. Soc. Aus. **29** 529 (2012); B. J. Carr and M. J. Rees, Nature **278** 605 (1979). The Anthropic Principle is sometimes associated with Intelligent Design. A discussion relating the two can be found at, V. J. Stenger, Skeptic **4** no. 2, 36 (1996).

- The requirement that the electric charge has a value close to its known value for life to exist is also discussed in numerous places. One example is the J. D. Barrow and J. K. Webb, Sci. Amer. 57 (June 2005).

- A nice summary of the use of blind analyses in the physical sciences can be found in Joshua R. Klein and Aaron Roodman, Annu. Rev. Nucl. Part. Sci. **55** 141 (2005).

- The asteroid in the story was motivated by the Oumuamua asteroid observed in 2017. The *strange facts* came from a Scientific American article published on Nov. 20, 2018. The suggestion that it is artificial is not a widely held view. Wikipedia has a nice summary description of the asteroid.

- An example of a follow-on to the Mohole project is Mohole to Mantle (M2M) described in a BBC Engineering story on May 6, 2019.

- The Changing Universe Society was inspired by the Heaven's Gate cult. Thirty nine members of this cult committed group suicide in March of 1997 in San Diego. They believed the arrival of the comet Hale-Bopp was a signal it was time to leave this world. Wikipeadia has a description of the Heaven's Gate cult.

- Yes, Pastafarianism is a thing.

About the Author

Steve Elliott is a nuclear/particle physicist with a primary research interest in the properties of the neutrino. Growing up in Albuquerque, he graduated from the University of New Mexico with honors. He attended the University of California, Irvine where his dissertation documented the first observation of two-neutrino double beta decay. He was a postdoc at Los Alamos National Laboratory where he worked on an experiment in Russia measuring neutrinos from the Sun and then a postdoc at Lawrence Livermore National Laboratory where he worked on ion trapping. As a member of the research faculty at the University of Washington, he worked on a solar neutrino experiment in Canada. After returning to Los Alamos National Laboratory, he turned his research back to double beta decay with an experiment sited at the Homestake gold mine in Lead, SD. He is presently co-spokesperson for the LEGEND experiment, a 260 person collaboration conducting a double beta decay experiment in Italy. He is a Fellow of the American Physical Society and a LANL Laboratory Fellow. *The Day Before Thanksgiving* is his first novel. He lives in Santa Fe with his wife Mary, where his daughter, Alexis, grew up. The author photo is by Mary Elliott.

Made in United States
Orlando, FL
05 March 2023